The Sister Pact

The Sister Pact

Cami Checketts

Bonneville Books
Springville, Utah

ISBN 13: 978-1-59955-267-5

Published by Bonneville Books, an imprint of Cedar Fort, Inc., 2373 W. 700 S., Springville, UT 84663
Distributed by Cedar Fort, Inc., www.cedarfort.com

Library of Congress Cataloging-in-Publication Data

Checketts, Cami, 1974-
    The sister pact / Cami Checketts.
        p. cm.
    ISBN 978-1-59955-267-5 (acid-free paper)
    1. Sisters--Fiction. 2. Falls (Accidents)--Fiction. 3.
Coma--Patients--Fiction. I. Title.
    PS3603.H434S57 2009
    813'.6--dc22
                                2009009871

Cover design by Jen Boss
Cover design © 2009 by Lyle Mortimer
Edited and typeset by Heidi Doxey

Printed in the United States of America

10 9 8 7 6 5 4 3 2 1

Printed on acid-free paper

Acknowledgments

To my sister and best friend, Abbie. Thanks for being there, Bubs, I shudder to think how I'd make it through the day without a phone call from you.

Thanks to the real Detective Keller of The Cache County Sheriff's Office for making sure I don't annoy any officers of the law.

And finally, thanks to my sweetheart, Stan, for putting the boys to bed far too many nights so I could write. I love you.

One

Wesley Richins dimmed the lights, inching to a stop across the street from his target's two-story house. The Hummer was loud. Too loud. He cut the motor and peered out his windshield. Light radiated from the interior of the house, spilling onto the porch and yard. He couldn't see the woman. He waited.

Minutes later he received his reward, a glimpse of her at the kitchen window. She filled a glass with water and handed it to her baby.

Wes licked his lips. His eyes devoured her: Dark hair, olive skin, sparkling brown eyes. His heartbeat increased. Three weeks. His fingers tapped a staccato on the steering wheel. Three weeks of watching and waiting. He wrapped his palm around the wheel. Tonight was the payoff.

She walked from the kitchen and moments later passed the panes of glass adorning her front door. A glance at the clock confirmed his wait was almost over—9 PM, bedtime for her son. He rubbed his hands together. He'd give her some time to relax and then make his appearance.

How would she react? He tilted the rearview mirror and grinned at his reflection. What a dumb question. How did every woman react to him?

She'd melt.

❦

Allison Mendez hefted her two-year old into his antique white crib. A spasm sliced through her upper back muscles. "Oh, my heavens, you're getting too big for Mommy to carry."

Joshua reached up and patted his mother's hand on the crib railing. "You's okay, Mommy." He pointed a chubby finger to his chest, crossed both arms, and pointed at her.

"Oh, sweetheart." Ignoring the ache in her back, Allison leaned down. She inhaled the warm scent of baby lotion and placed a kiss on his soft cheek. "I love you, too."

Josh's dark head bobbed. A soft smile played on his lips. He closed his eyes and curled around his fleece blanket.

Allison stole one more kiss and slipped from the nursery. Plodding down the stairs, she sank into the leather couch and rescued Cussler's latest novel from the claws of a construction vehicle. A dozen pages later, the jangling of the phone jolted her back to reality.

She replaced the bookmark, tossed her black hair over her shoulder, and retrieved the phone with a sigh. The caller ID read: Savannah Compton.

"Hey, little sister," Allison said, her sigh turning to a smile.

"Hey, skinny momma," Savannah said. "How's my favorite nephew?"

"Your *only* nephew?" Allison shook her head. "Adorable and hopefully asleep. I'm not good at this single mom jig."

"Missing Ryan pretty bad, huh?"

"Yeah." Allison eased from the couch, sauntering to the bank of windows that overlooked the lush Cache Valley. "But I never tell him I miss him." A harsh puff of air escaped through her teeth. "I'm turning into a bitter old woman. Every time he calls I nag him about being gone."

"Ouch. At least he makes good money."

Allison looked around her home. The great room had a two-story vaulted ceiling. The doors and windows were trimmed in alder, a perfect compliment to the soft beige walls. The cabinets were cherry, and the granite in her kitchen and bathrooms had cost more than a mid-sized sedan. The house was gorgeous, yet worthless without Ryan here.

"Money isn't everything, Savvy," she said.

"I don't know. I'd settle for a fine Latino lamb-chop . . ."

Allison laughed. "A Latino *lamb-chop*?" Although Ryan's grandparents resided in Argentina, he'd been raised in America. The only part of his heritage he'd retained were his dark good looks and his passion for soccer. "I like that."

"Of course you do. I thought of it. I'd take a Latino lamb-chop who lets me go to the gym and park all day with my little boy and never asks me to balance my checkbook."

Allison tossed her head. "Oh, give me a break. You know I'm too retentive to not balance my checkbook." She plucked a truck off the floor and sauntered to the toy closet. "Speaking of lamb-chops, who's your favorite lately?"

"We're not serious enough for pet names, but Samuel's probably at the top of my list."

"When are we going to meet him?" Returning to her view of the valley, Allison ran her finger along the granite windowsill. A trail of grit appeared. Hadn't she dusted yesterday?

"Right. If I brought a man around you guys, Dad would find out and the poor sucker would face the horror of dismemberment."

Allison chortled. "Please tell me you don't talk like that around my son." Looking closer at the windowsill, she recognized the sugar from a pixie stick. Oh, Josh.

"You'll think twice before asking me to baby sit again, won't ya?"

"I know you'd never scare my baby." Brushing the candy into her palm, she walked to the kitchen and dumped it down the disposal. "The pact extends to our children as well."

"Did you get that in writing?"

"Written in my own blood," Allison said. "When you poked me with a needle."

"Oh, don't be such a wimp."

She smiled. "Well, at least I know the pact is binding. We stick up for each other. We protect each other."

"We love each other," Savannah finished. "I know the pact, but I didn't realize I'd have to keep it up for generations."

The doorbell rang.

"Oh, Savvy, can I call you back? Somebody's at the door."

"Sure, it's not like I have a life."

"Yeah, right. How many men did you have to tell no tonight?" Allison smiled, picturing her beautiful, dark-haired sister.

"Sometimes a girl needs a night off."

The doorbell rang again.

"Get your door," Savannah said.

Allison disconnected, tossing the phone onto the couch. She rushed to the front door and flung it open. A gust of fragrant, summer air flowed into the entryway. She studied the man dominating her doorstep. Her brow furrowed. *What is he doing here?*

Wesley Richins. The guy from the gym with a body like a shredded NFL quarterback and a face that could've graced the glossy pages of a magazine. Several weeks ago she'd decided to keep her distance when he crossed the boundary line from discreet glances to blatant flirtations. She was lonely enough without Ryan around. She didn't need to be near someone who flippantly disregarded her marital status.

Even if that someone was the best-looking man she'd ever seen. She couldn't stop herself from staring. His khaki shorts and white polo shirt achieved a pure contrast to his dark hair and skin. She'd thought he was perfect at the gym. Allison took a deep breath. He looked even better tonight.

"Wes? What-what's going on? Why are you here?"

"Allison." His smooth face creased with a smile. "Can I come in?"

Without waiting for an answer, he swept past her and into the foyer. "Nice house." He kept walking, poking his head into the office and formal dining room.

Allison trailed behind him, wondering what he was doing and how she would get him to leave. He shouldn't be in her house. Her husband would have a conniption fit—a justified conniption fit.

Wes sauntered into the great room, gave the decorations an appreciative nod and settled onto the leather couch. He relaxed against the brown cushions like he owned them. The large couch seemed to shrink to a loveseat. Pinching her novel between his long fingers, he studied the title with a smirk.

"Good thing I came by. Looks like you were getting bored here all by yourself."

She retrieved the book from his hand; he smoothly encircled her fingers before she could pull them away.

"I haven't seen you at the gym for a few weeks," he said.

Allison snatched her hand and the book from his grip. She set the book on a nearby sofa table. "I'm training for a marathon."

Wes's eyes trailed up and down her frame several times, studying her white T-shirt, heart-stamped pajama bottoms and everything her clothing didn't cover. She crossed her arms in front of her bosom to prevent his perusal of every part of her.

"Running's been good to you." He winked. "You look amazing."

She tried to ignore the warm rush his words gave her. "What are you doing here, Wes?"

He smiled. "Like I said, I haven't seen you for a few weeks. I've missed you."

Most red-blooded women would fling themselves at him. His dark eyes twinkled with innuendos. His white teeth gleamed against tanned skin. Her breath caught; she wasn't immune to that glance or smile.

"I think you'd better leave," she said. "My husband is playing soccer tonight. He should be home any minute."

His grin was positively wicked this time. "We both know that's a lie."

Allison backed away. She banged into an overstuffed chair. Her chest tightened. "How do you know that?"

He shrugged. "I've been watching."

"Watching what?" Her breath came in short puffs.

His lips curled as he leered. "You."

"Me?" She squeaked. Her eyes roved the room in search of the cordless phone. She should call the police. But what would she say? She'd opened the door to him. He hadn't done anything to her—yet.

Wes chuckled. He picked up the phone resting next to his thigh and held it out to her. "Looking for this?"

She rolled onto the balls of her feet, preparing for a sprint up the stairs to Josh's room. She could barricade herself in there until he went away.

He pushed the phone underneath his leg with a wink. "You can come and get it whenever you're ready."

Allison's eyes widened. She couldn't formulate an answer.

His gaze trailed over her. "Your husband flew out yesterday and if he follows his normal pattern, he won't be home until tomorrow night."

Blood drained from her face. How did he know that?

Wes smirked. "I've got you all to myself. Come over here, sweetheart. You've flirted with me enough at the gym. It's time we got to know each other better." He patted his lean thighs as some sort of invitation.

Allison backed farther away. "What do you mean I flirted with you at the gym?" Just because it was true, didn't mean she had to admit to it.

"Come on, don't play innocent. I'm sure you miss your husband and maybe you feel guilty for being attracted to me, but I think we're both adults here. Your husband will never know about me and if he finds out . . ." He shrugged sculpted shoulders. "Isn't it his fault for neglecting you?"

Allison shuddered. Ice cascaded down her neck. She forced herself to speak calmly, "You need to leave."

His brow furrowed. "I'm not going anywhere." He stood.

Allison scurried around the chair.

"You can't deny you've been flirting with me at the gym," he said. "You've been tempting me for months. One day I followed you home."

She jerked. "No."

Wes nodded. "Yes, I did. These past few weeks I've been watching you—while you were playing with your boy, going to the grocery store, running. Every day I've fallen harder for you." He licked his lips. "I need you, Allison."

The room started changing shades of gray. She grabbed the chair for support. "You've been stalking me?" Her eyes shifted, gauging the distance to the stairs.

"Stalking?" Wes rolled his eyes. "*Watching*, sweetheart. But I'm sick of watching." He held out his hand. "Won't you give me a chance?"

She shook her head. "No, Wes."

His eyes darkened blacker than her granite countertops.

"No," she repeated, trying to keep her voice level. "I would *never* cheat on my husband." She prayed he wouldn't see how scared she was. It didn't appear to matter whether she was willing or not.

His jaw clenched. He looked like a tiger ready to pounce.

Allison drew a shaky inhalation and managed a few more steps. "I need to go check on Josh. Let me walk you out."

Wes covered the distance between them, looming over her. "What if I don't want to leave?"

A shiver tingled down her whole body. "Sorry, that isn't an option." She whirled from him, speed walking toward the front entry and winding staircase.

He followed.

Allison said a silent prayer, *Please protect me. Please make him leave.*

Wes grabbed her arm before she reached the entryway and spun her to face him. "I know you want me, Allison. Let's be rational about this."

She shook her head. "My husband is all I want."

He grinned, tilting his head to the side and dissecting her with his eyes. "You just don't realize what I'm offering." In one fluid movement, he captured her in his sinewy arms.

She twisted, trying to free herself. Her heartbeat resounded in her ears. She couldn't escape. "What are you doing? Let go of me."

He bent. His lips grazed her neck. "I want you, Allison."

She shook her head. "Back off, Wes."

"Allison." Wes rested his forehead against hers. "I want you and I know you want me."

She jerked her face away. Placing both hands against his chest, she pushed with all her strength. "No. I don't. Believe me, I don't."

Wes's grip didn't slacken. He pressed her head against his chest with one hand. Holding her close, he massaged her back with his long fingers, working his way down, down.

Allison struggled to free herself. He was too strong. "Let me go, Wes."

"And let you miss all the fun?" He leaned back to glance into her face, wiggling his eyebrows. "You know you've thought of this before."

"No, I haven't. Let me go." She strained against his arms.

Wes didn't respond, just kept rubbing her back and molding his body to hers.

She squirmed, but couldn't budge. She had to try something else. Tossing a quick prayer through her head, she changed tactics. "Look, Wes. I'm flattered you would be interested, really I am, but you don't need to be wasting your time with me. I'm a Mom. You should see my stretch marks."

He chuckled. "I can't wait."

Allison gulped. "I didn't mean . . ." Oh, heaven help her, how was she going to get free? "What are you doing? I've seen the way women look at you at the gym. There are dozens of them dying for you to notice them."

He leaned close to her ear, his mint-flavored breath hot against her face. "But *you're* the one I'm interested in."

"No!" She screamed.

His eyes narrowed to dark pen slashes. He jerked her closer.

Allison freed one hand. She clawed at his face, trailing red marks down his cheek.

He yelped and clutched his cheek, releasing her. She rushed to the stairs. Her right foot connected with the first step. He grabbed her arm and twisted, pulling her onto level ground. "What's wrong with you?"

"Stop it," Allison cried out. "That hurts." She hit at his hand, pulling to free herself. "Let me go."

Wes's jaw clenched. "Calm down."

"No," she screamed.

Using her body weight as leverage, Allison strained against his grip. Wes tried to pull her in. Praying for strength, she fought. She couldn't let him wrap her up again.

An angelic cry pierced the air. Wes flinched, relaxing his hold.

"Josh!" Allison ripped her arm free and sprinted for her boy.

She took the steps two at a time. Wes pounded after her. She was one step from the top when she tripped. The wide staircase pitched and rolled.

"Allison!" Wes tugged at her hand, casting her further off balance.

Her left foot slipped off the carpeted stair. Her head banged into the wall. She screamed in pain. Her fingers jerked from Wes's grasp. He screamed her name and through the haze Joshua cried, "Mommy."

Allison tumbled down the steep stairs. Her head bounced against the banister and then the stairs. She grabbed for stability and caught air. The brown tile entry filled her vision. She slammed into the rough surface. Darkness enfolded her.

Two

Savannah flipped through *Shape*. "Redefine your thighs, ten great new moves." Ha. She tossed the magazine back on the coffee table. "Great new moves. Yet another version of lunges and squats? What's new about that?"

She jumped off the couch and walked through her small living room to the kitchen. Opening the refrigerator, she grabbed a water bottle. Why hadn't her sister called back? Who could've been at Allison's door at 9:30 at night? Some neighbor needing butter? Not likely. She hit speed dial one. Impatiently tapping her short nails on the tan and white speckled Formica, she waited for the call to go through. The busy signal screeched in her ear.

After a few sips of water, she tried again, then again. The busy signal buzzed. "I hate that sound." She slammed the phone down. "I'm going over there. Talking with Ally beats reading *Shape*."

Retrieving her purse from the counter, Savannah hurried from the condo to her Honda Accord. She sped through Logan City and into the quiet town of Hyde Park, belting out George Strait to pass the drive time. Pulling into the driveway, she glanced at the brick and stucco two-story home. Several lights were on.

Savannah parked next to the garage, leaving her purse and keys in the car. The peaceful hush of Ally's neighborhood and the scent of pine trees enveloped her. She typed in the garage code then walked through the garage and into the laundry room.

"Ally? I thought we could hang out, since we're both loners tonight."

No response.

"Ally? Allison?" She called. She entered the vaulted great room. What was that noise? She listened closer, someone or something wailed. Six strides later she identified it. Josh was screaming uncontrollably. Allison was nowhere to be seen. Something wasn't right. Savannah's legs moved faster.

"Ally? Where are you?" She ran through the great room. "Calm down, Josh," she called. "It's okay, sweetie. Aunt Savvy's here now. Allison?"

She entered the foyer. Her legs stilled. Her heart paused. Her eyes soaked in the scene, but her mind couldn't comprehend what she saw.

Darkness began to cloud her vision. Staying upright wasn't an option. Savannah sunk to her knees, her eyes riveted to the spot where blood pulsated from her sister's forehead.

"Ally!"

Savannah ripped off her T-shirt and pressed it against the head wound. The compression staunched the flow but didn't stop it. Blood seeped through the shirt. Folding it several times, she pressed her hand into the wound.

"Oh, Ally, oh, Ally," she moaned. Fear knotted inside her. The tile was painted crimson. How much blood had her sister lost? *Please, please, Ally, don't be dead.*

She leaned closer, a whisper of her sister's warm breath touched her cheek. Savannah breathed a sigh of relief. "Thank you, Lord, thank you."

She brushed matted hair from Allison's neck. Gulping past the fear, she checked for a pulse. It was there, though not as strong as it needed to be.

Mopping the red liquid away from Allison's face with the sleeve of her makeshift dressing, Savannah couldn't stop the tears racing down her cheeks. Her head spun. She was having a hard time remembering what she was supposed to do.

"Mommy, Mommy," Josh cried from his room.

Savannah could hear him rattling the bars. He couldn't escape his crib, could he? She couldn't let him see his mom like this. "I'll be right there."

"Savvy, Mommy," Josh repeated the names over and over again.

"Oh, Josh." Savannah shook her head and quickly prayed for help. Taking a long breath, she detached herself from the situation and recalled her CPR training courses. Survey victim. *Oh, help. Her only sister was the victim.* Check breathing. *This can't be happening.* Check pulse. *Not Ally. Please let her be okay.* Call 9-1-1.

She straightened. Call 9-1-1. Of course. With the amount of blood Allison had lost, she needed medical assistance—now. Savannah would call for help.

Her cell phone. Dangit. It was in her purse in the car. She gritted her teeth, searching for Ally's cordless. It wasn't in sight. She'd have to go find it.

But how could she leave her sister's side? The T-shirt compress had slowed the bleeding, but not enough. She knew Allison was in danger of bleeding to death if she didn't keep pressure on the wound. The fear for Allison's safety compounded as she listened to Josh's frantic screams in the otherwise silent house.

She felt, rather than heard, a movement. The hair on her arms stood. Was someone in the house? Her breath caught in her throat. She prayed like she'd never prayed before. Her eyes scanned the foyer, formal dining room, and office. The shadows danced. Was that breathing she could hear?

The stairs creaked. Savannah jumped; her heart thudded against her ribcage. She whirled to face the sound. No one was there. Had she imagined it? "Houses make noises," she said to herself. She swallowed a ragged breath, then held it and listened. She shook her head. It was futile to listen for an intruder, impossible to hear anything over Josh's cries.

"Josh," she called. "Aunt Savvy's here. I'll come get you in a minute."

She couldn't do this. She had to leave her sister, find a phone, and call 9-1-1. Wrapping the shirt around Allison's head, she rose to her feet and ran to the great room.

The cordless lay on the counter. Grabbing it, Savannah hurried back to the foyer, dropped to her knees and pressed her hand into the wound again. Warm blood oozed through the shirt and trickled onto her palm. She gasped and forced herself not to retract her hand.

Pushing the talk button with her free hand, she dialed 9-1-1, resting the phone in the crook of her neck. It wasn't ringing, what was wrong?

"Hello?" A voice said.

"Who is this?" Savannah demanded.

"This is 9-1-1 emergency. Who is this?'

"Oh, thank you. I didn't think the call went through. My sister's hurt. She's hurt bad. Can you send somebody?"

"An officer is already on his way. He should be there any minute. Can you tell me the extent of her injuries?"

"She's got a head wound and she's lost a lot of blood, but she's breathing on her own. Her pulse is weak but steady."

"Okay. Ma'am. Your name?"

"Savannah Compton."

"I want you to stay on the line. I'm going to dispatch an ambulance and update the officer who is en route."

"Okay," Savannah whispered, holding the phone with one hand and her sister's head with the other.

"Savvy, Savvy! Mommy, Mommy!"

"I'll be right there, Josh. I promise." His pleas tore at her heart. "It'll be okay, Josh."

She wanted to cry. She didn't know if it would ever be okay again. She pushed the saturated T-shirt into the wound, her hand sticky with her sister's blood. *Please let Ally be okay.*

The door five feet away shuddered with a violent pounding. *Oh, thank you, Lord.* Someone had come to help. She gripped the phone and leapt to her feet.

Rushing to the door, Savannah jerked it open. She gawked at the sight of a broad-shouldered, well-dressed man filling the entryway. She backed away slowly. The lady had said an officer was coming, but this was no policeman. Was this the man who had injured her sister? Had he come back to finish the job?

The man smiled gently, flipping open a badge and displaying it for her: *Detective Noah Shumway. Investigator. Cache County Sheriff's Office.* The air returned to her lungs.

"Did you need some help, ma'am?"

Savannah nodded. "Oh, thank you. You're the officer she said was coming. Is the ambulance on its way?"

She rushed back to her sister, letting him trail behind. Kneeling again, she pressed the T-shirt into Allison's head and glanced up at him.

His cell phone rang. He opened it, towering over Savannah.

"I'm at the house. Ten minutes? Tell them to hurry. I haven't had a chance to check her, but she's unconscious and there's a lot of blood." He paused. "Possibility of a spinal injury?" He glanced at Allison. "Definitely."

He nodded. "We won't move her until they bring the backboard."

He hung up the phone and bent down, taking the cordless Savannah clutched in her left hand. "That was the dispatcher. The ambulance is on its way. We can hang this up and I'll get the rest of the info they need from you later." Pressing the end button on the phone, he set it on the entry table and glanced at Savannah. "How long has she been unconscious?"

"I don't know," she said. "I found her like this."

He knelt beside her and began checking Allison's vitals.

"I've already done that," Savannah snapped. "Her heartbeat's weak but steady. She's breathing on her own. I don't know how long she's been unconscious, but the head wound appears to be the only serious injury. She needs an ambulance."

The detective stared at her.

"She needs an ambulance right now!" Savannah screamed.

He arched an eyebrow. "I understand that ma'am, and they're moving as fast as they can. There was a bad wreck out on the highway. The patrol deputies and first responders are all there. The dispatcher said they'll send an ambulance from Logan." He shook his head. "It could be ten or fifteen minutes before they get here."

Savannah's eyes widened. Her stomach clenched. "She could bleed to death."

He took a deep breath. "No." He checked Allison again. "You've got the bleeding under control and she's breathing on her own. She'll be okay until help comes."

She glared at him. Was he trying to convince her or himself? She gestured to the floor. "Look at how much blood she's lost. She is not okay!"

"All we can do is wait." He paused, frowning at Allison's still form. "What happened?" His gaze lifted from Allison and trailed over Savannah's spaghetti-strapped undershirt.

Her eyes narrowed. Her sister was hurt, and he was checking out her tank top? "I'm up here detective."

His head snapped. He blushed. "What happened?" he asked again, his sapphire gaze soft with compassion.

Savannah tossed her long hair. She glanced at her sister and tightened her grip on the saturated T-shirt. Allison's dark hair was caked with blood, her sparkling eyes closed, her full lips soft. Tears stung Savannah's eyelids. Her sister was really hurt. Her Ally. Would Allison make it through this?

"I don't know," she whispered. "She was supposed to call me back and she didn't. Her phone was off the hook forever, so I came over here. I found her like this. I don't know if she fell or if someone hurt her."

The large man nodded. "All right. Why would you think someone hurt her?"

"Because . . ."

"Mommy!"

"Oh, Josh. I'm sorry, baby." She grabbed the officer's hand. "Hold this. We need to keep the pressure on it."

His large hand covered the blood-soaked shirt. Savannah noticed the warmth of his fingers against her own. She looked into his clear, blue eyes. He met her gaze, nodding. She was comforted for the first time tonight. This man would take care of her sister until she returned. She ripped her hand away, forcing herself to leave Allison in the policeman's care so she could comfort her nephew.

Detective Noah Shumway watched the young woman go. He exhaled as her shapely form disappeared into a door at the top of the stairs. She was almost too thin, but still extremely attractive. He pulled his concentration back to the woman on the floor. Through the blood he could see the same oval face, dark complexion and naturally pink lips. Twins?

He wished the ambulance would arrive. When he'd heard the request for help over the radio he'd responded because he was only a few blocks from the scene, but he was an investigator, not a first responder. He didn't deal with bloody, unresponsive women until after the EMT's had come.

The sister emerged at the top of the stairs with a toddler in her arms. She buried his face into her firm shoulder to keep him from seeing his mother. The young boy sniffled, gulped for air, then cried out again.

"I've got to take care of Josh," the dark-haired beauty said. "Is Ally doing okay?"

"I'll take care of her," Noah said. "The ambulance shouldn't be much longer."

The little boy looked to be about two with a full head of dark hair. He tried to squirm from his aunt's arms. "Mommy, I want Mommy," he sobbed between sniffles.

"Shh, it's okay, love. Aunt Savvy has you. We'll find Mommy in a minute."

Her name was Savvy? Noah watched her cradle the small boy and rock him back and forth. She kept his face planted into her bare shoulder so he couldn't get a glimpse of his mom. After a few minutes Savvy turned and entered the bedroom door, reappearing without the boy.

She pounded down the steps, knelt beside her sister, and felt for a pulse. "It's still there," she said.

"She's doing okay." Noah turned to face her, ignoring the scent of her fresh-smelling hair. "Savvy?"

"Savannah." She met his eyes with a cool gaze. "Only my family calls me Savvy."

Noah pressed his lips together. She was intent on keeping her distance. "*Savannah*. You think someone hurt your sister?"

Her head bobbed up and down, then side to side. "I think . . . maybe. I guess she could've fallen." She stared at her sister. "But it doesn't make sense." Her dark eyes rose to search his face. When she spoke it was a whisper, "I almost felt like someone was in the house when I got here, or maybe they had just left. You know how you can sense or smell something different?" She shrugged. "I could be imagining it. I was pretty messed up when I saw her."

Noah took her hand, placing it on Allison's head. He stood. "Stay here."

He checked each room of the house. Finding nothing amiss, he returned to Savannah's side. "I didn't find anything."

She nodded. "They must've already left."

Noah studied her, wondering about the validity of her story. If she'd called 9-1-1, why hadn't she spoken at first? What wasn't she telling him? "Maybe," he said. "Is there someone you can call to stay with the little boy? I'm assuming you'll want to go with your sister to the hospital."

"Oh." Her brow wrinkled. "I can call her friend, Amy, from next door."

She left Allison in his care and moments later he heard her talking into the phone to what he assumed was a neighbor, but then he heard her redial. Her voice caught as she said, "Daddy." Noah tried not to listen to the conversation, but her overwrought voice and sniffles tugged at him.

Sirens wailed in their direction. Noah caught a full breath. Savannah reentered the foyer as the neighbor, the EMT's, and several other officers arrived.

Noah gratefully turned Allison's care over to them. He walked to his truck, but instead of driving home he decided to follow the ambulance and Savannah to the hospital. He kept telling himself it was out of concern for her sister and because he needed a statement, but part of him knew—he wanted a chance to see her again.

Savannah made tracks in the waiting area adjacent to the emergency room, pleading silently for help. The beige walls closed in. Nibbling off every fingernail she possessed, Savannah focused her stare on the receptionist, hoping the woman would have some news for her. The surly blonde ignored her, popping her gum and scouring *People* magazine.

An infant screeched in his mother's arms. The young mom tried to comfort him with his pacifier while her two-year old jockeyed for position on her lap. The baby's cries tore at Savannah. She started toward them, but stopped at a familiar voice, "Where's your shirt, young lady?"

"Oh, Daddy." Savannah turned to her tall, lean father, ignoring the reprimand. She took two steps and crumpled into his arms. Words tumbled out, "Allison's hurt, and I don't know how it happened. She's been unconscious for too long, they think it's a coma. It's my fault. I shouldn't have told her to answer the door and . . ." A sob worked its way up her throat and cut off her rambling.

"Okay, sweetie." Frank patted her back like a small child. "Everything's going to be okay. I've just talked with the doctor. Ally's going to come out of the coma soon."

Savannah wondered if he believed what he said. His angular face was normally as dark as hers, now his skin was the color of sand on a sun-drenched beach.

"You talked to the doctor?" she growled. "I've been waiting forever and they haven't told me a dang thing."

Her dad smiled grimly, holding up his phone. "They called. I'm listed as her emergency contact. I met with the doctor in his office before I came to find you."

"Oh. So, he was encouraging?"

Frank shrugged. Instead of answering her question, he settled Savannah into a chair. "I need you to calm down and tell me everything that happened."

She took his offered handkerchief, wiped her eyes, and related the events of the night. Her father's arm around her shoulder and the smell of his familiar handkerchief calmed her.

She relished the warmth of home until she sensed someone studying her. Her back stiffened. Any man who had the gall to check her out right now would get a piece of her mind. She glanced up to see the huge cop from Allison's house. Her shoulders relaxed. He offered her half a smile. Maybe she wouldn't tell him off.

Her father followed the direction of her gaze. He stood. "Yes? Can we help you?"

"Sir."

Savannah rose, leaning into her dad. For the first time that night, she appreciated every visible part of the detective. His white dress shirt was stretched thin over his wide shoulders. His sandy-blond hair was cut short. His startling blue eyes studied her with an unsettling penetration. His large form towered over her 5'5" frame. His face had the rugged appeal of someone who worked hard out of doors and never wore sunscreen. He wasn't eye candy like a lot of the men she dated, but he was definitely worth looking at a few more times.

He extended his hand. Her dad shook it.

"I'm Detective Shumway with the Investigative Department of the Cache County Sheriff's office."

Her dad nodded. "Frank Compton."

"I realize this is a hard time, but I need to ask your daughter a few questions."

Frank eyed Savannah. "Are you up to answering questions right now, sweetheart?"

Detective Shumway winced, frowning. "I'm sorry, I could come back later. Savannah just mentioned that she thought someone was in the house and if that's the case we want to start investigating."

Savannah spoke to her father, but focused on the detective. "I'm okay. I can answer his questions."

Her dad nodded his encouragement. His cell phone rang. He pulled it from his pocket, glancing at the display screen. "It's Ryan."

"Go talk to him. I'll be fine," Savannah said.

Frank squeezed her hand, nodded at the investigator, and walked outside to answer his phone.

Detective Shumway gestured toward the gray chairs. Savannah perched on the edge of the seat, wishing she were anywhere but here.

He didn't recline into the chair, but leaned forward resting his elbows on his thighs. "Are you doing okay, Savannah?" His blue eyes studied her.

Savannah blew all her air out. She shook her head in response to his question.

The detective raised an eyebrow. He fiddled with the small notebook that looked miniscule in his large fingers. "I'm sorry. I can't imagine how hard this must be."

"I'm sure you can't." She shouldn't have been so sharp, but her reaction to his hulking form was not appropriate when her sweet sister would possibly never wake again.

He nodded, his expression solemn. "I understand. I'll make this quick."

Savannah looked away from his azure gaze. "Thank you."

He flipped open his notebook. "Can you please tell me what happened tonight?"

She resisted the urge to rip off another nail with her teeth. She rested her hands in her lap, rotating her thumbs around each other. "I wish I knew. I was on the phone with Ally. She said someone was at the door and she'd call me back. I waited a few minutes and then I tried to call her. It was busy. I kept trying, but it was still busy. I didn't have anything better to do so I thought I'd go to her house and hang out."

"What time did the phone call and your arrival at the house occur?" He scribbled in the notebook, not looking at her.

"I hung up with her about nine-thirty and I didn't get to her house until ten."

His eyes locked on hers. "Ten?"

"Yes."

His eyebrows lowered. He tapped the pen on his paper. "You're sure about that time?"

Savannah drilled her fingers against her forearm. "I have a clock in my car. It glows green at night."

The detective pursed his lips, writing something. "Okay. What happened when you arrived at the house?"

"I came in through the garage because she usually has the front door locked at night. I couldn't figure out . . ."

"Wait." He held up a large hand, raising his eyes from the paper again. "She always locks the front door at night?'

"When Ryan's gone."

"Her husband?"

She nodded. "He's a car buyer for a wholesaler out of Salt Lake. He's gone a few days a week and she doesn't like being alone at night."

The detective rested his fingers on his chin, rubbing his jaw with his thumb. "Hmm . . . Okay."

Savannah waited. There was something he wasn't saying. "What?"

He rotated his head from side to side. Several seconds trickled by before he answered. "I didn't see any signs of a forced entry. If someone did hurt her, it was someone she knew. Someone she would've opened the door to."

Savannah digested the information, clenching her hands together. "Sorry I interrupted. You came in through the garage?"

She shivered and wrapped her arms around her stomach. "I came in calling for her. I couldn't figure out where she was, but then I heard Josh crying. Actually, he was screaming out of control and that scared me because Ally would never let him cry like that."

She swayed back and forth as if she were rocking Josh again. "So I headed for the stairs, that's when I saw Ally . . ."

The tears came again. The thought of her sister lying on the tile covered with blood overwhelmed her. Savannah shook her head, squeezing the wetness from her eyelids. "I'm sorry."

He wrapped his huge fingers around her clasped hands, giving her hands a brief squeeze. "It's fine. Take all the time you need."

Savannah studied the contrast of their entwined hands. His rough, broad fingers encompassed her small, tanned ones. She cleared her throat. He removed his hand and glanced at the notebook. She wiped the tears from her face. He waited.

"When I saw Ally." She swallowed against the thickness in her throat. "I took my shirt off and used it as a compress."

"That was your shirt?"

She arched an eyebrow. "Yes. I don't usually go around dressed like . . ." She flushed with embarrassment.

He lowered his head and focused on writing something. Savannah wondered what he could be scribbling about her shirt. She continued, "Then I checked her vitals and ran to call 9-1-1, but they were already on the phone."

His head jerked up. "You didn't call 9-1-1?"

"No."

The detective watched her for several, long moments. She shifted on the uncomfortable chair. Her honesty was on trial.

After a few seconds he pursed his lips. "Would you excuse me, Savannah?"

"Sure."

She watched him walk away, glad to be free of his questions for a minute. It reminded her of the time she got in trouble in high school—the policeman, the guidance counselor, the judge, even her dad—everybody questioning her and blaming her. She shook her head, pushing the memories away.

Her dad appeared in the doorway. The detective squeezed past him with a brief nod. Detective Shumway was a serious dude. Probably exactly the kind of person she should want investigating how her sister got hurt, but not someone who would be any good in a relationship. She shook her head, wondering why she cared. He probably had a pretty, young wife at home and three or four well-behaved children.

Savannah's thoughts returned to her sister's plight: unconscious, serious head trauma, too much blood lost. The doctor said her vital signs were good, but she still hadn't woken. What was going to happen to her Ally? How was Ryan taking the news? Had Josh stayed asleep or was he even now crying for his mom?

Savannah shuddered. Allison had to be okay. This couldn't happen to them again.

Her dad settled into the chair next to her, reaching an arm around her.

"How's Ry?" she asked.

Frank clucked his tongue. "Not good. He's hurrying to the airport. He'll try and find a flight home tonight. You know how he is. I hope he doesn't commandeer an airplane to get here."

Savannah almost smiled at the image. Ryan was a great guy, but very much in control. Not being here to care for his wife and comfort his son would drive him nuts.

She leaned against her dad's shoulder. They waited in silence for more news from the doctor.

Detective Shumway returned fifteen minutes later, his face grim. He settled onto a chair next to Savannah. "I've been checking on some things. They aren't adding up."

Savannah's eyes widened. "You think somebody hurt Ally?"

He didn't answer her directly. "Someone dialed 9-1-1 at 9:46, but the dispatcher said no one ever spoke. The dispatcher waited so they could do a call back and make sure everything was okay, but the line never disconnected. She called for a drive-by, but thought the call was a prank." He paused, staring at her. "That is until you started talking."

Savannah returned his gaze. The detective searched the thoughts she didn't reveal to anyone. She wanted to squirm. She didn't look away.

"Are you sure you didn't arrive until ten?" he asked.

Savannah straightened. "Yes. Besides, I wouldn't have called 9-1-1 and not said anything. That's idiotic. I would've told them to get help."

The detective knuckled his pen and notebook. His lips pressed thin. "Allison dialing the number and leaving the phone on the counter doesn't seem like a possibility."

Her head bobbed twice. "No way."

Frank had been silent throughout the exchange, but obviously couldn't hold his questions any longer. "Are you saying that someone did this to Allison?"

Detective Shumway shook his head. "I won't know anything concrete until they dust for fingerprints and check for a forced entry, but it looks like there could've been foul play."

Savannah looked at her dad. His jaw hardened. Fury radiated from his eyes. Whoever hurt Ally better be running—fast and far.

"What can we do?" Frank asked.

The detective lifted one palm. "I'm sorry, but at the moment the best thing you can do is wait. The neighbor has taken Josh to her house. She told one of my officers she would keep him as long as you need."

Savannah nodded. "That's nice of Amy."

The doctor entered the room. Savannah rose to her feet, standing next to her dad. The detective stood beside her. With her dad on one side and this strong police officer on the other, she felt incredibly safe.

"I'm sorry," the doctor began.

Her breath caught in her throat. Her heart ceased pounding. *Sorry? Was Allison . . . ? Oh, please help me, Lord, I can't make it without Ally.*

"She's in a coma," the slight man continued.

The air whooshed from Savannah's lungs. She caught her dad's hand and pressed hard. He squeezed back, but didn't glance at her.

"Her vital signs are good, but she's sustained a contusion to her brain and we won't know the extent of the damage or how long she may remain unconscious until the pressure alleviates. We've given her blood to replace what she lost and medicine to reduce the swelling. We're monitoring her brain activity, but there's not much else we can do right now."

"The brain activity is good?" Frank asked.

The doctor's lips compressed. "As good as can be expected."

"Do you know when she'll wake up?"

"I'm sorry." He lifted one hand, palm up. "We'll keep you informed, but all we can do right now is wait."

Her dad looked like he wanted to demand they do more, but he finally nodded. "Thank you Dr. McQuivey. We'll be waiting right here. Please let us know if anything changes."

"We'll move her into ICU within the hour. If you want to stay you'd probably be more comfortable in that waiting area. It's more private." He gripped Allison's file against his chest. "But I would strongly suggest you go home and get some rest."

Savannah swayed. "Go home?"

"We can't leave her," Frank said.

The detective moved his hand to Savannah's elbow, steadying her. She glanced up at him, grateful for his silent support.

Dr. McQuivey cleared his throat. "In cases like this it could be days or weeks before we see any change. The best thing you can do is give us your cell and home phone numbers, then go home and rest. You'll be no help to her if you're exhausted. Sleeping in a hospital waiting room is not a good experience for anyone."

The pressure of her dad's fingers increased on her hand. Savannah glanced over at him. Frank's eyebrows formed a V on his forehead.

The doctor jerked his chin down. "I understand you don't want to leave her, but please listen to me and get a few hours of sleep. If there's any change or she wakes up we'll call you immediately."

Her dad didn't say anything, but the lines around his mouth deepened.

"Can we at least see her?" Savannah asked.

The doctor frowned. "Well, maybe for a few minutes. This way." He turned on his heel and strode away.

Frank followed him, dragging her along.

Savannah rushed to keep up. She glanced back at the detective. He raced after them, extending his card. "Call anytime. I'll let you know if I've found anything."

She offered a weak smile, reaching for the card. "Thank you, Detective."

They burst through the double doors. Savannah looked over her shoulder for one last glimpse. He lifted a hand in farewell.

Three

They flew through the busy emergency room and down a short hall. Savannah raced to match Dr. McQuivey's pace. The doctor reached a curtain and pulled it aside, gesturing for them to move into the room. Savannah's feet froze, unable to walk through the portal. Her sister lay there as though her spirit was already gone. An oxygen tube invaded her nose, and several IV's protruded from her arms. The sterile area was uncomfortable and cold, silent except for the beeping of monitors and the whisper of nurse's feet rushing to help the most recent victims.

Savannah shivered, catapulted into a memory she had tried to forget. Allison looked exactly like Mom had looked . . . Savannah shook off the thought and tiptoed past the curtain. Touching Allison's hand, she recoiled in shock. It was freezing. She gulped for oxygen, but couldn't get enough. Oh, Ally. How could this happen to her sister? Her trembling fingers reached for her sister's hand again. This time she held on, the skin cooling her fingertips.

She looked at her dad, expecting him to say or do something. His eyes were locked on Allison's face. He teetered. His lips flapped open but nothing came out. He'd been so strong and assured earlier, but this was the first time he'd seen Ally. Were memories of Mom assaulting him too?

Savannah glanced at her sister's pale face, rubbing her fingers across the lifeless hand. "Ally? It's Savvy. I'm here. Everything's going to be . . ." She gulped and lied. "Everything's going to be okay. Ryan's on his way and we'll take care of Josh. You just get better, 'kay?"

Although it was heartbreaking talking to her sister, knowing there

24

would be no response, Savannah plunged on, "I love you, Ally. Daddy's here with me. Everything's going to be all right."

Savannah noticed through her tears that her dad had broken his trance. His head bobbed with every phrase she uttered. He gently touched Allison's cheek with his forefinger.

"That's right, love," he said. "You'll be okay. We're all praying for you. I love you . . ." His voice broke and Frank could say no more.

They sat in silence for several minutes, gazing at the once vibrant form. Savannah alternated between pleading with the Lord for her sister's safe return and the questions that popped into her head. When would Allison open her sparkling black eyes and tease Savannah again? Or give her little boy piggyback rides? Or kiss her husband? Or snuggle next to her daddy on the couch? The answers might never come. Savannah pressed her fist against her mouth, but couldn't withhold the sob that tore from her throat.

Her dad glanced at her. He didn't offer any comfort.

"I'm sorry, but we really need to prep her for her move to the ICU," the doctor said from behind them.

Savannah swiped at her eyes. The tears didn't abate. "Okay, um, we'll see you soon, Ally." Her voice caught. "Love ya," she whispered.

Frank nodded his agreement of Savannah's words, unable to say anything. He wrapped his arm around Savannah's shoulder and they left the room with several backward glances.

Fifteen minutes later, after running by Savannah's apartment to retrieve clothes for the next few days, they arrived at Allison's house. Savannah's depression deepened. The eerie red and blue cast from several police cars gave the whole situation an unreal feeling. Her dad wanted to hold Josh. Savannah walked through Allison's front door by herself while Frank plodded across the front lawn.

Savannah returned the stares of several police officers. The entryway smelled of men, blood, and metal. Another volley of tears fought to break through her eyelids. Allison's house always smelled like Mr. Clean and Downey. Savannah sniffed, barely holding the tears back. Allison was no longer here to create that smell.

"Excuse me, ma'am," a young deputy said, "but this is a crime scene, I'm going to have to ask you to leave."

Detective Shumway appeared, assuming command of her field of vision and the entire entryway. "Leave her alone, Sharks. This is her sister's house."

Warmth washed over Savannah like a flannel blanket fresh from the dryer.

"Excuse me, detective." The young man averted his eyes. "Sorry, lady," he mumbled.

"Just keep your eyes on the evidence, Sharks."

A swarthy, compact man strutted toward them. He smiled at Savannah and extended a hand. "Jason Keller, ma'am." He inclined his head toward Detective Shumway. "I'm his friend, sometimes."

Savannah shook the warm hand. "He looks like he'd be a lot of work to be friends with." She grinned at the detective to show him she was teasing.

Jason hooted. He winked at her, and turned to Detective Shumway. "Looks like you get the fun duty this time."

Savannah would've been offended, but there was nothing threatening about the smiling officer.

Detective Shumway shook his head. "I'll talk to you in a minute, Keller."

Jason winked at Savannah. "I'd rather talk to her." His smile disappeared as if he'd just remembered why they were there. "I'm sorry about your sister."

Tears threatened, guilt rushed in. She shouldn't be laughing. "Thank you."

Turning from his sympathetic gaze, Savannah glanced up at Detective Shumway. He smiled down at her. Taking her by the elbow, he led her down the stairs to the basement family room, a sanctuary without the intrusive smells and sounds of the policemen. The room was cavernous with only a couch, Lazy Boy, and a big screen TV to fill the space.

Savannah cast the detective a tired smile. She appreciated both his comforting touch and the reprieve from the stares.

After they'd settled onto the tan couch, he turned to study her. "How are you?"

The simple question brought unwanted tears. Savannah tossed her head, blinking back the sign of her weakness. "I've been better."

He nodded his understanding.

"What have you found out?" Savannah sniffed, touching the tip of her nose with the back of her hand. "Was there an intruder or not?"

Her father appeared on the stairs, cradling the sleeping Joshua in his arms. The toddler's dark head lolled forward. His soft cheek squished against his grandpa's cotton shirt. Savannah's heart ached at the sight. The poor little baby. What if his mom didn't make it? The woman in danger was not only his mom but her sister and best friend.

Frank closed the recliner and began rocking gently. He glanced at the tears staining Savannah's cheeks, blinked, and looked away. Savannah dried her eyes. Usually her dad would have comforted her, but she knew he was close to breaking and her tears weren't helping.

"What have you discovered?" he asked the detective.

The detective's lips pressed together. "We can't find any matches to the fingerprints in the house."

"Which means?" Frank asked.

Detective Shumway shrugged. "Nothing, really. The people who have left fingerprints in this house have never committed a crime or been fingerprinted through a government organization. Basically, anyone who has been here is not in any of the databases we can legally search."

"What about the ones you can illegally search?" Savannah asked.

He gave her a gentle smile. "I'm sorry, but this isn't a TV cop show. We can't illegally search any databases."

Savannah frowned. "Did you check if one of the neighbors was here?"

"We've checked the close neighbors. Most were home in bed."

"They could be lying," Savannah said.

The detective looked at her with narrowed eyes. "It's possible, we'll keep checking into it in the morning. Also, if the two of you and her husband could make us a list of anyone that held a grudge against Allison or might have been here and had any reason to hurt her."

Savannah shook her head. "You don't know her. Nobody would hold a grudge against Allison. She's the nicest person you'll ever meet." *Allison is the nice one, maybe her little sister should try and be more like her.* How many times had she heard that phrase? If anyone deserved to be hurt, it was Savannah, not Allison. She blinked. Detective Shumway was studying her.

"Well, you never know," he said. "Think about it."

"Okay," Frank said. "We'll talk to Ryan as well."

The detective glanced at Savannah again. "You're positive your sister heard someone knock on her door at nine-thirty and you didn't place the 9-1-1 call?"

Savannah closed her eyes for a second. She opened them to glare at the detective. "I'm positive."

He shifted away from her. "I have to make sure everything is accurate."

She nodded, turning her gaze to the wall. Her eyes settled on a framed picture of Ryan, Allison, and Josh on the beach. Ryan was buried in the sand; Allison and Josh knelt next to him, grinning. Savannah blew out a long breath. "I understand."

Josh squirmed in his grandpa's arms.

"I'd better go lay this guy down," Frank said. "You okay for a second, love?"

"I'm fine, Daddy," Savannah lied. She watched as he ascended the stairs and then turned her attention back to the strong man seated next to her. "So, Detective . . ."

"You can call me Noah." He looked away after making the request.

Savannah raised an eyebrow. "Noah, after the prophet?"

A half-smile lifted his lips. "Yep."

"Okay, *Noah*, what happens now? Is this being treated as a criminal case or a simple accident?"

His massive shoulders elevated, then drooped. "I don't know what to tell you, most of the evidence points to an accident. The only inconsistencies are the 9-1-1 call and the fact that you say your sister had someone at her door previous to the accident."

"I say?" She glared at him. "Wait, are you checking into me too?"

Noah studied the pictures on the opposite wall.

Her stomach tumbled. She clenched her ragged fingernails into her palm. "So, you aren't going to look for the person who hurt Ally?"

His gaze swung to connect with hers. "I'll do everything in my power to solve this case, hopefully Allison will wake up soon and be able to help us with the mystery."

The reference to Allison brought back all the fear and sorrow of seeing her sister lying on the tile floor covered in blood, then unmoving and cold, swallowed up in the stiff hospital bed. Savannah's shoulders trembled and the tears she'd been holding in ran down to her chin.

"Hey," Noah said. "Don't cry."

He placed an arm around her shoulder and drew her against his side. Savannah didn't know this man. She didn't care. She turned her face into his chest and sobbed. He gently stroked her hair. He didn't say anything. She appreciated his silence as much as his strong arms. Moments later, she heard her father clear his throat.

"Savvy, you okay?"

Savannah jumped. She extracted herself from Noah's embrace, too embarrassed to look at his face. She hurried to her dad's side, placing a kiss on his cheek. What must he be thinking, catching her hugging a near stranger? Her dad didn't say anything—didn't reveal to the detective his worries about Savannah's lack of discernment with men.

"I'm fine." She glanced at Noah. "Excuse me, please."

He nodded, his blue eyes filled with understanding.

She fled up the stairs, leaving her dad and the detective to discuss Allison's case or lack thereof.

Wes sat in his darkened apartment. He'd driven straight home, drank several wine coolers, and hadn't moved since. What had he done? He couldn't remove the image of Allison broken and bloodied on the tile floor.

He'd called the hospital. The nurse said Allison was in a coma. That was bad, but in a way it was good. At least she wasn't telling the police who had hurt her. He sniffed, wringing his hands together. He couldn't let his dad find out what he'd done. It was an election year—a big one—his dad was a candidate for governor.

Wes tossed his head. He couldn't sit here, hoping Allison wouldn't remember him when she woke up. He had to do something, had to protect himself. He shoved her beautiful face from his mind and picked up the phone. He'd call Charlie. His pharmacist friend should be able to help. Wes's face broke into a smile. Everything was going to be fine. Charlie would think of a way to make sure Allison forgot about Wes being in her house—something permanent.

Ryan Mendez glowered at the perky blonde standing behind the Delta Airlines counter. "So let me get this straight," he said. "You're telling me I won't be able to fly out of Phoenix until tomorrow morning?"

"Actually this morning." Her annoying perma-grin broadened.

Ryan leaned across the desk. "I realize it's already morning. I want to leave *now*!"

She typed with a flurry of exaggerated hand movements.

He knew she wasn't looking up anything new, just avoiding his gaze.

"I'm sorry, sir. Like I've already told you the earliest flight I have leaves at 5:13 AM"

He shook his head in disgust. "There aren't any other airlines open that I can check with?"

She raised a painted-on eyebrow, pursing unnaturally red lips. "No, sir."

Ryan pounded a fist on the counter. The woman jumped. Her styled hair didn't even bounce.

"I'm sorry," he muttered. "I really need to get home."

Her head pumped up and down. "I apologize for the wait, sir." She pointed at the digital clock behind her. "The flight leaves in less than four hours."

Ryan scowled. She was right, but it didn't make him feel any better. Four more hours of waiting and pacing. Four more hours of not seeing Allison. *What if something happened to his wife? How could he survive?* His vision blurred.

"Sir," the woman interrupted his fears. "Are you interested in booking a seat on that flight?"

Ryan tried to focus on the bottled-blonde in front of him. "What about a chartered flight?"

She harrumphed, rolling her eyes. "We are a commercial airline. We don't offer chartered flights."

"Do you know someone who *does*?" Ryan asked through a slit in his mouth. He clenched and unclenched his fist, wanting to pound on the counter again.

"Sir. I can see that you really need to get to Utah, but let me explain something to you."

Ryan didn't respond, just watched her tinted mouth through narrowed eyes.

"Even if you could find someone," she paused, glancing pointedly at the clock on the wall, "at 1 AM, who would be willing to fly you to Utah, you would have to catch a cab to another airport. The pilot would have to meet you there. They would have to ready their plane, file a flight plan, and so on. All these things take time and lots and lots of money."

Ryan folded his lean arms across his chest. The money wasn't an issue. Nothing could have been less of an issue in his quest to be with his wife.

"Then if by some miracle you were able to get airborne *before* our scheduled departure time of 5:13, you have to realize that the 747 you would be flying on with our airline will travel much faster than a chartered jet."

He inhaled then slowly blew out all his breath. "You're telling me the fastest way to get home is to wait for your stinking flight."

The woman nodded. She'd lost her smile and now eyed him with a mixture of contempt and uncertainty. Ryan knew she'd be more helpful if he told her why he needed to get home, but he wouldn't volunteer personal information to strangers.

He plunked his credit card down on the counter. She slid it toward her with the tip of a perfectly manicured red fingernail. Fingers and cheap jewelry flew over the keyboard, resulting in the following pronouncement, "The total is $819, sir."

Ryan shook his head. More than triple the cost of the round-trip ticket he purchased to come to Phoenix. He didn't say a thing, just signed his name on the receipt and moved aside for the weary customer behind him.

He trudged through security and down the terminal to the waiting area for his flight. Carrying his bag to a seat, he paced back and forth in front of it. He stared out the bank of windows without seeing the lights of the planes outside. Questions plagued him. Would Allison recover? Who had hurt her? Why? He sighed. There were no answers.

Pulling his cell phone from his pocket, he scrolled down to Frank's number. He glanced at the time and pocketed his phone. His father-in-law had said they would reach him if anything changed. Frank, Savvy, and Josh were probably trying to get some much-needed rest. Ryan jammed a hand through his black hair. Oh, man. His little Josh. His cute, funny wrestling buddy. Frank said Josh was sleeping through it all. It was the only good news he'd had so far.

Ryan clenched and unclenched his fists. He needed to be there. He hated this—couldn't stand thinking about Ally, unconscious, hurt. His legs stopped pacing. He tried to swallow and couldn't. His Ally. He could picture her dark eyes, her full lips turning up as he teased her. Could she really be lying in a hospital bed, eyes closed, lips not smiling?

Ryan sank onto a hard plastic chair. He braced his arms on his legs, burying his face in his palms. Closing his eyes, he prayed. He didn't stop until they called for his flight.

Unsettling dreams filled Savannah's night and a worse reality presented itself when sleep fled. Her cell-phone buzzed at 5:30 AM. She called the hospital, but the ICU nurse said nothing had changed. Dragging herself from bed, she slipped into a comfortable T-shirt and shorts and put her long hair up in a ponytail.

Arriving at the gym ten minutes later, her scattered brain waves couldn't coordinate an aerobics routine. Why hadn't she thought of getting a sub when they were waiting at the hospital last night? Now it was too late.

The class dragged. Frustrated mutters were discernible as the thirty early-risers trickled from the aerobics room. The smell of sweaty bodies dissipated. Savannah reinserted the CD's into their cases. The aerobics room door opened and shut. She didn't turn around. She could hear Shawn fidgeting behind her.

"Savannah, do you have time for an extra client this morning?"

She groaned. "I don't have time for any clients this morning. I just want to go back to bed." She pivoted to face her wiry boss. He was forever trying to bulk up with little success.

Shawn nodded his spiked, white-blond head. "Don't we all? Seriously, is your schedule full today?"

She shook her head. "No, but my sister was hurt last night. I was hoping to clear my schedule for a few days and take care of her little boy. I need to be there when he wakes up." She scowled. "I need to be there when she wakes up."

He elevated an eyebrow. "Wakes up? Whoa. That sounds serious."

Savannah closed and locked the music cabinet. "It is serious."

"I'm sorry about your sister, but will you please spare me an hour?"

She glared at him. "Give me a break, Shawn. I never ask for time off. This is my family. I've got to be there for them."

He gritted his teeth. His gaze slid to the hand weights stacked haphazardly in the corner. "I understand."

"Thanks." She hefted her bag and stood to leave.

Shawn's hand on her arm stopped her. "Listen for a second. If you'll give me an hour I'll clear your aerobics schedule and train your clients myself."

She came face to face with him. "Why?"

His pale eyes gleamed. "There's a dude downstairs who says he wants a trainer, but it has to be you."

Savannah blinked. "Who is it?"

He shook his head, the spikes stayed firm. "I don't know. I think his last name is Richins. I can't remember his first name, but Savannah this guy is begging for you. Seriously. He said he'll pay three hundred an hour."

She straightened. "Even for the initial evaluation?"

Shawn rubbed his hands together. His eyes shone. "Yes."

"What? Why would he pay four times what we normally charge?"

"I don't know."

She glared at him.

"Sorry. You know I think you're a great trainer, but this guy already looks fit. Really fit. He came in asking for you and said he would pay whatever he needed to get you. I guess he's been a member since we opened and one of the front desk girls said his family owns most of the valley." Shawn begged her with his watery eyes. "Please, one hour. Your nephew probably isn't even awake yet."

She glanced at her watch. She could be done by eight. Josh would still be asleep. Sadly, so would Josh's mom. Savannah shook her head. "Okay, one hour, but I get 80 percent instead of 60 and you're clearing my schedule for a week."

Shawn nodded. "Done. I'll clear your schedule of everyone but him for the next week."

Her mouth dropped open. "I just told you I need to be with my family."

"Come on, Savannah, three hundred an hour? You can make it in a few times this week for that kind of money."

She closed her eyes, knowing she could use the money. "Okay, but everything else is cleared until next Wednesday."

Shawn grabbed her elbow. "You got it. Come downstairs, I'll introduce you."

Leaning against the receptionist desk was a face and body that reeked of an unlimited expense account, long days in the gym and longer days by the pool. His dark hair was wavy and hung around his perfect face. His brown eyes were framed with thick lashes. His firm mouth beamed a welcome as Savannah approached. He extended a tanned hand.

"Savannah, thank you for making time for me." He pressed her hand instead of shaking it, grinning to reveal straight teeth that gleamed brighter than the whites of his eyes. "I'm Wesley Richins."

Four

Savannah went through the paces with Wesley. Her thoughts kept sliding to her sister. It had been two hours since she checked on her. What if she woke up? Savannah wished she were with her. She wouldn't be here training if it weren't for Ally. Her sister had taught her to love exercise, turning Savannah's life around and giving her confidence she never had as a child. Now Ally was in a coma. She shuddered and turned her attention to Wesley.

As she tested him, Wesley took every opportunity to brush closer to her. Savannah kept her distance. Even his cologne wrapped itself around her without consent. No one should smell that good when working out.

His strength was impressive, rivaling any of the men she'd worked with before. She noted the usual imbalances: chest stronger than back, quadriceps overpowering hamstrings —easily fixed if you knew what you were doing.

They finished the testing and moved into the personal training office. Savannah gestured to a chair across from her desk. His dark gaze burned into her.

She shifted in her chair and cleared her throat. "So, somebody mentioned you've been a member since the gym opened?"

He shrugged striated shoulders, maintaining that unnerving stare.

Savannah forced herself to hold eye contact. "It's strange I've never seen you in here before."

Wesley smiled. "It is strange. I know I would've noticed you."

Savannah ignored that. "How did you find out about me?"

He looked out the office window. "A friend recommended you."

"Oh. Who was that?"

Wesley pursed his lips, his eyes returned to studying her face. "Looking at you, I've completely forgotten his name."

Savannah rolled her eyes and changed the subject. "Can you meet me early in the morning?"

"Anytime's fine as long as I get to see your pretty face."

Savannah clenched her notebook. "When do you usually work out?"

"On my lunch break, around twelve-thirty."

"That's when my sister usually comes . . ." Savannah caught herself. Her stomach rolled. *Her sister.* She had to wrap this up. "Can you tell me your goals please?" She looked down at her notes.

"You mean besides getting a date with you?"

Great, another one, just what I need. She didn't even raise her eyes off the paper. "Your exercise goals."

"Oh, those." He paused, waiting until she gave him the courtesy of a glance, then he winked. "My exercise goals are to be ready for the Mr. Utah competition this spring."

Savannah cocked her head to the side and glanced over his body. "You're broad enough and your face is passably good-looking." His face was light-years beyond passable, but she wouldn't give him that boost. "I think with me as your trainer you might stand a chance."

He trailed his tongue along his bottom lip. "So you approve?"

"I don't see why my approval matters. If you want to enter the competition . . ."

Wesley reached over and brushed long fingers over her hand. "Not the competition. You approve of the way I look?"

Savannah flinched, disengaging her fingers. "Once again, my approval doesn't matter. This is a client-trainer relationship. Do you understand that Wesley, or do you want to terminate it now?"

She held his warm glance with a cold glare. The last thing she wanted or would encourage was another muscle-headed gym rat hitting on her. All the come-ons built her confidence, but they annoyed her as well. She found herself wondering how these shallow men would react to her childhood nickname, "Chub-cake."

He flashed an easy smile. "I understand completely. But please, call me Wes."

Savannah shoved a medical report into his hands. "I need this filled out by your primary care physician and returned when we meet tomorrow, *Wesley.*"

She stood and reached for her bag. Wesley rose with her, taking her arm and guiding her from the office. Savannah wanted to wrench her arm from his long fingers, but she needed to be careful. She was having a hard time watching her tongue and she shouldn't offend a client, a well-paying client at that.

They made it to the front door. She turned to face him. "I'll see you in the morning." She swallowed. "It was nice to meet you." *Oh, the things I'll say for a little money. I should tell him where he can take his three-hundred an hour.*

Wes grinned, pumping his eyebrows. "Believe me, the pleasure was all mine."

Savannah grabbed the front door, jerked it open, and raced for her car before she had to endure one more of his smug smiles.

❧

Ryan drove into Cache Valley just as the sun crested the towering eastern mountain range. Instead of enjoying the brilliant red and orange hues, he cursed the glare off his windshield. He flew through Wellsville and into Logan. Skidding into the Logan Regional Hospital parking lot, he raced through the hallways and stairs to his wife's room.

"Excuse me." A woman at the nurse's desk with gray, butchered hair who outweighed him by at least fifty pounds held up her hand. "Where do you think you're going?"

"I'm going to see my wife," he said, searching past the woman for Allison's door.

The nurse stood. She was almost as tall as him. "And who might that be?"

"Allison Me . . ." his voice caught. Ryan turned from the nurse's stern gaze, clearing his throat. "Excuse me, Allison Mendez."

The etched lines in her face went slack, softening her features. "Oh, you're the husband. I see." She nodded brusquely. "I'm Ilene."

Ilene took his elbow, ushering him down the hallway. Ryan could see Allison's slight form through an open doorway at the end of the hall, surrounded by blankets and monitors. Oxygen tubes rested near her nose. She didn't move. Her dark hair framed her face like a halo.

His feet stilled. *Like a halo.* Like her vibrant spirit had already vacated

37

her beautiful body. He couldn't move another step. He didn't want to see her like this. The nurse dragged him along. She continued to prattle, telling him about Allison's condition, saying how sorry she was, on and on. Ryan needed to stop. He needed to breathe. He didn't want to go into that room. He couldn't do this.

"Well, here she is." Ilene edged him next to the bed. "Take all the time you need." Gently, she shut the door.

Ryan looked at the closed door. The nurse had left him alone. He forced himself to turn to his wife. But it wasn't her. It was only a version of Ally, a lifeless version who didn't open her eyes to see him. Who didn't run and throw herself into his arms. Who might never laugh with him again.

He sank onto a hard chair next to the bed. Reaching over, he took Allison's hand in his. It was limp and cold. He wanted to drop it. He squeezed it instead. "Hi, Ally girl. I, um, just got here. But everything's going to be . . ." His voice broke. He coughed, tried again. "Everything's going to be all right now, baby, I'm here."

He swallowed hard, blinking. He had to force himself to look at her, to see her like this. She looked okay, like she might wake up anytime. There were some red marks on her face and a bandage around her head, but besides those two things it seemed probable that she could open her eyes.

Ryan waited—hoping, praying. But she didn't open her eyes. She didn't move at all.

He rolled his head, working out the kinks in his neck. Giving his heart a break from looking at her, he dug his wallet out of his back pocket, retrieving the picture. Just looking at it made him smile. His little family on the beach in Puerto Vallarta. His head poking out of the sand. Ally and Josh bending over him with huge grins splitting their faces. They'd spent an hour burying him. Josh couldn't stop giggling the entire time. Allison had danced around in her swimsuit. She'd looked so good to him. He could picture it all now.

He glanced back at his wife. Her tiny frame was swallowed up in stiff sheets and thin blankets. Her soft lips, her smooth cheeks and forehead, the cloud of dark hair. Above the bed were stenciled the words, *Faith, Hope, and Love*. Ryan grunted. Where was his faith? Would he ever see her dancing again?

He clamped his jaw closed; his eyes narrowed. It shouldn't be like this. His Ally, the one who baked treats for every neighbor, even the rotten ones whose dogs pooped on their lawn. The woman who volunteered at the nursing home, watched everyone's kids without complaint, and loved her son and her husband.

Ryan exhaled. Who had done this to her? Why? He clenched his fingers. Something dug into his palm. He opened it, staring at the blob of paper—his picture. Oh, no. He tried to smooth it. Allison's face was distorted. Her body wrinkled. No.

He'd crumpled her past recognition.

※

"What is your relationship to the patient?" the petite, round nurse asked.

"I'm her brother-in-law."

"Okay." She glanced up at him with small, dark eyes. "I'll need some ID."

Wes opened his wallet, producing the ID a friend had made for him minutes earlier.

"Jonathon Mendez." The nurse nodded, her black curls swaying. She wrote for a moment then looked up at him with a smile. "You look like the rest of them. Ilene said your brother was just here. I think he went to meet with Dr. McQuivey and discuss her condition."

Wes smiled. "Oh, Ryan was in? I'm glad he got back from Phoenix so quickly."

The nurse's shoulders relaxed, her smile widened. "Yeah. That would be awful to have your wife severely injured and not be here."

He sighed. "I know. The whole situation is awful."

Her smile left. "Yes. I'm so sorry. Hopefully, she'll wake up soon."

Wes hid his thoughts. "Hopefully," he said. "Which room?"

"Three-eighty, around the corner, first door on the right."

"Thank you," he said. "And I'm sorry, I didn't catch your name."

Her smile returned. She self-consciously patted her curls. "It's Rosie."

"Rosie." Wes nodded. "It's nice to meet you." He leaned over the desk. "Can I ask you a favor?"

She grinned like a kid being offered a bubble-gum filled lollipop. "Anything."

He got closer, lowering his voice. "It's kind of personal and a little bit embarrassing."

Her grin grew. "You can trust me."

Wes winked. "I feel like I can."

Rosie blushed.

He pressed on. "I don't know how to say this so I'll come right out with it. I don't have the best relationship with my family. Allison is the only one who really cares about me."

Rosie's mouth fell open. Her dark eyes softened. "Oh, Jonathon. I'm sorry to hear that."

Wes nodded. "It's been hard." He waited to build sympathy. "I wonder if you would not mention my visits."

She bit her lip. "Um, well…"

"If they find out I'm coming they would try and make it so I couldn't see Ally. I need to help her out of this coma."

She looked stricken. "Oh, that would be awful if you couldn't be here for her. Of course I'll do that for you."

Wes reached down and patted her hand. "You're the best, Rosie. Could you write down a copy of your schedule? I want to make sure I see you again."

Rosie's hand trembled as she wrote with a flourish, including her home and cell numbers.

Wes pocketed the note with a grin. He sauntered away. The plump nurse was exactly what he needed this morning. She'd believed everything he said and thought he was interested in her. Perfect.

Seconds later, he opened the door to Allison's room and the smile dropped from his face. Was it only last night she had been beautiful and alive? It seemed a century ago. Her pale face and limp body shocked him; guilt shot over him like a fire hose. He stood, uncertain for a moment, then pushed the guilt away and plunged ahead.

He bent over her, his nose wrinkling at the disgusting hospital smell. "Oh, Allison. I'm sorry about what happened. I didn't want you to get hurt. But now I'm even sorrier about what I have to do." He withdrew a syringe from inside his shirt. "I can't have you waking up. My father would pitch a fit."

He glanced around and out the open door. Perfect. No one within visual range. Following his friend's instructions, he inserted the needle in the IV.

"Enough injections of this and you won't even remember your name when you wake up. Sorry about the drama, but I need you to forget, and

I need some time to get to know your sister better." Wes sighed, picturing the gorgeous Savannah. "You know, I really thought you were the one I wanted, until I saw her."

He finished emptying the medicine into the tube. "I couldn't sleep last night. I felt bad about what happened, especially when I called and they said you were in a coma. I went to workout to try to forget. Savannah was teaching an aerobics class."

He hid the empty syringe inside his shirt. "I knew instantly she was your sister—the one I'm meant to be with. That must be why I was drawn to you in the first place, to bring me to Savannah."

He smiled, thinking of Savannah made all the deception and effort to obtain the drug worthwhile. If he could keep Allison asleep, Savannah could be his. His lips twisted. "She's a feisty one. I think she'll be enough challenge to keep me interested for a long time."

The pudgy nurse walked by the window, craning her neck for another glimpse of him. Wes reached out and gently caressed Allison's hand.

"Sweet dreams," he paused and chuckled, "Sister."

Savannah, her dad, and Josh, pushed through the rotating front door of the hospital. A dark-haired man in a deep blue shirt and plaid tie hurried past them. Savannah recognized him. "Wesley?"

Her voice stopped him. Wes whirled to face her. His eyes darted from her to her dad and then settled on Josh. Glancing back at her, he favored her with a smile. "Savannah. Imagine seeing you here."

"Yeah." She inhaled and regretted it—he smelled better than he had at the gym. She hefted Josh higher on her hip.

Her dad met her eye. She nodded. "Dad, this is Wesley Richins. He's a client," she added so her father wouldn't worry.

Frank reached out a hand. Wesley returned the handshake. "Nice to meet you, sir."

Her dad nodded. "You too. Any relation to Senator Richins?"

"My father."

Frank frowned and took Josh from her arms. "This little guy is anxious to see his dad.

"Daddy," Josh called out, clapping his fingers happily.

Frank smiled. "We'll meet you in the waiting room by the ICU, Savvy."

"Okay, thanks Dad." She watched them until the elevator doors closed, not surprised at her dad's coolness toward Wes. If a man seemed interested in her, her dad expressed instant disapproval.

"Savvy, huh?"

Savannah turned back to face him. "Only to my family."

"Oh." Wes flashed his straight, white teeth at her. "Guess I'll stick with Savannah."

She folded her arms across her chest. "Guess you will. What are you doing here?"

Wes looked up and down her frame, lingering on her legs in that intrusive way of his. Savannah wished her shorts were capris.

"You look good in clothes," he said.

Savannah rolled her eyes at the line she'd heard twenty times before. She could easily return the compliment but refused to. "What are you doing here, Wesley?"

His eyebrows scrunched together in the center, but he didn't try any more cute comments. "I'm visiting my Grandma. She broke her hip a couple days ago."

"That's too bad."

"Yeah. She's supposed to be housebound, but that doesn't stop her from trying to shop. She's so independent and she keeps firing everyone I hire to take care of her. What do you do?" He gestured with his hands as he talked, sending his tie off kilter. "She fell down her garage steps, trying to get to her car. I feel like it's my fault because I wasn't there."

Savannah cringed. "Don't blame yourself." She wondered if she could make herself believe those words. Maybe she'd been wrong about Wes. It was possible the man did possess a heart. "I'm sorry she got hurt."

"Me, too." He shrugged his shoulders. "It was awful when I found her."

Savannah thought of her sister, lying on the tile—bloody, unconscious. "Yeah, that is awful."

"Why are you here?" he asked.

"My sister was hurt last night; she's in the ICU."

"No." His dark eyes opened wider. His black hair swayed as he shook his head. "I hope she'll be all right."

Savannah's chest constricted, and she couldn't breathe. She felt like she'd been pinned under a three-hundred pound wrestler. "Me, too," she squeaked.

Wes reached out and she automatically extended her hand. "I'll let you go be with your sister." He latched onto her fingers.

"Thank you," Savannah whispered.

"I'll see you in the morning?" he asked.

Savannah nodded. She tried to focus on training Wes. It would get her thoughts away from her sister and hopefully alleviate some of her stress. She inhaled, withdrawing her hand from his. "Six still okay?"

"Whatever works for you is fine with me."

Savannah walked away from him and opened the door for the stairs. She glanced over her shoulder to find him studying her with a soft smile.

Five

Noah took a sip from his water bottle, reclined into his chair, and closed his eyes. He was exhausted. He and Jason had spent hours questioning the neighbors and anyone who might have had a reason to be in Allison Mendez's house. The only person they could place at the scene was the sister, Savannah. He sighed. She didn't seem like the type. He hated to think she could be capable of pushing her sibling down the stairs and then lying to him about it.

Jason sauntered up to his desk. "Guess who was a juvie?"

Noah straightened. "No."

"Yep." Jason held the paper just out of reach. "Got the proof right here."

Noah leaned over the desk, snatching the paper from his friend. He read it quickly. His jaw hardened.

"You get to go visit the hottie again." Jason whistled. "I can't believe you go on a prank 9-1-1 call and end up getting to question a woman that fine." He exhaled. "Maybe we should do a role reversal on this case. I could get the truth out of the lovely Savannah. I'd take her to dinner first, then a little lip action . . ." He winked. "After I work my magic, she'd confess everything to me."

Noah focused on the decade old court case, with superb willpower he could almost destroy the vision of Jason romancing Savannah.

Ryan had been ushered out of Allison's room while the staff ran tests on her. He waited in the small lounge area adjacent to the ICU, his fore-arms braced on his legs. His head hung toward the floor. His shoulders bowed under the pressure.

"Daddy!"

His head snapped up. Air whooshed into his lungs. Josh struggled from his grandpa's arms, pumping his short legs in Ryan's direction. Ryan knelt on the floor, catching his son in his embrace.

"Bubba!" Ryan buried his head in Josh's warm neck. It smelled of maple syrup and happiness. Ryan bit his lip. He wouldn't cry. He'd enjoy this perfect moment with his boy.

Ryan turned to his father-in-law. Frank put an arm around his shoulder. "Glad you made it here, son."

Ryan nodded. He opened his mouth to speak, but nothing came out. He leaned into Frank's strength.

"Daddy, where's Mommy?" Josh asked innocently.

Ryan stared at the dark eyes that sparkled like Allison's. Josh was a mommy's boy who didn't have a mommy right now. He shook his head. Oh, Ally. They couldn't survive without her.

"Me want Mommy."

Ryan buried his face in Josh's hair. Frank squeezed his shoulder awkwardly.

"Daddy! Me want Mommy!"

Ryan could take it no longer. He closed his eyes and sobbed.

<hr />

They waited over twenty minutes until a nurse with butchered gray hair and an endearing smile came to inform them they could each see Allison for a few minutes. Savannah held Josh while her dad and Ryan used their allotted time. When the nurse informed her it was her turn, she took half steps the entire way.

She entered the room, gazing over Allison and the benediction imprinted above her head. The words *Faith, Hope, and Love* beamed over her sister. Peace oozed into Savannah's soul. She prayed the feeling and words were a good omen.

Sitting next to the bed, she brushed the hair from her sister's neck. The nurses must've washed her hair. It wasn't caked with blood anymore. Savannah shivered.

"Hey, Ally girl. It's me." She studied the huge bandage across Allison's forehead. Oxygen tubes lingered below her delicate nose, other tubes protruded from her toned arms. "Don't worry about Josh. We'll all take care of him until you wake up. I think the little man is doing okay. He keeps calling for you . . ." She paused. "He wants you, but I don't think he has a clue what's going on. It's Ryan who's struggling, and Dad, and me . . ."

Savannah stared at her beautiful sister, willing her to wake up. "This really bites, Ally. I need you to be okay. We all do."

She stroked her sister's smooth cheek. "I know we made that sister pact, but it was always you watching out for me, not the other way around. I need you to be here for all of us. You're the one who takes care of everyone. You're the nice one. I'm not the nurturer. I can't do your job and I just . . . I just miss you."

Unable to bear the scene any longer, she looked out the window. In the parking lot three stories below, leaves on the poplar trees fluttered with the soft breeze. The day was warm and perfect, but Savannah couldn't enjoy it any more than she would a traffic jam.

She spoke hesitantly. "You always do anything I ask. Please just do one more thing for me, Ally, and I'll never ask for anything else again—ever."

Savannah's gaze swung back to her sister's still form. She clutched the cool hand between both of hers. "Can you please, please wake up? Josh needs you. Ryan needs you. Dad needs you. Heck, I hate to be the selfish bugger, but I need you."

Savannah released Allison's fingers, wiping at the wetness on her cheeks with the back of her hand. She reached out to touch her sister's forehead. Ally was still so cold. Savannah exhaled slowly. "Okay, girl, I hate to do this, but you're not giving me any other option."

"If you don't wake up soon you know what's going to happen. I'm going to let your house get trashed." Savannah smiled to herself. "That's right, big sister. Ryan and Dad have no clue how to keep it clean, and I'll try my best, but you know I fail at cleaning. There'll be dishes piled in the sink, hard water buildup on the faucets, plants wilting, dust everywhere, and I swear I won't wash the sheets. Just think about all those skin cells resting on your crisp, white sheets."

She searched her sister's face, praying for something, anything. After several minutes she whispered, "I was kidding, Ally. I'll take care of everything." She leaned in closer. "If you'll wake up I'll pay for a cleaning service and I'll make sure they do windows." Savannah waited. Allison didn't flinch.

"Forgive the interruption," the nurse said from the doorway, "but we need to rotate her in the bed, and then you can come right back in."

Savannah acknowledged her with a wave of her hand. She tried to smile, but failed. "It's okay, Ilene. Come on in. I'm done." She didn't want to tell the truth: she was relieved to have an excuse to escape the silent room and her more silent sister.

She leaned close and kissed Allison's cheek. "Love you, sis. I'll talk to you . . ." she choked on the words. "I'll see you later."

Savannah walked to the door on trembling legs. She tripped. Ilene caught her in a motherly hug. "It'll be okay, honey," Ilene said. "We're going to take great care of her and she'll come out of this, you'll see."

Savannah looked up with a weary smile. She pulled back. "Thanks, Ilene."

The nurse grinned, her face crinkling like a Lay's potato chip. "And if we can't get her to wake up, you keep promising to get her windows cleaned."

Savannah laughed. "Think that might work?"

"I don't know about her, but it'd work for me."

The older woman ushered Savannah back to her family, making her yearn for her own mother.

Josh tired quickly of junk food and the too-quiet hospital. Frank and Savannah volunteered to take him home for lunch and his nap. No amount of talking could pry Ryan from his wife, and they didn't push the issue, both understanding his need to stay by Allison's side.

Her dad's Isuzu followed a white four-door truck into Ryan and Allison's circular drive. The truck stopped and Savannah glimpsed Detective Shumway easing his long legs from the vehicle.

Parking next to the garage, they walked around to greet the detective. Frank transferred Josh to his left arm and shook Noah's hand. Savannah sensed the detective wasn't here with good news. Her stomach curdled like cottage cheese. She didn't know if she could handle anything more today.

She turned her head, staring into sapphire eyes. His brown lashes almost touched his eyebrows as he returned her gaze. Her father cleared his throat and they both jerked guiltily to face him.

"Excuse me, Detective, did you need to tell us something?" Frank asked.

"Um, nothing really new." Noah shifted his weight from one foot to the other. "I've questioned all the neighbors. No one saw any unusual cars or activity, but it was late and most of the people I spoke to were either in bed or watching television when the incident happened."

Savannah winced. Her heartache was reduced to an incident.

"So they weren't much help?" Frank asked.

"No, sir." Noah glanced from her father to her.

"You don't have a suspect yet," Frank said.

Noah's eyes never left her face. He shook his head. "No."

Her dad coughed. "Could you excuse me for a minute? From the aroma this boy is exuding I'd better get inside and change him."

Savannah noticed a gleam in her father's eyes that had been missing for the past twenty-four hours. Her over-protective father *wanted* to leave her alone with the detective. This was a first.

"If it's all right with you, sir, I'd hoped to spend some time alone with Savannah and ask her a few questions."

Frank raised his eyebrows. "No problem at all. Why don't you two walk out back? The flower garden is beautiful this time of year."

Savannah's eyes widened. Weren't fathers, especially her father, supposed to *prevent* their daughters from spending time alone with strange men? Her dad was encouraging the detective? *Unbelievable.*

Noah nodded. "Thank you, sir."

Frank smiled and sauntered up the steps to the wide front porch.

Noah opened his hand and gestured. "Do you mind?"

"I guess not," Savannah murmured. "Long night?"

He turned her way and smiled. "You could say that."

"Did you even go home?"

He shook his head. "I studied the info from this case all night, then spent the day ruling out suspects. Haven't had a chance to go home yet."

They settled onto a wooden bench amidst Allison's overflowing flower garden. The zinnias and sunflowers waved merrily at them.

Savannah shifted her body so she could look at him. "You couldn't wait to see me, so you rushed over here without even taking the time to shave?"

"Something like that." Noah cleared his throat. "I need to ask you some more questions."

Savannah couldn't hide the pang from herself. She flirted with him and he couldn't care less. "Of course you did. Why else would you be here?" It suddenly hit her why he wasn't responding to her. The sun's heat intensified. Her face reddened. "You're married."

Noah smiled her, his eyes twinkling. "No."

Savannah tucked her arms around her midsection "Oh, well, that's . . . good. Why are you here?"

His smirk left. "I'm here to find out what happened to your sister."

The air left her lungs. Her sister. "Of course," Savannah whispered. "That's all I care about too." How could she be thinking of anything else? "What other questions do you have?"

Noah studied a patch of begonias. "I hate to keep hammering on this, but we're concerned about the timeline. Do you have any proof you didn't arrive at your sister's house until after the incident?" He rubbed his large hands together. "I guess what I'm saying is, do you have an alibi?"

Savannah bit her cheek. The temperature in the sun-drenched garden dropped twenty degrees. "Do you think I'm lying to you, Detective?"

He licked his bottom lip, lifting a hand in a helpless gesture. "I don't know what to think."

Savannah gasped. He might as well have said she was lying. Seconds puttered by with agonizing slowness. She tried to think of some way to prove she was telling the truth. "What about the phone? Isn't there some record that proves I was talking to Ally?"

Noah searched her eyes. "Qwest faxed us your phone record. It shows you were on the phone with Allison from 9:22 to 9:29, but there's nothing after that."

"Didn't it show that I tried to call her and it was busy?"

He shook his head. "The records only tell us when a call is connected."

She gulped. "But it still proves I'm telling the truth about the phone call."

Noah raised an eyebrow, studying her. "The first phone call, yes. But after that? You had plenty of time to make it to her house before she was injured and . . ." He shrugged. "I'm sorry, but unless I get concrete proof of where you were, I'll have to take you in for questioning."

She jumped from the bench. "What! You think I would hurt my own sister?"

Noah stood. "Well, nobody wants to think that. It's just . . ." He looked like he'd been caught with his finger in a newly frosted birthday cake. He coughed once, a fake, hollow sound. "I've done everything I can to prove you innocent. My partner and I have searched and questioned and ruled out every possible suspect. We can't find evidence that points to anyone else."

An exhale burst from Savannah's lungs like she'd been punched in the stomach. Her lips parted, then pursed in an angry circle. "Oh, so nobody thinks I hurt my sister, but the evidence proves I did. What kind of crap is that? You want to arrest me, Detective Shumway?"

He appraised her, his blue eyes solemn. "No. I don't want to arrest you, I, um . . ." He shrugged. "Don't leave the valley, okay?"

Savannah's hands trembled. She raised her right arm, jabbing it at him. "I did not hurt my sister."

Noah's forehead wrinkled. "Yeah. You know I want to believe that, but the evidence."

"You want evidence," she whispered. "Find the jerk who hurt my sister. Someone was in the house." Her voice rose several octaves. Her hands flung everywhere, punctuating each word. "Someone called 9-1-1. Whoever did it was smart, they wiped off their fingerprints or wore gloves, or something like that."

Noah shook his head. "The only reason someone would hurt Allison and *then* call 9-1-1 is because they felt guilty—because they cared about her." He didn't study the flowers now and he no longer appeared uncertain. He stared into her soul trying to locate each and every fault. "I don't know why you hurt your sister, Savannah, but I'm hoping it wasn't intentional. Things will go a lot easier for you—"

"It wasn't me," she screamed. "I would never hurt my sister, never!"

"You're the only person we can place at the scene. I hate to do this to you and your family, but if you don't have an alibi we'll have to charge you with the crime."

Savannah clenched her teeth, speaking calmly took greater effort than curling twenty-five pound dumbbells. "I didn't commit any crime," she said.

"If you were a first-time offender, I might believe that." He took a deep breath before continuing. "When we ran the fingerprints taken from the house through the juvenile court system we found it."

Sweat dotted her forehead. "Found what? What are you talking about?"

"Why didn't you tell me about the incident in high school when we talked last night?"

The blood drained from her face. High school. Jenalee Schmidt. "That has nothing to do with this."

He raised an eyebrow. "You sure? Another girl. Pushed down the steps."

"No. You don't know what you're talking about."

He folded his arms across his chest. "Yeah, I do. You've committed a violent crime before. Criminals tend to repeat the same offense. Maybe with some counseling . . ."

He kept talking, but Savannah couldn't hear the words because of the blood roaring in her ears. Her fists balled, she could hardly see him through the slits in her eyelids. Spinning on her heel, she ducked under a tree and speed-walked away from him. His hand wrapped around her arm and spun her to face him. Savannah tripped on a root and fell against his hard chest. He put an arm around her to steady her.

"Let me go, you, you, Jackie."

Noah gave her an amused look. "Jackie?"

"Yeah, Jackie. Ally thought of it . . ." Savannah stopped, tears filling her eyes. She buried her head against his thin dress shirt. Noah's arms softened around her.

"Ally and I made it up so we wouldn't have to swear," she whispered. "Please, Noah. I can explain about the thing in high school." She gulped. Could she really? She didn't want him to know why she'd pushed the rah-rah.

She continued. "You have to believe I wouldn't hurt my sister. I love her. She's my best friend." Leaning back, she looked into his blue eyes. "Trust your instincts on this one. You can see how much I love my family. Think about when you found me. Did I look guilty? Did I look like I could've possibly hurt Ally like that?"

Noah stared at her. She wanted to look away, but she held his gaze, willing him to know her, to believe her.

"Please believe me," she whispered again.

He shook his head. "I want to believe you, Savannah. But . . ."

"No, buts, please." She placed a hand on his chest. "Look, I understand the position you're in. You can't let someone loose who you think might have committed a crime, but you can't do this to my family right now."

"I wish I could go on emotion," Noah began.

She cut him off. "Listen to me for a minute. Why couldn't you follow me around? Stay by my side twenty-four hours a day until you find the person who hurt Ally. Couldn't you do that? I need to be here with my dad and Josh. I need to be able to go visit Ally and Ryan at the hospital. If you think I hurt her . . ."

Savannah paused, swallowing against the pain. Her Ally was hurt and now this. Noah's accusations sliced her. How could he think she would hurt her sister? She had to convince him otherwise.

"I understand you need to be cautious," she said, "but please don't take me in. You don't know how bad we're all hurting right now. If you accuse me of this it'll kill my dad and Ryan. They need me and they can't take care of Josh like I can. He needs me. Think of that precious baby."

Noah studied her, he released his arms from her back and Savannah removed her hands from him and put a few inches between them.

"Okay," he said.

Savannah's head whipped up. "Okay?"

He nodded and smiled. "If you'll promise not to call me a Jackie again."

Savannah smiled, though her stomach still rolled. "I can try. We'll see how you act."

Noah arched an eyebrow. "You know this is a little different than how we normally handle a case like this."

Savannah grabbed his forearm. "Please, Noah. Please make this work. I can't be taken from my family right now."

Noah glanced down at her hand on him, slowly raising his eyes to hers. "I'll see what I can do. If you aren't our suspect someone should be protecting you and your family until he's found."

"I'm not the suspect."

"I guess we'll see."

Savannah didn't answer. She released his arm and squirmed under his scrutiny.

Noah cocked his head to one side. "Are you sure you want me watching over you?"

Savannah backed up half a step. "I—I think so."

He took a full step toward her. He towered over her. The sun's rays were blocked. Savannah didn't dare move.

"You understand that if my boss agrees to your idea I'm going to stay right with you wherever you are. It'll be worse than going to jail."

Savannah arched her head to study him. Her body tingled. She gulped a breath and retreated a few inches. "Anything's better than going to jail."

Noah knew he must be crazy. He stared at Savannah, wishing he knew how to read her, wishing he were a better cop. He was known around the department as Stone Face. He never displayed emotion or let himself trust his instincts, but one plea from the pretty girl in front of him and he cracked like a windshield hit with a baseball bat.

He ran a hand through his hair, glad she'd moved away from him. He'd never been so tempted to wrap someone in his arms. He thought about what she'd talked him into doing. He sighed. His sergeant would never go for this idea. The case wasn't a high priority. Sergeant Malm would chuckle at the phone call and tell Noah to get back to work.

Savannah stared at him. He wished he could hold her again. Noah had to talk his sergeant into her idea. He couldn't charge this beautiful woman with a crime she might not have committed. "Can you give me a few minutes to contact my supervisor, and then I'll come inside?"

Savannah nodded. She placed a hand on his arm. "Thanks for doing this. Once you get to know me better, you'll see I'm telling the truth."

His eyes flicked to her hand, then back to her eyes. "We'll find out soon enough."

She dropped her hand, spun on her heel, and strode away. He watched her go, admiring everything about her physical appearance, but unsure what to think of her character. Was she playing him for a fool? Was she devious enough to hurt her sister and then try and place the blame on some unknown assailant? And what about the assault charges filed against her when she was only seventeen? She'd gotten off with community service and a fine, but the charge planted more doubt about her innocence. For some reason, staring into her eyes had mesmerized him so that he'd agreed to exactly what she'd wanted.

He pulled out his cell phone, dialed, and exhaled slowly. Yeah, he was an idiot. He'd never been such a sucker for a pair of dark, long-lashed eyes.

"Hello, sir," he began without preamble. "I have an interesting proposal. I'd like to try something on the Mendez case."

"What'd you have in mind Shumway?"

"I'm worried about the sister. Either she is the perpetrator or she may be in danger. She looks enough like the injured woman that if the assailant is still around he might come after her. I want to stick by her side for the next few days and watch over her and the sister to see what I can turn up."

Sergeant Malm didn't answer right away. Noah could hear him tapping on something—probably his pen against his jutted chin, like usual.

"I don't know, Shumway. I can't see spending too many hours on this case. We don't have proof that Allison Mendez didn't just fall down those stairs."

Noah sauntered between rose and dogwood bushes. "Sir, with all due respect, I know she didn't fall without some help. She couldn't have called 9-1-1 by herself. There would've been a blood trail if she even attempted it."

"I'm having a hard time believing this is an important enough case to assign you to it exclusively."

Noah rubbed the back of his neck with his hand. He thought of Savannah. Beautiful, possibly dangerous. "Well, sir, I feel like it is. I have a lot of vacation and sick leave stored up. I'll use whatever of that I need until the case is solved."

"Shumway, you need to use that time to actually go on vacation!"

"By myself?" Noah regretted the words the second they were out. "It's fine, sir. I'd rather use the hours to solve this case. It kept me up last night."

His sergeant guffawed. "The case is keeping you up or the sister?"

Noah halted. "Sir?"

"Shouldn't have said that. Keller informed me she's quite attractive."

"Trust Keller to report the important facts."

"So, it's true?"

"Yes, sir, but that's not what this is about." *Now I just need to convince myself of that.*

Sergeant Malm paused, then exhaled. "All right. I'll give you forty hours on my clock and then you'll have to use your leave. Make sure your other files are taken care of and keep me informed. If that sister is the culprit, I don't care how pretty she is or how hard it is on the family, I want her put away. Understood?"

Noah gripped his phone. "Yes, sir." He disconnected the call, and then dialed again.

"Keller here," the cheery voice sang over the line.

Noah exhaled, the comfort of an old friend relaxing his neck muscles.

"Hey, Jase," he muttered. "It's me."

"Don't sound so excited. Oh, I forgot. You're saving all your excitement for our gorgeous little suspect."

Noah couldn't stop his smile. "Something like that."

"Come on, dude. Even Stone Face has to crack once in a while. She's nice." He whistled. "Very nice."

"I didn't call about Savannah."

Jason chuckled. "Oh, so it's *Savannah* now. Why would you waste my time calling about something else?"

Noah shook his head. He paced the fragrant flower garden. The air was dead without a hint of a cooling breeze. The hot sun beating on his long-sleeved shirt made him stickier than a beehive. "I need you to take over my other cases for a few days."

"Awesome. You're going to finally take some vacation time. Are you taking the hottie with you?"

Noah kicked at a clump of dry grass clippings. "Keller! I'm staying right here with the hottie to figure out if she hurt her sister."

"Now that's progress. You admitted she's hot."

Noah snorted. "I'd have to be a monk not to notice that."

"Even monks have eyes, dude."

Noah blew out a long breath. "Am I seeing this right, Jase? She seems so . . . great. Do you think she could've pushed her sister down those stairs?"

There was a pause. "I don't know man. One thing I do know—beautiful women are good at messing with our minds."

"That's the truth. Seriously, we couldn't find another suspect. We've been through every possibility. She has a history. Am I jumping to conclusions?"

"It's one of those things we'll have to wait and see. You stay with her, and I'll keep checking any leads I can. Quiz her on the sister. See who would've had motive to hurt Allison. Get in tight with the family, claim you're there for their protection and see what's really going on with all of them. Hopefully I can turn something else up and you can enjoy checking Savannah out."

Noah rotated his neck. "Thanks for your help. I couldn't do this without you."

"Sure you could. It would just take you forever because you're not as smart as me."

Noah laughed. "Can you take care of my other files too?"

"I'll do it or assign Sharks or one of the other overambitious newbies, but you have to promise me one thing."

Noah smiled. Leave it Jason to delegate. "What do I need to promise you?"

"Call me after the first time you kiss her."

Noah squinted against the unforgiving sun. "I'm hanging up now."

"No, you're not. You promise me a phone call or I won't help you."

"Keller." Noah tossed his head like an angry bull. "She could be the suspect. I have no intention of becoming involved with her."

"Did I say anything about becoming involved? I'm not asking for a commitment here, buddy. I asked you to call me after you kiss her."

Noah swatted the leaves on a nearby maple tree. "What makes you think I'm going to kiss her?"

"A girl that beautiful, by your side twenty-four hours a day. You may be a boring church boy, but you're not an idiot. If you don't kiss her before this is over I'm booking plane tickets to the Cayman Islands for the two of us. We'll stay on the beach until I'm certain you're straight."

Noah shook his head. "I'm hanging up now."

"After you promise."

Noah gritted his teeth. "I swear one of these days you're going to grow up."

"You wouldn't have any fun if that happened. Don't forget you called asking me for a favor. Now I'm waiting for that promise."

Noah ripped a leaf off the tree, hurling it away from him. It fluttered gently to the grass, reminding him of how soft he was becoming. "I promise to call you *if* I ever kiss her."

"That's my boy. Now get to work, and I'm not talking about the case."

Noah did hang up then, wondering how Jason had ever convinced him to start attending church in the first place. The man didn't take anything seriously.

Moments later, he knocked on Allison's front door. Scenes from last night flashed through his head: Allison beat up and bloodied, the tile soaked with her blood, and the memory he never wanted to replace: Savannah looking so tempting in that tank top. The door swung open. Savannah's endless, obsidian gaze asked the question he knew she'd been waiting for.

"He agreed," Noah said, thinking of what Jason had said, not his boss. His skin felt warmer than the hot sun's rays could make it. He hoped his antiperspirant was functioning. "My only priority is you."

Savannah's pink lips smiled, and her eyes sparkled. "I like the sound of that."

Noah couldn't respond. Sweat trickled between his shoulder blades. He was going to kill Keller for planting these ideas in his head.

"Thank you," she said.

He cleared his throat. "I'm trying to figure out how much to tell your dad."

Her smile froze. "Can we claim you're here for our protection?"

Noah thought for a minute, remembering what Jason had suggested. "Do you think he'll buy half the story?"

"My dad thinks you're interested in me." Her olive complexion darkened. "But he might think it's odd that your boss would have you stay with us all the time." She inclined her head. "Maybe you could claim you're doing some of the work on your own time. That will help him believe you're telling the truth."

She didn't know how close to the truth she was. The words played through his mind: *My dad thinks you're interested in me.* Was he? He kept trying to shove any feelings for her into the trash. She was beautiful, feisty, and much too confident. He needed to be extremely wary.

Noah placed a hand on her lower back, guiding her into the living room. It was the most natural movement in the world, but Savannah absorbed his heated touch through her thin shirt and his closeness confused her thought process.

Her dad stared expectantly at the two of them. Josh played on the floor with his favorite monster truck.

Noah cleared his throat. "I've been assigned to this case full time until we find out who hurt Allison. I'm also here to protect your family, especially Savannah. With your permission I'll stay here at the house and go everywhere Savannah goes."

Frank approached Noah and shook his hand for the second time in an hour. Savannah was grateful her dad had bought Noah's excuse. She couldn't imagine his disappointment in her if Noah explained she was a suspect. Would her dad believe she'd hurt Ally?

"Thank the Lord," Frank said, his dark eyes bright. He shook his head. "Thank you, Detective. I'll feel much better knowing you're around. I keep worrying that the guy will come back and either hurt Allison worse or come after Savannah. Most people think they're twins."

Noah swiveled his head in Savannah's direction. "They aren't twins?"

Savannah gasped. "She's four years older than me."

Her dad chuckled. "Allison loves it when people think they're twins and as you can see, Savannah . . ."

"Oh." Savannah glared at her dad. "I'm not offended that someone would think we're twins. It's a compliment. Allison is gorgeous." She turned to Noah. "But she *is* older than me."

Noah raised an eyebrow. "Four years is a lot older. I can see a huge difference in your age now that I think about it."

Savannah tried not to smile. Her dad chuckled.

"We are a lot like twins," she said. "Allison's my best friend and I'd never want anything bad to happen to her."

Frank nodded his agreement. "They're really close, even though Savannah's always been my feisty one."

Savannah's neck tightened. She was sick of being labeled. Why couldn't her dad say she was the nice one, just once? Noah studied her. He didn't say anything. Her phone rang. She looked at the caller ID: Jefferson Reed. She pushed a button to silence the ringer.

"Aren't you going to get that?" her dad asked.

She shook her head. "He'll call back."

Noah arched an eyebrow. He turned and spoke to her father, "I'll make sure to inform the hospital that only family is permitted to visit Allison. If there's a breach, we'll have them contact security immediately."

"That will make me feel a lot better," Frank said. "Thanks for being here. You can't understand how hard it is to see your daughter like that and not know why someone hurt her or who could do something so horrible."

Savannah caught Noah staring at her. Her eyes squinted until she could barely see him through the slits. *What a jerk.* He was convinced she'd hurt Allison. Well, she'd prove him wrong. She'd find out who hurt her sister and make the calloused detective feel like shower scum.

Six

Savannah, Ryan, Frank, and Noah spent the afternoon and evening at the hospital. Savannah arranged for Allison's neighbor to watch Josh. She thought Noah would make her uncomfortable, but he was pleasant and helpful and thankfully said nothing to her dad or Ryan about his suspicions.

Looking at Noah whenever she got the chance was the only thing that succeeded in taking her mind off her sister's condition.

Her cell phone buzzed against her waist. She sighed. It hadn't stopped ringing all day. At least this time it was a client and not Samuel bugging her to go out to dinner again. She pressed the button to answer.

"I ate ice cream last night," Isabelle cried over the phone. "I hate myself."

Savannah stood. "It's okay to eat a treat once in a while."

Her dad's head snapped up, and he raised an eyebrow. She walked away. "Don't beat yourself up."

"I feel so guilty when I put something fattening in my mouth. I just know I'll gain my weight back. I know it!"

"Calm down," Savannah said. "Maybe we need to get you into a psychiatrist who specializes in nutrition issues."

"No. I've tried that. You help me more than he ever did. All I want is to be like you. Can't you help me?"

Savannah shuddered. *Why would anyone want to be like her?* She was always hungry. She lived for her next workout. She weighed herself twice a day to make sure she didn't gain any of the weight back. She relished every compliment given by word or glance, but then pegged those men as shallow. It wasn't healthy, and she knew it.

She continued soothing her client, knowing she was a hypocrite. She didn't follow any of the words coming out of her mouth. She returned to the waiting area a few minutes later and tried to forget the conversation by studying Noah. He leaned back in the chair with a Newsweek magazine between his long fingers. She liked the angular curve of his jaw line and his straight nose, but his full lips, deep blue eyes, and strong body were the things that most intrigued her. He must've felt her stare. He looked over and raised his chin in acknowledgment.

Savannah tore her eyes from him, glancing at the clock. It was almost eight. If she had to go into Allison's room and see her sister lying comatose one more time today she would scream loud enough to wake her sister. She almost smiled. It might be worth trying.

She lumbered to her feet and tapped Ryan's arm. "I think we'd better go get Josh. It's almost bedtime, and you know he won't go to sleep unless he's in his crib."

Ryan peered up, but his reddened eyes didn't focus on her face. "You guys go. Do you mind bringing Josh to see me in the morning?"

Savannah shook her head. "You need to come home too."

He closed his eyes. "I'm not leaving her."

Savannah looked to her dad and Noah for help. They both glanced away. Frustrated, she planted her hands on her hips. "Ry, you need to eat something, sleep in your own bed, and take a shower."

Ryan shook his head stubbornly. "I still have my bag from the trip. Ilene said they have an empty room down the hall. She promised to get me settled before she goes off duty." He shrugged. "It's not like I could sleep anyway."

Savannah squeezed his shoulder. "But what about Josh? It's hard enough not having Ally around. He needs . . ."

Ryan jerked from her touch like she was a campfire. "Don't Savvy. Josh will be okay. He won't remember this. I have to be with her."

"You need to rest."

Ryan jumped from his chair and glared down at her. He was only six inches taller than her, but it felt like a foot. "How could I live with myself if she woke up and I wasn't here? How could I?"

Noah and Frank moved to Savannah's side. Her dad put an arm around her. "Savvy's just trying to take care of you, Ryan."

Ryan deflated. His shoulders dipped. "I'm sorry, but you have to understand why I can't leave."

Savannah gulped down the guilt. She didn't want to desert her sister, but she needed to flee from this sterile, depressing building. "I guess. So, what do you want me to tell Josh?"

Ryan's mouth twisted. "I don't know. I'm sorry." His head hung forward, his hands limp at his sides. "Just bring him to see me in the morning, okay?"

"Sure," Frank said. "We'll take care of him."

After sneaking dinner past Josh's picky lips, Savannah gave him a long bath. He squirmed when she tried to massage him with lotion.

"No smelly stuffs," he said.

Savannah laughed, slipping his toes into soft cotton pajamas.

"Aunt Savvy?" Josh asked. "What Mommy doing?"

Savannah pursed her lips together, gathering him into her arms. "Mommy is . . . sleeping right now, honey. When she wakes up she's going to come hug you, okay?"

Josh heaved a sigh. "Me miss Mommy."

Savannah hugged him. "Me too, baby. Me too."

She sang songs to Josh. Lullabies and then songs about Jesus like her mom used to do when she was a little girl. It took half an hour to rock the precious boy to sleep. She didn't mind. It was the first time she'd felt at peace all day. She laid him in his crib and listened to him softly snore. Bending down for one more kiss, she had to wipe away the tear that splattered on his cheek.

⁂

Wes watched the house from across the street. He couldn't see Savannah clearly, but he had a good view of the detective. He gritted his teeth. He had to find a way to get rid of that guy. Shumway was the one person in high school and college who never cowed to him. He and his stupid friend, Keller, always acted like they were as good as Wesley. *What a joke.* Everyone knew better.

Allison was sleeping soundly at the hospital thanks to another injection of Versed. Rosie helped Wes slip in while Ilene settled Ryan into an empty room. After visiting Allison, Wes left the hospital and drove straight to Allison's house. He'd wait a few more minutes, and hopefully get a glimpse of Savannah.

Savannah was every bit as pretty as her sister and much better suited for him. He grinned as he thought of her. The grin slid down. *How close were she and Shumway in that house?* He forced the image away. What did it matter? Even if Shumway was doing more than his job, he was no match for Wes. Convincing Savannah to choose him over the detective shouldn't be any problem. He rubbed his hands together. He couldn't wait to do the convincing.

Now if he could just find a way to get her alone.

Noah rested on a barstool next to Savannah's dad. They said nothing, both drowning in their own thoughts and worries. A light tread bounced down the steps. Noah whirled and watched Savannah descend. Her fluid movements reminded him of a ballerina. He loved seeing her black hair swish along her back and her dark eyes flash at him when he made her angry, which he seemed to be an expert at doing.

He wished he'd met her in another situation, but maybe it was good he knew what she might be capable of. *Could she have hurt Allison?* He didn't like to think about it. Any woman who could injure her own sibling and then pretend she didn't was definitely not someone he wanted to be around.

She glanced at him with dark, somber eyes. He almost decided he could spend forever with a deceiving temptress if she looked that good. Her phone rang before he could say anything. She flipped it open and walked into the laundry room.

"Tyler! No, sorry, not this weekend." A pause. "Sure, I'd love to go to Café Sabor with you, but I've had some family trouble . . ."

Noah grimaced, gripping the counter. He'd heard Savannah repeat similar words into her cell phone throughout the day. How many men was she currently dating? Frank studied him. Noah mustered a smile.

Frank elevated a shoulder and sighed. "Her phone rings a lot."

Noah nodded. "So I've noticed."

Savannah reentered the room.

"I'm going to bed," she said to her dad. "I got no sleep last night."

Frank's eyes darkened. "I know. At least we can sleep in tomorrow."

"Not me." Savannah clutched the back of a barstool. "I've got to train a client at six. Then I'll have the rest of the day off to be with Ally."

Noah sat up straighter. That meant he'd have to get up early as well.

Was the client just an excuse for Savannah to go to the hospital without her family around? If she was alone no one could stop her from injuring her sister.

"Do you have to go?" her dad asked.

"Unfortunately, yes. The guy is paying three hundred an hour."

Her dad whistled.

"Yeah. He insisted on me training him and offered to pay a few hundred an hour to get me. I'm not going to kick the dumb horse in the mouth, isn't that how the saying goes?"

Her dad grinned. "Something like that."

Savannah sauntered past Noah. Her vanilla-scented perfume swirled around him. He inhaled slowly.

She kissed her dad's cheek. "I'll see you in the morning."

Noah rose from his perch. "I think I'll head to bed too. Do you mind showing me what room I'm using?"

Savannah's gaze was cool. "No problem. Goodnight, Dad."

"Goodnight, Savvy, Noah." Frank didn't seem to be able to wipe the smirk from his face as Savannah marched toward the stairs leading to the basement.

Noah retrieved his bag from the laundry room and nodded goodnight to Frank. He loved how Savannah's dad made him so comfortable. He should've been the outsider, but Frank didn't treat him like that. Too bad the beauty in front of him didn't extend the same acceptance.

He followed Savannah down the stairs. She led him through the living room and down a short hall. They entered a spacious guest room. A field of green and pink flowers overran the bed. Dancers folded in grotesque positions were adorned by antique white frames. Noah halted. How could he sleep surrounded by that? "Do you have anything less girly?"

Savannah tapped her fingers on a dresser, amazingly it didn't fall apart. "It's this or the couch, Bub."

He smiled. "Okay. I guess I'll get in touch with my feminine side."

Her eyebrows arched. "Good luck with that."

She walked past him. Noah caught her hand, pulling her closer than he'd intended. She looked up at him with large, dark eyes, her small hand warm and inviting where it cradled against his palm.

"I'm not putting someone else out of a room, am I?" he asked, his breathing strangely erratic. "I don't mind the couch."

Savannah's eyes trailed up and down his frame. She didn't take her hand away. "I don't think you'd fit on the couch."

She took a step closer. Noah couldn't catch a breath. He lowered his head toward hers. Her sweet scent flooded his receptors. He could almost taste those rosebud lips.

"There are four guest bedrooms down here," she said, her breath hot against his lips. "This one has the best mattress. Enjoy it." She pulled away from him and breezed toward the door.

Noah gasped for air. He straightened in an attempt to appear unfazed. "What time do we need to go in the morning?"

She whirled to face him. "Do you have to be with me every second?"

"That's my job."

Her face fell. Noah wished he could have said something nicer—maybe, *I want to be with you every second*, but that wouldn't be like him.

"Be ready at 5:40," Savannah said.

Noah nodded. "Okay."

She didn't budge. "You don't really think I hurt my sister, do you?"

Noah rotated from her dark gaze. He hoisted his bag onto the bed, undoing a zipper. "What I think doesn't matter."

"What if it matters to me?"

Noah's head swung up. He released the bag and crossed the distance between them in two long strides. He forced himself not to gather her lithe form into his arms. "Well, that would be a completely different subject."

Savannah placed a delicate hand on his chest. Noah took a quick breath. He reached up and cupped her face with his palm. She leaned into his touch. Her hand on his chest trembled. He drew closer.

"It doesn't matter to me," she whispered. Dropping her hand, she pivoted on her heel and flew down the hallway.

Noah sat there, stunned. This woman was a contradiction in every sense of the word, and he knew he was falling for whatever game it was she was playing. It took him hours to forget the sensation of her hand on his chest. Images of her dark eyes smiling at him stayed with him as he drifted to sleep.

Savannah heard a strangled cry in the night. She rolled over with a groan, her body aching for more sleep. She grabbed the baby monitor, waiting for another sound. Nothing from the nursery. It wasn't Josh. She froze. What was it?

It came again. Definitely a human voice. She trembled, sharp fingernails pricked her arms and scalp. *Was somebody in the house? Had whoever hurt Ally come back?* She tossed off the covers and scrambled from bed. She flipped on the light and hurried down the hallway, worry for Josh's safety propelling her forward. Ten feet from her room, she heard it again.

Savannah listened closer. A deep voice called from the end of the hallway, "Mom, Mom."

"Mom?" she whispered to herself. She crept through the sleeping house, toward the noise. Her heart thumped. Within seconds she was poised outside the guest bedroom Noah slept in. She raised her hand to knock.

"Mom, Mom," Noah moaned.

She dropped her hand and slowly turned the doorknob. The door creaked open. The light from the hallway filtered into the room.

Noah lay on the bed, his T-shirt drenched in sweat. His head twisted back and forth, hands clenching the comforter, bare arms taut with tension.

"Mom. I'm sorry. Please don't. No. Mom!"

Savannah moved to his side, even though she knew she should close the door and walk away. "Noah," she whispered.

"Mom. Mom, come back."

Savannah shivered. This huge man whimpered like a puppy dog. The sight was scarier than an intruder. She'd never imagined Noah could look so weak. She leaned over him and grabbed his arm. It was burning.

"Noah. Wake up. You're having a nightmare."

"Mom. I shouldn't have. No!"

"Noah!"

His eyes flew open. He blinked at her face inches from his own. He drew in and exhaled several ragged breaths.

She moved her hand to his shoulder and leaned closer to him. "Noah. You were dreaming. Are you okay now?"

He grabbed her arm, pulling her onto the bed. "What are you doing in here?"

"I think you were having a nightmare."

"Oh." He released his grip on her.

Savannah waited for him to say more. His heartbeat thundered against her. "Do you have nightmares often?"

Noah didn't answer. Awkward in the silence, she moved from his side and stood. Even though it was the last thing she wanted to do.

"I'm sorry if I scared you," he said, watching her.

Any signs of vulnerability were gone. He was back to the tough, hardened detective who thought she'd hurt her sister. She covered the distance to the door, clinging to the handle. "It's okay. Can you sleep now?"

He exhaled. "I'll see you in the morning."

That was obviously a no. Savannah turned from his gaze and walked back to her room.

Seven

Noah struggled to sleep but didn't succeed. When the alarm on his cell phone buzzed at five-thirty, his body rebelled against the movement he forced upon it. Neither he nor Savannah said much on the way to the gym. He wanted to apologize for waking her last night, but he didn't want her to have the opportunity to ask more questions about his mom.

The one thing he wouldn't apologize for was pulling her close to him. He wished he were more like his best friend. Jason could've taken a moment like that and made something out of it. Oh, well. Last night would've been a disappointment to Jason, but it was a good reminder to Noah. He needed to be careful with this woman. She could chew up an inexperienced man like him.

They pulled up to the large white building. Noah held the glass door for Savannah. She left him without another word, organizing weights for her client. Noah sauntered to the cardio section. He climbed onto an elliptical machine to warm up, keeping one eye on Savannah.

"Hey, Shumway," a loud voice called, "I thought the cops all worked out at the *other* gym. Doesn't Steve give you a discount there or something?"

Noah looked down from the elliptical machine. "Richins?" He nodded. "Yeah, we try to avoid the rich boy gym if we can."

Wesley Richins chuckled. "Bet you do. It's good to see you, Shumway. How's life?"

Noah mustered a smile, refusing to lie and say it was good to see Wes. "Doing all right. You?"

"Couldn't be better." Wes lifted the inner part of his eyebrows. "Hey, I'd love to chat, but I've got a training appointment with that beautiful little thing." He jerked his head in Savannah's direction.

Noah's jaw dropped. His eyes narrowed. *Unbelievable.*

Wes noticed. "Wait, please don't tell me you're after Savannah as well?"

Noah looked at the display module of the cardio machine. "Have a good workout, Richins."

"Don't worry. I will." Wes chortled. "If only you could afford to hire her, eh?"

Noah didn't respond. Wes laughed louder, slapping him on the back and walking away. Noah's legs rotated faster. He upped the intensity. Wesley Richins. Of all the people for Savannah to be training, it would have to be the guy who'd stolen every girlfriend Noah ever had from high school on up. He hated the jealousy eating at his insides, but as he watched Wes greet Savannah his stomach curled and anxiety raced through him. Noah's breathing increased, but the workout machine had little to do with it.

Savannah had a hard time concentrating as she met Wes for his first training appointment. She could see Noah going through the motions on an elliptical machine. He caught her peeking at him and jerked his chin up. Why couldn't he wink or show some interest in her? She rolled her eyes. Maybe because he had none.

She puller her ponytail tighter. Why did she care? Did every man have to fall at her feet? Savannah shook her head and looked down at her client. "Okay, Wesley, I know you've got ten more in you."

He grunted. "Good thing you know that, because I'm not so sure."

She smiled. "Never gonna improve if you can't kick your own tail-end."

Wes chuckled as he lay on the bench and grasped the fifty-five pound dumbbells she placed in his grip. "Never tried to kick my own butt before, though my dad did it a few times." He pushed the weight straight into the air. His chest muscles bulged from the movement.

"I'm sure plenty of people have wanted to try," she said.

He shook his head at her, focusing on the movement.

Savannah counted, "Eight, Nine . . . Come on, Wesley. Make me proud. Ten, that's it." She retrieved the weights from his trembling fingers one at a time, struggling to re-shelve the heavy dumbbells. "Impressive, not many people could superset fifty-five's on chest press after doing three sets of flies."

Wes slowly rose to a seated position. "I'm not like many people."

She raised an eyebrow. "So, I've noticed. Okay. We've done chest and delts pretty well. Let's hit your tri's and we can call it a day."

He was in his third set of triceps dips, his hands on one bench, his heels propped on another, when Savannah grabbed a forty-five pound plate. Wes grunted, "Please say you're not going to put that on my lap."

"And here I was thinking you aren't very bright."

He groaned. "How about you just sit on me?"

Savannah dropped the weight on his thighs. He jerked, but kept rising out of the dip.

"I weigh a lot more than forty-five pounds," she said.

"Yeah," Wes panted, lowering into another repetition. "But it'd be a lot more fun."

She glanced up to see Noah several feet away doing a lateral raise. He watched them with a clamped jaw. When he saw Savannah looking at him, he jerked his head forward and concentrated on his form in the mirror. A wave of guilt rushed through her abdomen.

"Are you going to take this thing off my lap?" Wes asked, hanging suspended between the two benches.

Savannah nodded dumbly, reaching down to grasp the plate. Her fingers brushed his leg.

Wes smiled. "It was worth the agony, just to have you do that."

Savannah didn't respond. She cast a sideways glance at Noah. Again she caught him scrutinizing them, a frown wrinkling his forehead. She quickly handed Wes a weighted bar for an overhead triceps extension. When he finished, she helped him stretch his chest, shoulders, and triceps. Every time she touched Wesley, Noah's reaction became more obvious.

"So," Savannah spoke to Wesley, but her eyes never left Noah. "That's all for the day." She grabbed her clipboard and walked away. Wes followed her.

"Thanks," he said. "I haven't pushed myself that hard in a long time."

"Well, I want to give you your money's worth."

Wes grinned. "You're worth every dollar."

Savannah felt she could smile, knowing Noah was far enough away he couldn't see her. "Thank you." They'd reached the locker room. "Same time tomorrow?"

"Anything is fine with me," he leaned closer, "as long as I get to see you again."

Savannah's smile froze. *The usual flirtations.* "I'll see you at six."

Wes raised a hand in farewell as she strode past him. Noah dutifully followed Savannah to the office space she shared with the other trainers and then out the front door.

The drive to Hyde Park passed in silence. Savannah wondered why Noah intrigued her. Where Wes worked so hard to cajole one smile from her, Noah seemed to be doing all he could to tolerate her presence. She glanced over at him. He was steering the truck with one hand and looking out the window with a bored expression. Why did he appeal to her? He was a dull cop, who showed about as much interest in her as a slab of concrete.

❧

Wes hurried to the hospital. Rosie would only be on duty until 7:30 AM. He didn't want to risk explaining his "situation" to another nurse. He took the stairs two at a time to the third story, hurrying down the hallway and buzzing into the ICU.

"Well, hello today," Rosie beamed up at him.

"Hello, yourself." Wes smiled. He tilted his head, pretending to study everything from her dark, frizzy hair to her unattractive nurse's uniform. "I didn't know they made scrubs in such pretty colors."

Rosie blushed. "I have lots of different colors and patterns."

He winked. "Do they all look as good on you as this one?"

Rosie faltered. "Um yes, I mean, no. I mean, thank you."

"You're welcome." Wes sauntered past the desk. "I'd better hurry and check on Ally. I only had a few minutes this morning, but I didn't want to miss seeing her or you."

Rosie grinned. Wes entered Allison's room, shut the door, and quickly administered the medicine. He bent down close, kissing the soft, cool cheek.

"Things are going well with Savannah. You might have to sleep for a long time because she's warming up a little slower than most women. But I'm sure you'll understand that's exactly the way I like it."

70

He straightened and left the room. A few more flirtations with Rosie and he was done with his unpleasant duties for the day. The rest of his time could be spent playing with his dad's money, watching Savannah, and thinking of ways to win her.

Ryan jolted awake in an uncomfortable and unfamiliar bed. The morning sun filtered through tilted blinds. He wasn't sure what woke him: The dull ache in his stomach, the sharp pain in his lower back, or the intense agony of knowing his wife might never wake again.

Climbing from the bed, he jerked on yesterday's clothes. He had to get to Allison's side. Maybe there'd been some change in the night. He didn't do much more than dress before he was storming down the hall toward the ICU. A dark-haired, well-built man, dressed in a tank top and shorts, brushed past him in a hurry to get to the elevator.

"Excuse me," the large man mumbled, looking into his face then quickly averting his gaze.

"Not a problem." Ryan watched the man hurry away. As he passed the nurse's desk, a new nurse asked what he needed. He wished Ilene was still on duty. "I want to see my wife."

"And who might that be?"

"Allison Mendez."

Ryan hurried past the nurse and rushed to Allison's room. Entering the room, Ryan searched Allison's face praying for something, anything.

The machines beeped periodically. If he listened closely he could hear Allison breathe, but there was nothing else. No indication that his thoughtful, loving wife still resided in the comatose form. If anything she looked paler and more limp than yesterday.

Ryan sank onto the chair. He didn't move. He studied her and waited. *Faith, Hope, and Love.* Was there any hope? The pain in his stomach and back increased the longer he sat.

He captured Allison's cold fingers between his hands. Lifting her hand, he brushed the back of it against his mouth. He remembered the first time they'd met. He could still picture her standing in the hallway of their high school. He'd been a senior and she was a sophomore. She'd looked uncertain and beautiful, trying to figure out which locker was hers.

Ryan had marched over and offered to help. She glanced up at him with sparkling black eyes and he was hooked. When the bell rang, he grabbed her hand and brushed it against his lips. His soccer buddies teased him, but he didn't care. From that day on, he stayed by her side every minute she allowed him to.

The memory faded. Fifteen years later and he still couldn't get enough of her, but did she know that? He spent too many nights in a meaningless hotel room instead of by her side.

He pushed a hand against his eyes. Pressure built and he couldn't hold back the sob ripping through his body. Ryan bowed under the pressure. He closed his eyes, his head pressing against her arm. Desperate to touch her, he stroked her soft skin and did the only thing he could. He prayed.

Noah and Savannah arrived at Allison's house to find it deserted. A note lay on the counter.

> Savvy,
>
> The doctor called with some test results that he couldn't inform us of over the phone, but he said not to worry. Allison is the same. I tried your cell, but you didn't answer. Come to the hospital after you get ready.
>
> Love ya,
>
> Dad

Savannah lifted the note off the counter, leaning against the granite. "I wonder what the doctor wants."

"It doesn't sound too urgent."

She stared at him. "I guess if it's not your sister it wouldn't seem like that big of a deal."

His mouth formed a circle. "Oh."

Savannah waited. She raised an eyebrow. That was it? She would love an ounce of emotion out of this man. Why didn't he try and discuss things like her dad or Ryan would, or apologize and grovel like all the men she dated?

Noah cleared his throat. "Your dad said not to worry. I'm sure everything is going to be okay."

Savannah rolled her neck, trying to release the tension there. "You're probably right." She closed her eyes, when she opened them Noah was studying her.

His look seared through her, but his words were in the same level tone he always used. "Where do you want me to shower?"

"Um." Savannah pulled her shirt away from her neck. Swishing it in and out she tried to create some cool air on her face. Noah watched her. Savannah stopped fanning, embarrassed. "You can use the guest bathroom downstairs," she said. "I'll use the one on the main floor."

"Okay. I'll meet you in fifteen minutes."

"Fifteen?" Savannah laughed. It sounded nervous even to her. "Better make it thirty. You don't have hair."

He grinned. "Hey, I have a little." He brushed past her and descended to the basement.

Savannah couldn't move. His glance and grin about did her in and the brush-by had completed the task. What was wrong with her? She had any number of men falling at her feet, trying to touch her and take her out on exciting dates and here she was smoldering over a burly detective looking at her and barely making contact. She shook her head. *This has to stop.*

Forty-five minutes later, they entered the waiting room to find her dad and Dr. McQuivey toe to toe.

"I am telling you that my daughter has never taken drugs and if you say that one more time—"

Ryan set Josh on the floor and grabbed his father-in-law's arm. "Calm down, Frank. Something weird is obviously happening with Ally. The important thing is getting her better. Let the doctor talk."

Frank turned away in disgust. "I'm through listening. My Ally girl is comatose and instead of making her better, he has the gall to—"

Dr. McQuivey backed away, clenching his clipboard.

Savannah rushed to her dad's side. Noah followed.

"Dad. What's going on?" Savannah asked.

"Aunt Savvy." Josh held up his hands. "What doing?"

Savannah swooped him up. "I'm here to see you, Josh."

He smiled, leaning into her shoulder. "Good, Savvy."

Frank jammed a hand through his thick, slate gray hair. He gestured to Ryan. "You tell her."

Ryan looked at the doctor then swung his gaze to Savannah. "They just tested Ally's blood and have found some kind of drug. They think she was taking it before the accident to make her relax or something."

Noah shadowed her, not speaking. Savannah was grateful for his solid presence.

Frank glared at her. "Do you believe that, Savvy? Would Allison ever do something like that? She was the best wife and mom and—" He spun and strode from the room.

"Dad?" Savannah called after him.

He lifted a hand. "In a minute."

She knew he must be close to a break down and couldn't let any of them see. But what were they saying about her sister? "I don't understand. What kind of a sedative?" she asked the doctor.

"It's called Midazolam."

Savannah's confusion must have been apparent.

"Midazolam is the generic name," Dr. McQuivey said. "You may have heard it called Versed."

Neither drug sounded familiar.

"I don't know how she could've gotten a hold of it," the doctor continued. "It's a prescription tranquilizer that only physicians have access to. It's similar to Valium and is typically administered prior to surgeries to help people relax. It's potent and a person who took too much would exhibit comalike symptoms. It can also induce amnesia, hypotension and a myriad of other side effects. It probably explains why she's still in a coma. Her concussion isn't serious enough to warrant the sustained lack of consciousness, but Versed would."

Ryan's head snapped up, his eyes filled with a childlike hope for the first time in the past two days. "So what you're saying is once this leaves her system, she'll wake up?"

Savannah waited for the answer impatiently.

The doctor frowned. "Yes, that's what I'm hoping, but I can't give you any promises. She did lose a lot of blood and sustain a traumatic head injury."

"But still," Ryan pressed on. "Ally could start recovering if this will just leave her body?"

"Yes, she could," Dr. McQuivey said. "But the other issue we need to consider after recovery is a detox program. This is a serious drug problem. An interesting one to boot. She must have been taking the medication to relieve anxiety." He scratched his chin. "Versed isn't well known, but it can be habit forming."

Savannah shifted Josh to her other hip and raised her hand. "Wait a minute. Why are you so quick to assume that Allison would've taken something like this? Maybe the person who attacked her put something in her system or maybe somebody at the hospital did it."

The doctor eyed her like she was insane.

She set Josh on the floor.

"Hold me, Savvy," he begged.

Savannah held up a finger. "Just a second, sweetie."

Fishing some lip balm out of her pocket, she handed it to him. He jerked the lid off and started applying it to his arms.

"Listen," she said to the doctor. "Isn't it possible that someone else could've given this drug to Ally?"

The doctor pressed his lips together. "I'm sorry. I know it's hard to believe that someone close to you could be addicted to prescription meds, but this sort of thing happens often. Did she have a recent injury or . . ." He glanced at Ryan. "Were there problems at home?"

Ryan's mouth tightened.

"Wait a minute," Savannah interrupted the doctor. She wanted to scream at the insensitive jerk, but didn't want to terrify Josh. "There aren't problems, and my sister would never take drugs. She rarely took Tylenol for crying out loud. Someone else had to have given her the drug!" She could see why her dad wanted to hit the doctor. The physician's look clearly said she was in denial.

Noah moved around to face her, grasping her forearm with one hand. "Why would someone want to keep her in a coma, Savannah?"

Her jaw dropped. She snatched her arm from his grip. "Well, I don't know, Detective Shumway."

He leaned closer. "Maybe you do," he whispered.

Savannah looked away. Ryan raised an eyebrow at her, his glance full of questions. She dropped her gaze to Josh, at least he wasn't blaming her for hurting his mom.

The doctor shook his head. "I don't know what you two are implying, but no one but a physician could get access to this medicine."

Savannah whirled on him. "Exactly. So, somebody at this hospital is drugging my sister, and you're trying to make it look like she did this to herself!"

The doctor harrumphed.

Ryan stepped toward her. "Savvy, maybe you should go find your dad."

"Maybe, nothing," Savannah retorted. "I'm protecting my sister."

"Savvy," he said. "She's my wife as well as your sister."

"She was my sister before she was your wife."

Ryan rocked back on his heels. His eyebrows rose high enough to touch his hairline.

"I know her better than anybody. No one is going to tell me that my sister was taking drugs. Wait a minute. Why are you just telling us this now? Is this the first time you've done blood tests?"

The doctor opened his file. "Well, no, they did a panel on her blood the night she arrived in the ICU. I'm not sure why I wasn't informed of the substance earlier. It should've been in higher concentration that first night." He paused, searching through the papers. His forehead wrinkled. "That's strange."

"What?" Savannah and Ryan said together, pressing closer to the doctor. Noah watched silently.

"The earlier tests showed no traces of Midazolam. But how could that be? No one on our staff would've administered the medicine and the only visitors have been family." He shook his head, looking up at them. "I'm sorry. Something isn't adding up. Will you excuse me, please?"

They all nodded.

"I'm sorry to have startled you. Something isn't right with one of these tests. We'll run another panel and get back to you." He was already exiting the room, but still mumbling to them, "I have your numbers. We'll be in contact."

Savannah turned to stare at Ryan. A chill pierced her. "What's going on, Ry?"

He put an arm around her. "I don't know."

She leaned into his shoulder. The only sound was the ticking of the wall clock.

Noah squatted down next to Josh. "You're covered in that stuff, little man."

Josh grinned in return, holding the Chap Stick aloft. Noah lifted the little boy from the floor. Straightening, he held out his arm and Josh went to work.

Savannah watched them, at least Noah was cute with somebody in her family. "Sorry about what I said about Ally being my sister before—"

Ryan cut her off. "I think you're permitted one snide comment in situations like these."

She grinned. "Can I have ten of those permission slips?"

Ryan shook his head, the corners of his lips lifting. "No way. You'd be burning me on every turn." He looked at Josh and Noah. "Would you mind taking Josh for a walk? He's sick of this, but I don't want to leave in case Ally wakes up."

Savannah nodded. "I'd feel better if you were here watching over her. It's almost like someone is hurting her on purpose."

Noah turned, careful not to upset Josh's work on his arm. He moistened his bottom lip, searching her eyes. "I think you're right."

Savannah stole her nephew from his grasp. "Do you want a doughnut?"

Josh's eyes lit up. "Yes, please, please, please!"

Noah moved to her side. "I'll come with you."

Savannah sighed, but was relieved that at least he wouldn't be sharing any of his theories with her brother-in-law. "Do you want anything, Ry?" she asked.

"No. I had some juice earlier."

"How about a bagel or something more filling?"

Ryan shook his head. "I can't eat."

Savannah felt guilty for her grumbling stomach. "Okay." She and Noah walked away. She waited until they were in the elevator to whisper, "Don't you trust me alone with my own nephew?"

"I don't know how you think I could," Noah said. He studied her. "Did you put drugs into your sister's IV?"

"Oh!" She cried out. "How could you think—?"

"You knew from the start that you were a suspect. Remember how you begged me to stay with you so you could prove me wrong?"

"Yes, and now that you know me . . ." He couldn't still believe she'd hurt her sister.

His eyebrow arched. The elevator door opened. Noah waited for her to go ahead, then caught up to her in two long strides. "All I know now is someone is still trying to hurt your sister. You were at the scene of the first accident and you're one of the few people who have access to Allison."

Savannah hated him. "I know now why they call cops pigs."

He didn't even give her the courtesy of a reaction. "Call me all the names you want. I'm going to figure out who's hurting your sister and if it's you I don't care how bad your family is hurting. I'll put you away."

"Why don't you quit wasting time badgering me and find the person who really hurt Ally?"

Noah's eyes narrowed. "My partner is following every lead we have in this case. If there's another suspect he'll find him."

"Good! Then you can leave me alone and prosecute the real Jackie."

"I'm afraid I'm looking at her."

Savannah swung her hair, stomping away from him toward the hospital cafeteria. "Let's both have a donut with chocolate frosting," she said to Josh, not caring how fattening they were. Sometimes a girl just needed some chocolate in her system.

Noah trailed Savannah and Josh to the cafeteria on the main floor of the hospital. She picked out a donut with sprinkles for Josh, skim milk and a banana for herself. Noah grabbed two bagel sandwiches and an orange juice.

"Thought you were going to have a donut," he said as they waited to pay for their food.

She shook her head, glaring up at him. "It's not worth it."

Noah raised an eyebrow. Did that mean a donut wasn't worth the calories or being mad at him wasn't worth ruining her diet?

They carried their food to the table. Noah was grateful Josh broke the silence. "Rosie, rosie," he begged.

"Why don't you eat your donut first?" Savannah asked.

"Rosie," Josh demanded.

Savannah sighed and half-heartedly sang, "Ring around the Rosie." Josh spun in circles, laughing. "Savvy loves to throw me," she continued. Josh held out his arms. Savannah lifted him in the air. "Ashes, ashes, we all fall upside down." She tipped him off her knees, so his head hung toward the floor.

He giggled. "Again, again."

Noah watched the way Savannah interacted with her nephew. He was having a hard time believing this warm, beautiful woman could have hurt her sister. He grimaced. At this point she was the only suspect in the case. If there was one thing he'd learned numerous times in his past four years with the sheriff's office—people were deceitful.

Josh tired of the cafeteria after an hour. Noah cleaned up their food and dumped it into the trash. They walked out of the cafeteria and toward the main entry. Savannah moved past the elevators and opened the door for the stairs.

"Do you ever take the easy way?" Noah asked.

Savannah glanced over her shoulder. "You can burn an extra forty calories running four flights of stairs."

Noah grunted in response. *Who cared about a measly forty calories?*

"Plus, Josh loves the stairs."

Savannah bounced and counted. Josh giggled. She exited the stairway at the second floor instead of going up to the third.

"Wrong floor," Noah said.

"I know." She flipped her hair over her shoulder. "We want to check if the babies' window is open. Is that okay with you?"

Noah was at a loss. "Um, sure."

Josh smiled. "Babies?"

Savannah nuzzled his neck, kissing him. "Yes, love. We adore babies, don't we?"

Josh's dark head bobbed. "Mommy have baby?"

She sobered and pulled him closer. "Maybe someday."

The nursery window's blinds were open. Savannah's face lit up as she exclaimed over the newborns. "Look at those little feet, Josh. That boy has the cutest bird legs."

"Pink one cutest." Josh poked the glass with his chubby finger.

Savannah sighed. "How could you ever decide which one is the cutest? I'd take them all home."

Noah barely saw the infants. His eyes were focused on Savannah's face as she gooed and gaahed. Was she putting on a show for him? Was she genuinely this excited over a bunch of shriveled newborns? Noah liked babies at much as the next person, their soft skin, their innocent eyes, but he'd never seen anyone so enthralled with them as Savannah appeared to be.

Noah walked twenty feet down the hallway and dialed Jason's number, still keeping one eye on Savannah.

"Hey, Keller. Any luck finding me a suspect?"

"You mean besides your girlfriend?"

Noah gazed at Savannah. She turned and met his eye, then quickly refocused on the babies.

"Anyone but her."

"Sorry, man, I got nothing. One neighbor said they heard a car peel out of the neighborhood a little before ten, but that could've been a teenager. Any lip action?"

Noah ignored the last question. "They found a sedative in Allison's blood. It didn't appear until after she was at the hospital, so somebody's injecting it into her." Noah turned his back and lowered his voice. "The first time I've trusted my instincts instead of the evidence and this case is a mess. I don't think Savannah could've done it, but she was the only one at the scene and now the drugs? The husband's been here nonstop. Hospital security is doing random checks, but their surveillance system is from the Stone Age." He shoved a hand through his hair. "I don't know what else to do but watch Savannah."

"I don't know what to tell you. I'll get an officer to do checks up there and drive-bys, but that's probably as far as I can stretch."

Savannah was walking in his direction.

"I've got to go," Noah said. "Let me know if you find anything else."

"You let me know when you get a piece of that woman."

Noah hung up the phone and reddened when Savannah stopped at his side.

Eight

The day at the hospital dragged. Noah spent most of the day questioning the nurses and other staff members, but he always made sure Savannah wasn't with Allison unless he was watching. She hated that. Savannah, Josh, and Noah visited the nursery again. The sight of those perfect babies lifted her spirit, but every time she thought of Allison her peace evaporated.

While they ate lunch in the cafeteria with her dad, she talked to several of her friends on her cell phone and fielded calls from a few of the men she was dating. Every time she hung up, she noticed Noah gripping his sandwich tighter. When the bread from his sandwich reconverted to dough, she smiled and turned the phone's ringer off. Maybe the hard-nosed detective was affected by something.

Savannah took her turns visiting Allison's room. Each one made her feel worse. How could they bring Ally back? Was someone putting drugs in her IV? Was her Ally even in that lifeless body? The words on the wall mocked her. She closed her eyes, silently asking, "Why can't I have the faith to bring Ally back?"

Noah waited outside Allison's door, arms folded across his chest. He'd dressed casually today. Savannah's eyes traveled the length of his frame. He looked as good in jeans and a T-shirt as he had in dress clothes. He returned her glance with an unblinking stare. What was in his eyes? Did he really think she could've done this to Ally?

She gritted her teeth, tossing her hair over her shoulder. Detective Shumway could think anything he wanted and monitor her every move, but he'd never see her do anything to hurt her sister. How would she convince him she wasn't a monster? She jerked in her seat. *Why did she care?*

She let her gaze swing to the window, longing to be free of the depressing room. It was a gorgeous day outside. If Ally were awake they'd probably be playing at the city pool with Josh. Savannah sighed. A pang of guilt hit her. She shouldn't crave freedom and the warmth of the sunshine when her sister was lying comatose two feet away.

She rose to leave. She'd run out of things to say minutes ago.

"I'll see you tomorrow, Ally. Love ya." She paused, there had to be something else, something she needed to tell her sister.

"Um, get some rest." She cringed. That was all Allison was doing: resting.

She walked from the room and Noah took her arm.

"I can make it on my own."

He turned to her with an easy smile. "I'm sure you can."

He didn't release his grip. Unfortunately, she enjoyed it.

Ilene stood in the hallway, arms crossed and a grin lighting her face. "Hello, you two."

Noah's cheek crinkled as he smiled at the nurse. "Hello, Ilene. Are you just starting your shift?"

"I'm here all night." She beamed at them. "If you aren't the most darling couple I've ever seen."

Savannah's mouth gaped open and Noah turned a shade darker.

The nurse chuckled. "Now I know there's no ring, so you're obviously not intended yet, but I just have to say you look perfect together. The detective is so big and handsome and you my dear, could be a model. You look like something out of a movie."

"We . . . we," Savannah stuttered.

Noah slid his hand down her arm, surrounding her fingers. "Thank you, Ilene."

Savannah gazed up at him in shock. Why hadn't he corrected the nurse?

Ilene patted Savannah's arm. "Now, don't you worry one bit about your sister. I'll take good care of her all night. You hurry home and rest. Oh, and take that brother-in-law of yours with you. He looks like garbage."

Savannah nodded her thanks, still unable to talk. Noah confused her.

How could he accuse her of hurting Allison and then minutes later pretend he liked her? He escorted her out of the ICU unit, releasing her hand before they reached her family. Ryan stood and set Josh on the ground. Savannah watched as Josh raced to Noah and Noah swung Josh up in his arms. Her own nephew had just run to the cop instead of her. Was she the only one who wasn't falling for Noah? Correction: Was she the only one who didn't want to be falling for Noah?

"You'd better get Josh home," Ryan said.

Josh whipped his head around. "Daddy come home?"

Ryan shook his head. "Sorry, bubba. Maybe tomorrow night."

"Ry, you have to get some sleep and eat something," Savannah said. "I'm fine."

Frank inclined his head toward Josh, who was happily chattering to Noah. "Your son needs you."

Ryan studied the floor. "I can't leave Ally."

"Wearing yourself out isn't going to help Ally," Savannah said. "Things will look a lot better if you eat something and sleep in your own bed."

Ryan's jaw hardened. "Things aren't going to look better until my wife wakes up!"

Josh whimpered, burying his head in Noah's shoulder. "Daddy, no yell."

Ryan held out his arms. Noah transferred the child to his father. He gently rocked his boy. "Sorry, bubba. Sorry. Daddy won't yell again." He moved Josh's head to the middle of his chest. His eyes caught Savannah's over the baby's head.

"How could I sleep in our bed without her?" he whispered.

Savannah compressed her lips. "I didn't think of that."

"I can't leave her alone." Ryan kissed Josh and handed his son to Savannah. "Thanks for taking care of him."

Josh cried for his dad and mom as they walked down the hospital hall. Noah strode to Savannah's side and held out his arms. Joshua dove for him. Noah swung him up onto his shoulders. Josh giggled and clung to Noah's ears.

Savannah stared at the detective. She breathed a sigh of relief. Maybe having Noah around was accomplishing some good, if only the sight of him didn't affect her so much.

Wes watched Noah, Savannah, and her family trudge from the hospital. It looked like another long day for the group. He ran his hand across his face. He hated causing Savannah pain, and he hated Shumway being close to her, but he couldn't fix either of those things yet. Once Allison had taken the drug long enough, she shouldn't be able to remember him even coming to her house. Until then, he'd have to keep working his way into Savannah's heart. He grinned. So far their encounters showed promise.

He started the motor of his Hummer. Rosie wouldn't be on duty until tomorrow morning; he'd have to wait until then to inject more Versed into Allison's IV.

His phone rang. He pushed the receive button. "Yes?"

"Wesley," Jamison Richin's booming voice matched the rest of his body. "Cynthia says you haven't been at the office much the past few days."

"I've been in and out," Wes said. "I've been busy, Dad."

"With what?"

Wes thought of Savannah. "I'm dating someone."

The older man snorted. "Like that's something new. You've dated the entire female population in the valley." He paused. "Well, the attractive ones at least."

Wes shook his head. "This one's new. She's special."

His dad laughed, causing a round of hacking coughs. "When do I get to meet her?" he finally choked out.

Wes turned right on Tenth North, wishing his dad would lay off the cigars. "Hopefully soon. I've got to convince her she can't live without me first."

His dad chuckled again. "Shouldn't be too hard, son. Well, try and spend some time at the office."

"Okay." Wes squinted against the setting sun. He opened the compartment for his sunglasses and put them on. "Hey, Dad. Hypothetically speaking, what would you do if I got into trouble?"

His dad cleared his throat. "I'd cut you off. I've told you that before."

Wes gripped the steering wheel tighter. "That's what I thought."

"You in trouble, son?"

Wes forced a laugh. Not yet, he wanted to say. "I'm not stupid."

"You're not stupid at all, but be careful. I've got enough worries with the ridiculous rumors being fabricated in this valley. We've got an election coming up, you know?"

"I know." How could he ever forget? There was always another election. He wanted to ask his dad about the rumors, but knew that would cause a tirade he didn't have the patience for.

"Come see me with that girl sometime," Jamison said. "What did you say her name was?"

"Savannah." Wes smiled. "The gorgeous Savannah."

"What is it, Keller?" Noah said into his cell phone as he strode to the room he was staying in.

"Have you made a move yet?"

Noah thought of the beauty upstairs. He thought of the brief contact they'd shared. He thought of the accusations he'd hurled at her today. He shook his head. "Nothing yet."

Jason sighed. "Thought I'd better get an update. Do you need me to take over your job? I'm willing and ready for the responsibility. You know what I'm saying?"

Noah sat down on the bed. He thought of his funny, good-looking friend flirting with Savannah. His grip tightened on the phone. "You stay away from her."

"Whoo-hoo. Now that is the best thing I've heard from you in a long while. Detective Stone Face getting emotional about a woman."

Noah exhaled. Of course Jason was teasing him.

"You still think she hurt her sister?" Jason asked.

"I don't know what to think. She doesn't seem like the type, but until we find another suspect." He shrugged. "I'm afraid she's playing me pretty hard."

Jason laughed. "That's great."

Noah leaned into the pillow, shaking his head against the softness of it. "Why is that great?"

"You're closer to that kiss than I ever thought possible. What's happening at the hospital?"

Noah sobered. "I already told you about the drug they found in Allison's blood."

"Uh-huh. So, whoever hurt her is trying to keep her in that coma."

"I can't imagine when Savannah could be injecting the drug."

"Only family is visiting?"

"The doctor promised me they would keep it to family. I've spoken with all the nurses but one. So far there's been no motivation to hurt Allison or a way to access the medication without the doctor's approval. I'll talk to the one I missed in the morning when she comes on duty. I left the ICU staff info on your office phone. Will you do background checks tomorrow for me?"

"Sure thing. Did you check the sign-in sheet and make sure you know who's been in and out of that unit? Maybe somebody's claiming to visit someone else and sneaking into her room."

Noah closed his eyes, rubbing his forehead with one hand. Why did Jason always think of these things? Where would he be without his best friend? He sighed. Sometimes he hated his job. "I'll do it in the morning."

"Okay. You trust the nurse on duty tonight?"

He laughed. "Yeah. I pity the person who tries to hurt Allison on Ilene's watch."

"Good, but we'll still do checks. You'll be there all day tomorrow?"

Noah exhaled. "Yeah. I can't believe I didn't think of the sign-in sheet."

"Don't worry about it. I can see why you'd be distracted." Jason whistled. "Get to work on kissing Savannah and I'll try to find us another suspect."

Noah wished they had someone else to pin this on. He couldn't stand thinking that Savannah might be a criminal. It didn't fit, and he didn't want it to. "Thanks for your help, Jase."

"My phone's always on, waiting to hear from you, man, especially if you get some action."

Noah smiled. "So if something happens in the middle of the night?"

Jason cackled. "Even better."

<hr />

"Mom, I'm coming," Noah called out. He flew toward her on shaky legs. She doubled over, a swath of blonde hair falling across her forehead. Grasping her stomach, she moaned. She glanced up at him, eyes drained of their dancing blue light. "Noah." One hand lifted to touch his cheek. Her fingers were drenched in blood. Noah shied away from the red limb. Who had done this to her?

"Oh, Mom." His voice caught. He sank to his knees. "I'll get an ambulance. You'll be okay."

He reached for his phone, choking on a sob. Her bloodied hand stopped him.

"No, Noah." She stroked his cheek, leaving trails of wetness. "I love you."

Her eyes closed. Her hand slipped away.

"No!" he screamed. "No! No!" He looked down at his hands. They were covered in blood. He gripped a sticky knife between his fingers. It was his fault. He'd killed her.

"No, Mom! I'm sorry."

Someone was shaking him, pulling him away. He fought the person. "I won't leave you, Mom. I won't. I'm sorry. No!"

Suddenly, she was gone. In her place a dark form hovered over him. His legs were entangled in warm sheets. A small hand massaged his shoulder. His mom was gone. He tried to clear his vision. A nightmare. It was just another nightmare.

"Noah? Noah? Are you okay?"

Reality entered. He was in his house, but he wasn't alone. *Who was this woman? What was she doing here?* Noah sat upright. He grabbed the intruder. Flipping her around, he crushed the woman against his chest. "How did you get into my house?"

"Noah," the woman whispered. "It's me. It's Savannah. We're at my sister's house."

He released his grip on her. She stayed on his lap, turning to face him. Noah couldn't help himself. He buried his face in her neck and tried to regulate his breathing. She wrapped her arms around his back, gently massaging the tight muscles in his shoulders and neck.

"It's okay, Noah. I've got you. It was just a dream."

Realization soaked into him. The nightmare was replaced by a reality he'd been fantasizing about. His hands surrounded Savannah's small frame. Suddenly all he could think about was the woman nestled in his arms.

His lips nuzzled against the warm skin between her collarbone and chin. He imagined himself trailing his mouth up to her face. "Oh, Savvy . . ."

"Savannah," she corrected.

The moment shattered. He lifted his head, and slowly released his grip on her. "Of course, Savannah."

She didn't appear to notice his withdrawal. "I didn't want to wake you, but it seemed like an awful nightmare." She paused then whispered. "What happened to your mom?"

Noah reclined against the headboard, drawing farther away from her. Savannah leaned closer to him. Her soft scent and the pressure of her weight on his legs was a pleasant torture. He wanted to wrap his arms around her and share every secret.

"I'm sorry if I scared you," was all he could manage.

The silence scratched at his ears. Finally Savannah lifted herself off of him.

Noah caught a ragged breath, grateful to find oxygen again. He wished he could be grateful she wasn't touching him anymore. He couldn't see anything but her outline moving toward the doorframe.

"I want to workout before I train. Do you want to come or can you trust me alone?"

He cleared his throat. "It's already morning?"

"Yeah."

"What time is it?"

"4:30."

Noah felt the softness of the bed beneath him, begging him to linger. "And the reason we can't workout after you train?"

"I want to be with my family."

Noah tossed the blankets out of his way. He stood slowly. He towered over her in the dimly lit room. "I'll be ready in two minutes."

Savannah backed away. She sighed. "That's what I figured. Bring stuff so you can shower there. Afterwards we'll go straight to the hospital."

Her voice was so cold, but there was nothing Noah could do about that. He couldn't trust her to be alone and he couldn't trust her with his secrets.

Nine

Noah and Savannah exercised in companionable silence. They started on the Stairmasters, pumping their machines up and down. Savannah studied the display monitor to pass the time, constantly changing the settings and looking to see how many calories she'd burned, miles she'd covered, and steps she'd taken.

She liked having Noah next to her. With scant entertainment available, her mind flitted to the feel of his large hands caressing her that morning.

"You about ready to lift?" he asked, wrenching her from her daydreams and reminding her how awkwardly their early morning encounter had ended.

"Oh, sure," she said.

She stepped off the Stairmaster and moved toward the free weights. She started piling weight on the Smith machine. Noah let her be in charge of their workout. They took turns doing sets of weighted squats with the machine.

"I don't usually train for free," Savannah teased, watching the muscles bulge in his quadriceps.

He grinned. "Maybe I'll have to find a way to make it up to you."

Blood rushed to her face.

Noah removed the plates he'd stacked on the Smith machine. "I was thinking dinner at Hamilton's once Allison recovers."

Savannah turned to retrieve a weighted bar, hoping he wouldn't realize what she'd been thinking. "That sounds great," she said, moving into a wide squat.

She loved watching the striated musculature in Noah's quadriceps and hamstrings as they did squats, lunges, dead lifts, extensions, and curls. She couldn't lift one-fourth of what he did. She decided to level the workout field by implementing a few Plyometrics. Setting up a sixteen-inch lift, she demonstrated their next move, leaping into a deep squat then stepping back.

Noah shied away from the step. "You expect me to jump around like a bunny rabbit?"

"Stop worrying about what people think. This is going to shred your calves."

He folded his arms across his chest. "I'm shredded enough. I'm not a dancer."

"Just try it, you pansy." Savannah leaped onto the bench, liking the pull in her quadriceps as she squatted.

Noah groaned, but seconds later he was jumping onto the bench beside her. They accomplished the first set of sixty seconds and in silent agreement walked shakily to the drinking fountain. After the second set, Savannah's legs were screaming in agony. She wasn't even sure she could do the third set, but was determined to beat him at something.

"Are we done?" Noah asked.

"One more set."

He groaned, but moved to the bench again. Savannah couldn't agree more. It hurt, but she wouldn't quit. They leaped onto the bench and stepped off in harmony. Sixty seconds passed and Savannah's legs trembled. After ninety seconds she didn't jump high enough. Her toe caught, tripping her. She caught herself, stepped down and jumped again.

Noah panted next to her, "You okay?"

"Yeah," she managed, willing him to quit, but he kept going.

They reached two minutes and Savannah finally gasped, "You had enough?"

"Yes." He stalked away from the bench toward the drinking fountain.

Savannah smiled to herself. He'd quit first. She collapsed onto a nearby bench.

"You done?" Noah asked, wiping a droplet of water from his lower lip with the back of his hand.

Savannah licked her own lips.

"You can do more?" she asked, struggling to her feet.

"No." He shook his head. "But I couldn't be the one who admitted it first."

Savannah sighed in relief. Noah grinned. He sank onto the bench, pulling her down with him. He wrapped his hand around her bicep. Laughing, she flexed.

Noah nodded appreciatively. "You're the toughest chick I know."

Savannah shivered from his touch and the warmth of his compliment. "Thanks, you're not such a wuss either." She leaned into him, slowly catching her breath, though her pulse refused to slow down with Noah this close. "We should cool down and stretch."

"Ah, that's a waste of time."

She whirled on him. "Stretching after a workout is one the most important . . ."

He grinned, raising his hands in defense. "I was kidding. Come over to the mat and I'll stretch you."

"That's the best offer I've had in a long time." They walked past the weight equipment to a large exercise mat.

"Lay down," Noah said.

"We can stretch at the same time."

He rotated his head. "I said I'd help you stretch, now lay down."

Savannah obeyed his command, lying on her back. Noah knelt next to her. His hands closed around her left calf muscle, raising her leg off the mat. Slowly, he pressed her leg toward her head. She closed her eyes, enjoying the stretch and the feel of his strong hands touching her.

Half a minute later, he lowered her leg and repeated the movement on the other side. She peeked at him through a slit in her eyes. He caught her watching and smiled.

"You're like a monkey," he said.

Savannah's eyes opened wider. "A monkey? I'm not sure that's a compliment."

"It is. I've never seen anyone so flexible."

She tilted her head on the mat, appraising him. She'd like to run her hand along the curve of his jaw and stare into those blue eyes without looking away. "You spend a lot of time stretching women?"

His tongue trailed along his lower lip. "This is a first for me."

She smiled as he lowered her leg.

"Roll onto your stomach."

She did as instructed.

Noah lifted her left leg by the ankle, his other hand gently pushing behind her knee, forcing her quadriceps muscle into the mat. His calloused fingers trailed along the back of her knee.

She giggled. "That tickles."

"I know you like it."

"Stop it," she laughed, slapping at his hand.

"Savannah?" A voice questioned from behind.

Noah released her leg, whirling to face Wesley. She flipped over, sitting up on the mat. Noah stood, his eyes darkened to a midnight blue, his grin slid to nonexistence. He offered Savannah a hand, gently helping her to her feet.

She forced a smile. "Good morning, Wesley. You ready to workout?"

He wrapped a towel around his neck, holding onto each end. His trapezoid muscles bunched around his ears. He nodded at Noah. "Looks like you're already done."

"I needed a good workout today. I don't get any exercise training you." She smiled and turned to Noah. "I'll see you in an hour."

He nodded. "I'll finish stretching and spend some time in the sauna, maybe I can undo some of the damage you caused."

Savannah grinned. "I can't wait to see how you're walking tomorrow."

He returned the smile. "See you in a bit." He jerked his chin at Wesley as he brushed past him.

Wes flashed a charming smile at Savannah, ignoring Noah. Savannah almost felt like she should introduce the two, but neither of them seemed interested. She got right down to business. An hour later, Wes was having difficulty walking as well. They picked their way through the weight machines, moving toward the locker room.

"Don't I need to consume protein after I workout?" Wes asked.

Savannah nodded. "It's the best way to recover and increase muscle mass. The general guideline is within half an hour."

"It's hard to want to eat after working out hard."

Savannah stopped in front of the women's locker room. She pointed up the wide staircase. "Try the counter upstairs. They make a great yogurt smoothie. Ask Jill to add two scoops of protein powder to yours and you'll be in business."

Wes leaned against the tan wall, folding his brawny arms across his chest. His dark hair curled with wetness. Savannah had to admit she couldn't find anything wrong with his looks.

"Wouldn't a good breakfast be better for me?"

She shrugged. "Maybe. You are trying to increase your mass, but I thought you just said it was hard to eat after working out."

"It's hard to eat by myself." He tilted his head to the side. "So, how about it?"

Savannah blinked at him. "How about what?"

"Want to go to breakfast with me?"

She shook her head. "I don't think so."

Wes leaned toward her. "Why not?"

"Um, I'm all sweaty."

"We can both shower quick and meet outside."

Savannah tried for another excuse. Noah would not like her going to breakfast with Wesley. "I really need to get to the hospital."

Wes's face grew solemn. "Yeah, but you really need to eat, too. You'll be a lot more help to your sister and family if you keep your strength up."

"I don't think Noah would like it."

Wesley reached out and took her hand. "You aren't going to let him dictate your life, are you? You're free, beautiful, and over twenty-one. Who's going to tell you what to do?"

Savannah looked up to see Noah sitting on a couch in the entryway dressed casually in a tan T-shirt and jeans. His short hair was darker than usual, still wet from the shower. His blue eyes studied her with a frightening intensity. His lips were so pouty he could've won a contest with Josh after the toddler had been told no. She looked away. What right did he have to act like she was in the wrong to be with her client? Wesley was right. She was hungry, and Noah wasn't in charge of her.

"Come on," Wes said. "I don't see you as the kind of woman who lets someone tell her what to do. Don't let him boss you around. Come with me to breakfast."

Savannah looked at Noah again. She thought of his hands on her legs as he helped her stretch. She couldn't ditch him, but maybe Wes's attention would make Noah realize what he was missing.

"Okay," she said to Wes.

He smiled.

"I'm sure Noah would love to go to breakfast with us."

His eyes widened. "Um."

"I'll meet you in twenty minutes."

Twenty uncertain minutes later, she exited the locker room dressed in a black cotton shirt, tan capris, and chunky-heeled black sandals that added a couple of inches to her height.

Noah was waiting just outside the locker room door. She brushed past him. "We're going to breakfast with Wes."

"What?"

"You heard me," she shot over her shoulder. "It'll only take an hour. You'll be right with me to make sure I'm not hurting anyone."

He grabbed her arm, dragging her to a stop. "I thought you needed to rush to the hospital and be with your family."

"What I do with my time is not your business."

Noah's eyes were hooded. His full lips thinned. "Oh, but it is. I seem to recall a little girl begging me to stay by her side twenty-four hours a day rather than put her in jail."

Savannah's jaw dropped, she glared at the spot where his hand seared her flesh. "You never said you were going to put me in jail."

He released her arm, spinning away. "I should have."

"I'm sorry." She crossed her arms over her chest. "I'll tell Wes we can't eat breakfast with him because my parole officer is jealous."

Noah whirled back, towering over her despite her high-heeled shoes. "I'm not jealous." He gestured toward Wes, standing outside the double exterior doors, dressed in a shirt and tie. "You think I'd be jealous of pretty boy? Let's go," he muttered. "But make it quick. I've got work to do."

Savannah sauntered toward Wes with a smile adorning her lips.

The awkward trio eased into a booth at Angie's Restaurant. Savannah ordered water, scrambled eggs, and fruit. Wesley ordered an orange juice, a hot chocolate, pancakes, a Denver omelet with extra cheese, and a plate of bacon on the side. Noah said he'd have the same, looking completely uncomfortable. The waitress was back in moments with their beverages.

"Men are so lucky," Savannah said, drooling over their hot chocolates mounded with whipped cream.

Wes set his mug on the table and winked. "Because we get to look at you?"

She shook her head, dismissing the empty flattery. "No. Because you can eat anything you like and you just look better the bigger you get."

He leaned back in his chair. "That's the closest thing to a compliment you've ever given me."

Savannah took a long swallow of her water. "I meant it in general." She looked over to see Noah with a clamped jaw. She searched for something to say that would ease the tension. "What do you do for a living, Wesley?"

He tapped his fingers on the table. "Can't you please call me Wes?"

"Maybe." She arched an eyebrow at him, ignoring Noah's scowl. "What do you do for work, *Wes*?"

He smiled at her. "Thank you."

"You're welcome. So, what do you do?" She swirled the water in her cup.

He slowly unwrapped his silverware from the paper napkin. "I manage the family business."

"Which is?"

The waitress delivered their food at that moment, saving Wes from a reply. He and Noah dove into their breakfast. Savannah took small bites, forcing herself to set her fork down between each nibble.

A dad with a little boy and girl were shown to the table next to them. Savannah smiled at them, lifting her fingers. The boy ducked his blond head in embarrassment. His younger sister grinned a mischievous greeting. Her round cheeks dimpled. Her red curls bounced. "Hi!" she shouted.

Her dad shushed her. "I'm sorry," he said to Savannah.

Savannah shook her head. "Don't apologize. She's darling."

"Thanks." The man smiled in return then settled his children into their seats.

Savannah turned back to find Noah grinning at the little boy and Wes chuckling. "What's so funny?" she asked Wes.

"You like little kids?"

Her eyes widened. "Of course. Who doesn't?"

Noah glared at Wes.

The little girl was waving frantically. Savannah returned the gesture and cut another bite of eggs.

Wes arched an eyebrow. "Yeah, who doesn't? Especially chubby ones."

Savannah's eyes widened. Her stomach dropped. "She isn't chubby."

He laughed. "She's definitely not thin."

"She's a little girl."

Wes didn't answer, drinking his juice instead. Savannah focused on her eggs. Her cheeks burned. The little girl wasn't overweight, but even if she were, she'd still be cute.

Noah lifted his chin at Savannah. "She's a cute, little girl."

She rewarded him with a smile.

Wes changed the subject. "You don't want anyone but your family to call you Savvy, huh?"

Her head whipped up. The rest of her body stiffened. "No."

Wes skewered half a pancake with his fork. "Is it nicknames you dislike or just that particular one?"

She looked at Noah. He studied her as if her answer meant everything.

"That one is for my family only." She'd let one unrelated man have the privilege of that nickname. It would never happen again.

Wes nodded. "Okay. How about I call you Anna?" He tilted his head to the side appraising her. "Savannah's too much of a mouthful for me and Anna is a perfect name for a woman as gorgeous as you."

Savannah snuck a glance at Noah. He rolled his eyes and shoved a bite of pancake in his mouth. If only he could take a few lessons from Wes. "Okay, I could let you try Anna for a while and see how I like it."

He washed down his pancakes with a gulp of juice. "Well, that's really big of you."

Savannah laughed. Noah's pinched face froze the merriment in her vocal chords.

"So, why are you following Savannah around Shumway?" Wes asked.

Noah stiffened. "None of your business, Richins."

Savannah smiled, but the effort was lukewarm. "He's here for my protection."

Wes waited, but she wasn't ready to divulge anything more. She tried another bite of cantaloupe: it wasn't any riper than it had been two minutes ago.

"I didn't know I was with such a big shot," Wes said. "You can afford your own protection and you're wasting your time training me for a measly three bills an hour?"

Savannah did smile this time. "I'm not paying for it. I told you about my sister being hurt."

Wes's features tightened. He jerked his chin down.

She shrugged, spearing a bite of eggs. "It's all related to that."

Wes's eyes narrowed. He swallowed two huge forkfuls of omelet. Noah didn't say anything.

The redheaded girl had escaped from her chair and was doing laps around the restaurant. The father almost caught her, but she was quick.

"Darcee," he called. "Come back here."

The little girl darted in and out of tables. She approached their booth, giggling, her blue eyes alight.

Savannah scurried from her seat and grabbed the little angel in her arms. "I caught you."

She laughed. "I'm too fast for my Daddy!"

Her father reached them. He took the child from Savannah's grasp. "Once again, I apologize." He wasn't looking at Savannah, but at Wes.

Savannah's eyes followed his. Wes's mouth was set in a thin line, his eyes colder than the wind gusting out of Logan Canyon on a winter's day. When he saw Savannah watching, he forced a smile.

Wes glanced at Savannah. "Don't apologize, she looks like a . . . fun kid."

Savannah turned to the little girl, tugging on one of her curls. "Darcee?"

"That's my name. How'd you know that?"

She smiled. "I heard your dad saying it. Can you do something for me, Darcee?" Savannah felt Noah watching her, his gaze full of warmth and approval.

"Okay," the little girl said.

Opening her purse, Savannah retrieved an unopened package of sugar-free bubble gum. "Do you think you could sit really still for your daddy and eat your breakfast and then share this with your brother?"

Darcee's eyes rounded. Her tongue touched the edge of her rosebud lips. She pumped her head twice. "Okay."

Savannah handed the gum to the tall, blond man. He smiled. "Thank you." He carried Darcee back to his table.

Savannah watched Darcee share the exciting news of their future prize with her brother. The blond boy looked shyly at Savannah and waved. She waved back.

"Speaking of your sister," Wes interrupted the exchange, placing his hand over Savannah's. "How is she doing?"

Savannah's heart clenched. "Not good."

"So what have the police found out? You think somebody hurt her, Shumway?"

Noah shook his head. "Even if I did, I wouldn't be talking to you about it."

Savannah opened her mouth.

Noah held up a hand. "Savannah isn't going to tell you anything."

Her stomach tightened. She stared at Noah. "Oh, really? I'm not going to tell him that you think I hurt my sister."

Noah's jaw dropped.

Wes's eyebrows shot up. "No way," he said, shaking his head. "How could anyone believe that someone as genuine as you would hurt anyone. Let alone her own sibling?"

His voice was loud enough for the whole restaurant to hear. Noah grimaced.

Savannah turned from him and refocused on Wes's chiseled face. "That's exactly what I told the detective, but you know how they are."

Noah rose to his feet.

Wes covered her hand with his. "I know how they are. Evidence is the most important thing to a policeman, but to me it's all about what's in somebody's heart, and I can tell yours is pure."

Noah threw a twenty on the table and glared at her. "I'll meet you at the car."

She watched him stalk away.

Wes grinned, massaging the back of her hand. She didn't return the touch, but she didn't move her hand either. She stared at his deeply tanned hands. They looked recently manicured. They were so different from Noah's large, calloused fingers.

Her cell phone rang. She jumped, pulling her hand from Wes's grasp. Searching through her purse, she retrieved the phone and flipped it open.

"Savvy? Are you coming to the hospital?"

"We're on our way. We stopped for breakfast."

Wes watched with interest, not touching his food.

"Oh. I see." Her dad paused. "I thought you wanted to get here early today, but I understand you need to eat too."

Savannah cringed. "Is there any change?"

He didn't respond right away.

She pushed her plate away, swallowing one more drink of water while she waited. When she couldn't stand the silence any longer she prompted, "Dad?"

"Truthfully, Savvy, she looks worse than yesterday. I think we should do something more aggressive. I'm going to talk to the doctor about it."

"Okay. I'll be there soon. Sorry it took me so long."

"We'll see you and Noah in a minute," her dad said.

"I've got to go," she said to Wes, dropping her phone in her purse. "I've got to get to the hospital."

"Is something wrong?"

Shaking her head, she choked down the fear in her throat. "My dad says Allison doesn't look very good."

His hand covered hers. "I'm sorry. I'm sure she'll recover soon."

Savannah wished she could be so confident that Allison would be okay. How was the drug getting in her system?

"Anna?" Wes stroked her hand. "Are you okay?"

"Fine." She blinked. "I'm just trying to figure out how to help my sister."

His fingers tightened. "Try not to worry. She's going to be all right."

Savannah stared into his dark gaze. He seemed so certain. His words, look, and touch comforted her. "Thanks. I'm praying she is."

He smiled. "Then I'll pray with you." He gestured to the door. "I'd better not keep you any longer. Let me walk you out."

They rose. He tossed a hundred on the table. Savannah arched an eyebrow. "Noah already left enough to cover our breakfast."

He shrugged. "I'm a good tipper."

Savannah swallowed back the worry over Allison and tried to smile. "I don't know if you've heard, but it's a standard in the fitness industry to tip your personal trainer."

He laughed, placing a hand on her elbow and directing her out the door. "I hadn't heard that, but I'm sure we could work something out."

Savannah waved one more time to her little friends and let Wes guide her to the door.

Noah fumed as he sat in the car. " 'That's exactly what I told the detective, but you know how they are.' " He muttered to himself, "We'll just see how the loudmouth likes it when I toss her butt in jail. See if her rich boyfriend can save her then."

He thought of how cute Savannah had been with the little girl. "Good thing she has some redeeming qualities," he said.

Savannah approached the car, laughing with Richins. Noah couldn't handle listening to Wes flirt with Savannah for another minute. He turned the key, pushed the radio button, and found a decent country song. Turning it up enough to shut out their conversation hurt his ears. He could've been at a rock concert and sustained less damage.

Finally, the passenger door swung open. Wes seated Savannah inside, touching her arm and then her leg.

Noah cringed. His jaw clenched until it ached.

Wes leaned across Savannah and smiled at him.

"Hey, Detective Shumway," he yelled over the music. "Take good care of her for me, and I'll make it worth your while."

Noah gritted his teeth, gripping the steering wheel until he lost feeling in the tips of his fingers. "I don't take money from average citizens."

Wes raised a plucked eyebrow. "Maybe you should. I'm sure you could use the fundage."

Noah started the engine and jammed the gear drive into reverse. Wes jumped away. The door nicked him. Wes cursed and limped toward his Hummer H3. Satisfaction seared through Noah.

Savannah scrambled to shut the door and fasten her seat belt. "Are you nuts?"

"What?" Noah sang out.

She reached over and pushed the power button on the sound system. Noah's ears vibrated. The lack of music was a welcome balm. Savannah's voice was not.

"Are you nuts?" she yelled.

Noah inhaled and exhaled twice before answering her. "I am not on this job to watch you flirt with Wesley Richins. Now let's get something straight—"

"Wait." She lifted a delicate hand in his face. "You two have some serious issues with each other. How do you know him?"

He sped up the street. A young mother with a double stroller sprinted into the crosswalk. Noah slammed on his brakes. Savannah braced herself on the dashboard. The woman reached the other side of the street. Noah jammed his foot onto the gas pedal again. "We went to high school together."

"Oh." She paused. "So, what was he like in high school?"

"Just your typical rich boy," Noah muttered. He turned to look at her, wondering how she could be so kind with children and so completely insensitive to him. *Couldn't she see her flirting with Wes was killing him?* "How is it you don't know him? Aren't you from the valley?"

"Transplants." She shrugged. "We're from Bountiful, but after mom died . . ." She waved a hand, dismissing the subject. "You don't need to know all that. What should I know about Wes?"

Noah's grip on the steering wheel tightened. He spun through an intersection. *Her mom was dead?* He'd just assumed her parents were divorced.

"Noah?" she said. "Are you going to tell me about him or not?"

Noah shook his head in disgust. "His dad's a millionaire. Running for governor. Wes manages his dad's finances which really means he plays around and gets paid for it."

Savannah nodded. "So, he has money."

Noah shook his head, disgusted with himself for thinking he had something in common with the arrogant beauty at his side. "I should've realized you'd think that was a plus."

A soft laugh escaped from her pink lips. "What's wrong with being rich?"

Noah cranked the wheel, turning left. Savannah grabbed the handle above the door to steady herself.

"Lots of things," he said. "But if you're into the sellout, smooth-talking, rich putz don't think that I give a crap." *Wow, he sounded like such a jealous idiot.*

She tapped her fingernails on her arm, raising an eyebrow at him. "Yeah. It sounds like you couldn't care less."

"That's right."

She winked at him. "So, what's with this irrational jealousy of Wes?"

Noah clamped his jaw, refusing to look at her.

"When are you going to tell me about it?"

His eyes slid to hers. "When are you going to tell me why you pushed Jenalee down the stairs in high school?"

She whirled away from him and folded her arms across her chest. A cloud of dark hair shadowed her face from his view.

Noah smiled.

Savannah stomped through the hospital. Noah trailed her to the ICU. They were almost to the nurse's desk when Savannah heard her dad's raised voice. She cast Noah a worried glance, their argument forgotten.

Noah placed a hand on her back and ushered her to where her family was gathered just outside Allison's room. For the first time that hour, Savannah was glad Noah was there.

"I want her moved to the University of Utah," Frank said. "You have no clue what you're doing at this hospital. We need someone qualified to help my daughter."

Dr. McQuivey patiently held up his hand. "With all due respect sir, there's nothing any other hospital or physician can do for you. It's just a waiting game at this point. There's no surgery that will help. No medicine that we aren't already trying." He looked at Ryan. "Your insurance would probably not pay for an unapproved transfer. Do you know how much a life flight ride costs?"

"I'll find the money to pay for it, if it can help Allison," Frank interjected.

Savannah stared at her dad. He'd barely paid off the medical bills from her mother's illness.

Ryan shook his head. "Frank, if we decide to move Allison, I'll be the one who pays for it."

Frank glowered at his son-in-law. "What do you mean *if*? We need to do something or Allison will be like that," he jabbed a finger toward her room, "forever!"

Savannah wrapped her arm around her dad's waist. "Daddy, what's going on?"

He whirled on them. "Savvy." He blew out a long breath. "Hey, Noah."

Noah nodded a hello.

"Did something happen with Ally?" Savannah asked

Frank didn't answer. Ryan mustered up a smile. "Actually, it's good news. The test this morning showed the Versed was almost out of her system."

Savannah caught Noah's eye. He smiled at her. Her stomach fluttered and her legs weakened. Ally was going to be okay.

Her dad jammed a hand through his hair. "Yeah, it's good news, except she looks worse today. If the drug is leaving, she should be improving. She should be awake. Dr. McQuivey," he glared at the man, "can't figure out why she's still in a coma."

Savannah's hands rolled into tight balls. Why wasn't Ally getting better? Was there some kind of internal injury they weren't catching?

The doctor sighed. "I understand your frustration, but if you move her to another hospital it would only cause more harm. She's stable, but a move like that can't help the swelling on her brain."

Ryan gestured down the hallway. He and the doctor walked away. "We appreciate what you're doing," Ryan said. "Please understand we're all worried and frustrated."

"Of course I understand . . ."

Dr. McQuivey and Ryan moved out of range.

Frank exhaled. "Ryan, the diplomat." He enfolded Savannah in his arms. "I should take a few lessons."

Savannah shook her head. "You're fine, Daddy. Everyone understands why you're frustrated, but she should be getting better now, huh?"

He shrugged. "You'd think so."

She changed the subject. "Where's Josh?"

"Amy has him again."

"That's nice of her. He still hasn't seen Ally, has he?"

"No, " he sighed, "but it seems like, 'Want Mommy' is the only phrase he knows lately. Are you going in to see her?"

Savannah pulled away from her dad, wrapping her hands around her midsection. "Yeah. Have you guys already been in?"

Frank nodded. "I'm going to get Josh. We'll play and have a nap, then come back later this afternoon."

"Okay. I'll go visit her for a while and meet up with you at home."

He hugged her again. "You smell like bacon."

She rocked from one foot to another, not looking at Noah. "I told you I went to breakfast with a friend."

"Some friend," Noah muttered.

"I thought you went with Noah." One look at Noah's face stopped any other questions her dad might have had. "Okay," Frank said, elevating an eyebrow. "Well, I can't handle much more of this hospital. I'll meet you at home. Call me if there's any news about Ally."

Savannah kissed him goodbye, then shuffled toward Ally's room.

Noah shadowed her every move. She whirled on him. "Can't I talk to my sister alone?"

"Actually, maybe you can." His shoulders relaxed. He squeezed her arm. "I've got a deal for you."

Savannah's pulse raced. The warmth of his blue eyes seared through her. "What kind of a deal?"

"I won't watch you every second, if . . ." He grinned and said, "If you promise to never make me go to breakfast with Wesley Richins again."

Savannah had to resist the urge to hug him. "I think we could work something out."

"Thanks." He directed her toward the desk.

They waved hello to the Spanish nurse who usually manned the desk when Ilene wasn't around. Savannah signed her name and walked toward Allison's room.

"Wait for me," Noah said.

He took the sign-in sheet from Rosie and glanced through the logs for the last few days. Shaking his head, he exhaled slowly. "Rosie. I need to talk to you when you have a break."

She looked down at the desk. "Okay."

Noah escorted Savannah to the room. "I've got to check on a few things. I'll be back in a couple of minutes."

Savannah nodded. "Thanks, Noah."

He smiled again. His cheek crinkled irresistibly when he really smiled. "It's great news that the drug is lower." He turned and strode away.

She watched him leave then crept to Allison's side. Her dad was right, Ally looked worse than yesterday. The lightheartedness she'd experienced with Noah dissipated.

"Hey, Ally girl." She lifted Allison's limp hand off the sheets. It was cold. She held it between her own. Maybe she could give her sister some warmth, but she felt cold inside. She had nothing to give.

"How are you?" She waited as if Allison would actually open her eyes and answer. "That's what I thought. You look bad, girl. Real bad. Sorry, that isn't what you need to hear." She brushed a dark strand away from Allison's cheek, repeating a prayer in her heart that Ally would recover.

"So the doctor says the drug is leaving and you should wake up. So that's good news, right? I'm praying it's true. I miss you. I really miss you."

She sighed and studied her sister's face for any sign of consciousness.

"Maybe I need to bring in your Keith Urban CD and dance for you. That might wake you up." She smiled thinking of Allison laughing at her dance moves. "I'll have to think of some way to get you out of this. Plus, I need to figure out who hurt you in the first place. Help me out here. What would Horatio do? There's got to be some way to find the evidence that somebody besides me was in your house that night."

Savannah talked through every episode of CSI she'd viewed. Finally it hit her. "Ally! That's it. Your clothes. They should test your clothes for some kind of . . . Well, I don't know. They could maybe find fingerprints or hairs or something on them, couldn't they?"

She bent down to kiss her sister's smooth cheek. "Remember the sister's pact, Ally. I'm going to take care of you and Josh, but you have to do your part and wake up." Allison's waxy complexion didn't offer any reassurance. Savannah lifted her sister's arm. It was dead weight. She looked around to see if anybody was watching. The coast was clear. She pinched the skin on the back of Allison's arm. Nothing. Not even a flinch. Savannah felt instant guilt when the skin reddened. It was a rotten thing to do, but she had to try everything she could.

Noah arrived at the door. Savannah's face darkened and she had to look away from his gaze or he would know she'd just pinched her unconscious sibling. She gazed at her sister's beautiful face. "Wake up soon, Ally. I love you." She walked to Noah's side, loving the warmth of his touch as he took her elbow and escorted her from the unit.

Ten

Wes watched Noah and Savannah drive away. He hated the way Shumway got her door. That should've been Wes's job. He drummed his fingers against the steering wheel. A few more days and Shumway would never touch his girl again.

He dialed Rosie's cell phone number. "Rosie, it's Jonathon Mendez."

"Oh, Jonathon." She sang out. "You just missed your family."

Wes smiled. "They're all gone?"

"Yes. Your brother is meeting with the doctor, they should be a while." Her voice dropped and deepened. "I'm here all alone. The other nurse is on break for twenty more minutes."

"Well, maybe I should come see you."

She giggled. "I'll be waiting."

Minutes later, he sauntered through the double doors. "Good morning, Rosie," he called, setting a bag of Einstein's bagels and cream cheese on the counter. "Thought you might be hungry."

Rosie's cheeks wrinkled. She grinned up at him. "Oh, thank you, Jonathon. That's so nice of you." She batted her eyelashes.

"Any change in Ally?"

"No. Dr. McQuivey met with Allison's dad and the rest of the family this morning. They were upset because even though the drug is clearing her system, she still isn't waking up."

Wes blinked. His body swayed. *They'd picked up on the drug?* He tried to appear nonchalant. "That's frustrating."

"Now that she's improving," Rosie continued, "you'd think we could relax. None of the staff can go in her room alone. Which is ridiculous seeing how shorthanded we are. What am I supposed to do when I go on rounds? Skip her?" She sighed. "Also, a detective has been quizzing all the nurses. I'm supposed to meet with him this afternoon. It's almost like he thinks one of us hurt her."

Wes fought to keep his face neutral. *Shumway was quizzing the nurses?* "Rosie, can I talk to you," he paused, "somewhere more private?"

Her eyebrows rose, and she nodded. She stood and walked around the corner. Wes followed. They entered the nurse's break room. The smell of coffee simmering mixed with the odor from a trash can overflowing with take-out containers and cookie wrappers. Wes backed Rosie into a wall. She looked at him with wide eyes.

"Rosie. Are you busy this weekend?"

"N-no."

"I would love to take you to dinner."

Her cheeks flushed a dark brown. "Okay. I mean, I'd love to."

He reached down and brushed his fingers across her cheek. "Can I ask a favor of you?"

She swallowed. "Sure, anything."

"I know I've asked a lot of you already."

Rosie shook her head. "Not a big deal."

Wes hid his grin. The woman was putty. "Please don't mention me to the detective."

She stared without blinking. "I can't lie to a police officer."

"No-no. I'm not saying to lie, just don't mention me. He'd have to tell the family I've been here and I've told you about our family problems."

Rosie's eyes shifted to the wall. Wes wrapped his fingers around her chin, forcing her to look at him. "I'd really appreciate it. Maybe I could make it up to you after dinner." He let the words linger.

Rosie trembled, licked her lips, and nodded.

Wes winked at her and walked away. "I'll call you to arrange something for Friday night."

She leaned against the wall. "Friday night," she whispered, raising her hand to her heart.

Wes smiled. He entered Allison's room, checked to make sure no one was looking and shot two syringes of the drug into her IV. A little extra couldn't hurt.

"This is getting to be a hassle," he whispered. "Please stay asleep,

Allison. I don't want to have to do something permanent." He patted her hand one more time and strode from the room. He saw Ryan and the doctor in the hallway by the elevator.

Turning into the stairway door, he caught Ryan glancing at him as if trying to figure out when he'd seen him before. The stairway door banged closed behind Wes. He took the stairs two at a time. The door clanked open above him. He increased his pace.

"Hey! Hold up."

Wes flew down the last few steps.

"Wait. Stop!"

Wes wrenched the door handle on the first floor landing, scurrying through the door and down the hallway. He raced past the cafeteria and another hall. He looked over his shoulder. Allison's husband exited the stairway, but Wes turned the corner before Ryan glanced his direction. He found a family bathroom, went inside, and locked the door. Seconds later he heard footsteps pound past the door. He waited ten minutes before exiting the bathroom.

How much longer he could keep this up?

⁂

Savannah waited until they were in the car to explain her break-through to Noah. Instead of responding to her amazing idea, he massaged his neck with his fingertips.

"What?" she asked. "They use the clothing thing on CSI all the time."

He pushed out all his air. Turning out of the parking lot, he headed east on Fourteenth North. "Savannah, you are aware that is a television show?"

She balled her hands into fists. He didn't need to act like she was an idiot. "So?"

"So, a lot of what they do is a farce."

"There has to be some truth to it. Please, we have to figure out some way to prove I'm not the one who hurt Ally."

He glanced over at her. "I'm working on it, but I doubt CSI is our answer."

"But it's a good idea," Savannah insisted. "Are you telling me you can't test the clothes to look for more fingerprints or hair fibers or some-thing?"

108

Noah shook his head, flipping his turn signal and moving into the left lane. He stopped at a red light and turned to face her. "You're right. We can check and see if there's anything on her clothes. The problem is where are her clothes?"

Savannah pursed her lips. "Do you think the hospital kept them?"

"Maybe. I could talk to ER and see where they stored them." Noah jammed a hand through his short, blond hair. "But we didn't find a fingerprint match. So, even if the assailant left proof on the clothes, if he's never been fingerprinted, chances are he's never had a DNA swab. So we wouldn't be any closer to knowing who he is."

Savannah's face fell. Her great idea wasn't so good.

Noah lifted her chin. Warmth radiated along her jaw line. "I'll make some calls. It is a good idea. We have to try everything we can." He smiled at her. "Thanks for sharing your idea with me."

She nodded dumbly. Noah thinking she hurt her sister and their angry words this morning seemed a thing of the past as she leaned into his huge hand. A horn blasted behind them.

Noah jerked his hand from her face, lifted his foot off the brake, and sped around the corner. "Guess they didn't like sitting at a green light."

"I didn't mind it," Savannah murmured.

Noah winked at her. She decided blue eyes were definitely her favorite.

Their afternoon visit to the hospital was more of the same, and the evening passed uneventfully except for Noah frowning each time Savannah's cell phone rang. Noah's sergeant called to inform them his officers had retrieved Allison's clothes from the hospital and sent them to the lab for testing.

Noah spent some time talking with Rosie, but he didn't share any of the details with Savannah or act like he'd gleaned anything useful.

Noah and Frank were discussing football when Savannah announced she needed to use the restroom. She looked at Noah.

He nodded once and kept talking to her dad.

Savannah pivoted and walked down the hallway, reveling in the freedom of not being followed. Noah really did believe she was innocent. She smiled to herself.

Savannah quickly used the restroom, washed her hands and depressed the door latch with a paper towel. She propped the door open with her hip and turned to toss the towel in the garbage.

She heard someone behind her. "I'll just be a min—"

A hand clamped over her mouth. A long arm encircled her waist. Savannah's eyes flew open. Her heartbeat thumped uncontrollably. Someone lifted her from her feet and carried her back into the bathroom. The door shut and latched behind them. She tried to scream for Noah, but couldn't get a sound out.

The person set her on her feet and released her mouth.

"Noah!" she yelled.

The hand covered her lips again. The man flipped her in his arms to face him. She blinked. *Wes?*

He put a finger to his lips. "I'm going to take my hand off, but please don't scream for the pain in the butt detective again."

Savannah swallowed. Her head trembled as it bobbed.

"Okay." He removed his hand.

She stared at him. "What in the world are you doing?"

He grinned. "Sorry for the suspense. I wanted to get you alone without Shumway around to watch."

Savannah took a deep breath and exhaled, her heart rate slowly returning to normal. "Ah," she said. "And you thought a bathroom would be a romantic encounter?"

Wes took a step closer, elevating one eyebrow. "Anything would be romantic with you involved."

She laughed. "Whatever." She brushed by him. "I've got to get back to my family."

He grabbed her arm, stopping her from leaving. Savannah stared at his fingers. He didn't get the hint.

"I hope I didn't scare you. I like seeing you and when I was leaving my grandma's room I saw you come in the bathroom. I thought it would be fun to surprise you."

"Some surprise."

His mouth thinned. "Granted, not a very good one, but you don't know how much I've wanted to be alone with you. This was my only option." He released his grip on her arm, trailing his fingers up her shoulder and to her chin.

Savannah wanted to pull away, but the look in his dark eyes froze her. Wes studied her like a piece of prime rib he'd happily devour.

"I'd like to see a lot more of you," he said.

She cocked her head to the side, trying to act natural. "In the bathroom?"

Wes chuckled. "No. Not in the bathroom, but somewhere without Shumway around. That guy won't leave you alone."

Savannah raised an eyebrow. She liked being around Noah. Wes, on the other hand, was giving her the creeps. She swallowed and backed up a step. Her back hit the door. Wes's arm dropped to his side.

He scowled, but immediately pasted a smile on. "When can I see you?"

Savannah bit her lip. "I don't know. Maybe after Ally wakes up and everything gets back to normal."

He moved closer again. "Couldn't you sneak away from your bodyguard tonight?"

She reached for the door handle, swinging it open and wishing Noah would come check on her. "I don't think tonight would work. My nephew needs me. I'm the only one who can put him to bed. Why don't we talk in the morning and I'll see what I have going the rest of the week."

She walked from the restroom, grateful when Wes didn't stop her.

He followed her out.

She raised a hand in farewell. "I'll see you in the morning."

His lips pulled down in a frown, and his brow furrowed.

Savannah didn't wait for him to reply. She whirled from him and hurried back to the safety of Noah.

Noah stared at her when she rushed into the waiting area. "You okay?" he asked.

Savannah's head bobbed. She wanted to tell him "no," but she couldn't say anything about seeing Wes. Noah was already upset about her going to breakfast with him. What a stupid move that had been.

"I'm all right. Fine." She glanced at her hands. She couldn't hold them still. She balled them into fists. "Sorry I took so long."

His eyes searched hers. She looked away before he could read her. Picking up her *Shape* magazine, she plopped onto a chair and feigned interest in an article on the newest lunge positions.

Noah and Savannah stopped at the grocery store on the way home from the hospital. An older gentleman was struggling to the car with his groceries. Noah rushed over to help him. He loaded the man's car and asked where he lived.

"Savannah?" he said. "Do you mind if we follow him and help unload his groceries?"

She closed her slackened jaw. "Um, no. That's fine. That's a great idea."

They climbed into her car. Noah drove. She stared at him.

"Do you do this often?"

He looked at her. "What's that?"

"Find somebody who needs help and go the extra mile."

Noah smiled. "I didn't think of it like that."

Savannah continued watching his strong profile. "You didn't answer my question."

He squirmed, adjusting the rearview mirror. "I try to whenever I see an opportunity."

"You seem like the kind of person who makes an opportunity where some people see none."

He didn't answer. He flipped on his blinker, following the man into his circular drive. They each took a load of groceries into the man's house, but Noah wasn't content with that. He put everything away and made sure there was nothing else he could do before they left.

The man thanked them profusely. Noah accepted his gift of four Oreo cookies, two for each of them, and tossed one into his mouth before he started the Accord.

Savannah fastened her seat belt, laughing at him. "Bionic Man eats Oreos?"

"Sure, don't you?" He extended the two cookies intended for her.

She shook her head, feeling her mouth salivate at the sight and smell of empty calories. "No way. I work too hard to waste calories on something like that."

Noah didn't start the car. He stared at her with an open mouth. He had a black crumb on the edge of his lips. "You never eat treats?"

She tossed her hair over her shoulder. "I eat birthday cake on my family's birthdays, pie on Thanksgiving, and chocolate at Christmas."

Noah gasped. "What a horrible way to live."

Savannah laughed, wiping away the cookie on his mouth.

He ducked his head and grinned. "Thanks."

She dropped her hand before her fingers could linger too long. "Maybe if I looked as good as you do at 225—"

Noah held up a hand, looking properly offended. "250."

She swallowed. "Wow, I didn't realize you were that big." She glanced up and down his frame, her eyes lingering on his striated arms. "Okay, if I weighed 250 pounds I guess I could eat like you." She turned forward in her seat. "Start the car. Let's get this grocery shopping done."

Noah still didn't move. "Please tell me you're kidding."

"Nope, I really want to go grocery shopping," she said.

He rolled his eyes. "Please tell me you eat treats once in a while."

Savannah folded her arms across her chest. "I can't gain weight."

He guffawed. "Why not? You could gain twenty pounds and still be teeny. What are you a size two?"

She shifted in her seat, hoping he'd never find out how big she'd once been. "Sometimes."

"And other times you're like a size nothing?"

Savannah laughed. "I'm a woman, not a child. What do you care what size I am?"

Noah finally turned the key in the ignition. "I don't. I just hate to see you squandering your life on healthy eating."

"Treats make life better?"

Noah bit an Oreo in half. He held the other half under her nose. "Come on, Savannah. You know you want it."

She inhaled the tantalizing scent of dry cookie and moist filling. Exhaling, she pushed his hand away. He set the half-bitten cookie on her leg. Moving the gearshift into drive, he slowly made his way back to the store.

Savannah pinched the cookie between two fingers. She pressed the window button, prepared to pitch the temptation.

"No!" He grabbed her hand, closing his fingers over hers. "Spare the cookie. He's an innocent victim in all of this."

Savannah giggled. "You're the one who set it on me."

Noah didn't release her hand. He moved it to her lips. "For me, Savannah. Eat the cookie. How many calories can there be in half a cookie?"

Savannah shrugged. "Thirty."

Noah arched an eyebrow. "It scares me that you know that. You'll burn more than thirty calories walking around the grocery store. When was the last time you had an Oreo?"

Savannah didn't have to think. She could remember the exact day.

The day she'd taken control of her life. The day she'd committed to stop wallowing in fat and follow Allison's advice. It was the year anniversary of her mom's death.

"Come on," Noah prodded, his blue eyes beseeching her. "Do it for me."

"For you?" Savannah laughed, shaking off the memory. "When you put it that way."

She could feel the firm cookie in her fingers. It was getting crumbled between her and Noah's grasp. Noah pushed her fingers and the cookie next to her lips. Before she could think about it anymore she opened her mouth and popped it in.

Noah cheered. He squeezed her hand. "Yes, now chew it slowly. Savor it. It might be ten years before we get another one down you."

Savannah smiled at him, but she wouldn't open her mouth. She did savor it, but she savored the look in his eyes and the feeling of his fingers on her more. She'd do anything for him, if only he'd ask.

Wes watched from his Hummer as Noah rushed around the Accord and helped Savannah from the car. He held onto her arm for one second too long. She glanced up at him and smiled. As they walked across the parking lot, Noah laughed at something she said.

Wes couldn't handle this. How he hated Noah Shumway. How he wanted Savannah Compton. They sauntered into the store and out of sight.

He shook his head. When could he get her away from Shumway for good? He didn't know if he could wait much longer.

Flipping the middle console open, he retrieved the new handgun he'd picked up at Al's Sporting Goods earlier that day. The cool metal felt good against his palm. Springfield XD .45, the salesman he'd ordered it from two days before said it was their most popular model. Wes didn't know if he'd have to use it when the right time came to steal Savannah from Shumway, but he wanted to be prepared.

Noah and Savannah glided through the automatic doors of the grocery store. He pushed the shopping cart as Savannah selected items. She chose a rotisserie chicken, a loaf of French bread, strawberries, and watermelon for dinner, and then filled the cart with other groceries.

The coolness of the dairy section raised the hair on her arms. Noah lifted an eyebrow at the twenty Yoplait light yogurts she piled into the cart. "You buying the store?"

"I want the fridge to be stocked with everything Allison likes when she comes home."

His lips twitched but he didn't respond. Savannah thought that wise. If he said what she was thinking, she feared she'd explode. The yogurts would probably be curdled before her sister made it home to eat them.

Her phone rang. She jerked it from her purse and glanced at the caller ID: Samuel Tibbits. She sighed. "I thought I told him to give me a few days before he called again."

She flipped the phone open. Noah snatched it from her fingers.

"Noah," she gasped, but didn't reach for the phone.

"This is Detective Noah Shumway with the Cache County Sheriff's office, I'm afraid I'm going to have to ask the nature of your call."

Her eyes widened. She grabbed for her phone. Noah wrenched his elbow away, smiling at her.

"Savannah is currently unavailable." He paused. "No, she's not in trouble. I'm just protecting her from all the men who seem to enjoy bothering her."

"Oh!" Savannah cried out. "Give me that phone."

"She's explained to you she needs time with her family, now I'd suggest you let her have that time," Noah said. "How much time? Oh, I'd say at least a couple of months."

He snapped the phone closed, handed it to her, and strolled toward the milk.

She rushed after him. "I can't believe you." She shook her head. "Why did you say that?"

Noah placed a gallon of chocolate milk into the cart. "Just trying to help you out."

Placing the chocolate milk back on the shelf, she grabbed two gallons of skim and a 2 percent for Josh. "But Samuel was one of my favorites."

His eyes turned a frozen blue. "How many favorites do you have to have begging for your attention, Savannah?"

She arched an eyebrow and playfully grabbed his shirt. "I have a whole list of them."

He shook his head. "I should've figured."

Savannah leaned closer. "Do you want to be added to the list?"

He looked down at her, the ice in his gaze melting on the fringes. "Maybe."

Standing on the tips of her toes, she ran her fingers through his blond hair. It was softer than she'd imagined it would be. "I'd put you at the top of the list."

Noah caught her hand as it descended from his hair. He pulled it into his chest. Savannah could feel his steady heartbeat.

"I don't want to be at the top of your list," he said.

"Oh." Disappointment coursed through her. She fell onto her heels, pulling back a step.

He held her hand firmly in his own, bringing her body into full contact with his. "I want you to throw the stinking list away."

Her eyes widened. His body against hers confused her thought process. She couldn't come up with a snappy reply.

"Why, Noah Shumway. I haven't seen you in ages and here you are flirting with a pretty girl in the dairy section."

Noah dropped her hand and spun to face a petite lady with a fluff of gray hair and a smattering of brown age spots and wrinkles. His face broke into a grin. He opened his arms and swallowed the little woman in his grasp.

Savannah was suddenly jealous of an eighty-year old grandma. She shook her head in frustration.

"How are you, Mrs. Chambers?"

"Doing okay for a crotchety old woman."

Noah released her.

She stepped back, glancing up and down his muscular frame. "You're looking good, young man. I think you've gotten bigger. You haven't been taking those steroids."

He shook his head. "No, ma'am."

Mrs. Chambers smiled. The lines in her face grew deeper. Savannah had never thought of wrinkles as beautiful, but on this lady there was no other way to describe the lines that revealed her life. She probably had thousands of fun and vibrant memories behind every crevice.

The lady tapped his arm. "Good boy. Now introduce me to this beautiful young lady."

Noah placed his hand on Savannah's back, drawing her into the conversation. "This is Savannah Compton."

Mrs. Chambers extended a hand full of blue veins and sagging with extra skin. Savannah was surprised at how warm and comforting the fingers were.

She pressed Savannah's hand. "Nice to meet you, dear."

"It's nice to meet you too."

Mrs. Chambers gaze swiveled to Noah. "Now wait a minute. Let's redo that introduction."

Noah arched an eyebrow. "Excuse me, ma'am?"

"Don't ma'am me. Reintroduce us and I want to hear who this Savannah is. I don't want to hear this is Savannah Compton. I want to hear this is my wife, Savannah, or my fiancée, Savannah, or at the very least my girlfriend, Savannah."

Savannah's mouth fell open. She turned to see Noah's reaction. He grimaced and blushed and looked absolutely irresistible. He seemed unable to answer. The lady turned to Savannah.

She laughed, turning her palm up helplessly. "We've only known each other a few days."

"That's no excuse. I married my husband two weeks after I met him."

Savannah's eyebrows shot up.

"And we were happy for fifty-two years." Mrs. Chambers shook her head, her green eyes bright.

Savannah didn't know if she should say congratulations on her happiness or she was sorry he was gone.

"Now you'll have to forgive me for embarrassing you, sweetheart." Mrs. Chamber's gaze traveled to Noah. "But how any woman could resist that rock hard body and those blue eyes is beyond me." She patted his cheek and smiled.

Noah cleared his throat. He looked at Savannah with an apology. "Mrs. Chambers always loved to tease me."

Her clear eyes twinkled as she looked up at Noah. She tapped him on the chest. "You come see me sometime. I've got cookies waiting, you know."

Noah nodded. He bent and kissed her withered cheek. Savannah's breath stopped between her throat and her lungs. She swallowed, but couldn't choke down the warmth she felt for Noah at that moment. Mrs. Chambers toddled away after one last smile at Savannah.

They sauntered through the grocery store together, neither mentioning Mrs. Chamber's comments or the conversation she interrupted. Savannah could almost pretend they were a couple like Mrs. Chambers had suggested and that they went grocery shopping together on a regular basis. He'd toss junk food into the cart, and she'd laugh as she restocked it on the shelf.

The only strange thing was Noah kept glancing over his shoulder. Savannah followed his gaze, but saw no one.

Noah left her in the produce aisle for a minute.

She was sorting through green leaf lettuce when she felt eyes on her back. She glanced over her shoulder. A middle-aged, brown-haired man with wide hazel eyes stared at her. It wasn't unusual to catch a man staring at her, but the way this man studied her made her want to hide behind the bags of potatoes. Suddenly, he disappeared into the diaper aisle. Savannah was cold. She moved away from the chilled stacks of greenery, wrapping her arms around her stomach.

Noah appeared around the corner with a clear plastic bag stuffed with Swedish fish. Savannah thawed. The weird guy meant nothing. Her protector was right here. She smiled, shaking her head at Noah's bag of candy.

He beseeched her with his eyes, like a little boy begging for a BB gun. "Please. Josh is going to love these."

She cocked her head to the side. "You would use my cute nephew to try and get your way."

Noah's lips twitched. "They're all for Josh. I don't even like the things."

"Uh-huh."

His hands clutched the bag. "I'll only eat a few if he insists."

Savannah laughed. "Put them in."

Eleven

Ryan watched as Ilene adjusted Allison's pillow and fanned her hair above her head. His wife was gorgeous, even in a coma.

"She's a beauty," Ilene murmured.

Ryan nodded. "I'm lucky to have her." He swallowed. "At least I used to be."

Ilene glared down at him. "Quit your whining."

He jolted. "Excuse me?"

"You heard me. Have you been looking at those words?" She pointed at the wall. "Do you know who put them there?" She jabbed a finger at her chest. "Me. And I've seen more miracles in this room than you could imagine, boy. Now buck up and believe. She'll come out of this."

She pulled him to his feet, wrapping him up. Ryan leaned into her strength. "Thanks."

"You'll thank me when she wakes up." She looked him up and down. "Now when was the last time you ate?"

He shrugged.

Ilene nodded. "That's what I thought. I brought in some chicken potpie for my supper. I'll warm it up and we'll share it on my break."

"You're an angel, Ilene."

She grinned. "Been called a lot of things in my day, but never that." She patted him on the shoulder. "I'll see you in a minute."

Ryan watched her go. He turned back to Ally and lifted her hand off the covers. Softly stroking it, he wondered why she wasn't getting better. If the drug was gone, she should wake up. She looked pale and withered like all the vitality had drained from her and only a shell of skin remained. Shaking his head, he offered a brief prayer, *Please, God. I can't live without her.*

The monitors beeped. The hospital hummed with quiet activity. He waited, but nothing changed except the sky outside the window which was getting darker and darker. He buried his face in Ally's chest and closed his eyes tightly.

Noah sat on the Lazy Boy across from Frank on the sofa. A baseball game was on the television, but only his eyes registered the action. His brain pictured Savannah. The pleasure on her face when she ate the Oreo. The feel of her close when she said she'd put him at the top of her list. Her soft smile for the little girl at the restaurant this morning. It had been a great day, except for breakfast with Wes. He frowned. And except for the fact that he couldn't find another suspect and was no closer to solving this case.

"I hate to ask this Noah."

Frank's voice interrupted his thoughts. He swung around to face Savannah's dad. "What's that?"

"You haven't found a suspect."

Noah shook his head. If Savannah wasn't going to tell her dad she was a suspect, he wouldn't either. Why would she keep that from her family? It made her seem guilty.

"I appreciate you not suggesting Savannah could have hurt Ally."

Noah swallowed. "We've looked into the possibility, sir."

"I'm sure you have, but I appreciate you not accusing her. She's been through a lot and something like that would kill her."

Noah's gaze swung to the television, unable to hold Frank's eyes any longer. What had Savannah been through? She seemed to him like a beautiful girl who'd always had everything go her way, until now. "I'll remember that, sir."

"Have you found any leads?"

Noah shook his head. "Not really."

Frank begged him with a glance. "Please don't give up, Noah."

"I won't."

It took Savannah forty minutes to rock Josh to sleep. He howled for his dad and mom. He fell asleep murmuring, "Want Momma. Want Daddy." It broke Savannah's heart. She wanted to cry, "Want Ally," herself. She missed her sister more than she would've imagined. She tucked Josh into his crib and stared at the sweet baby.

She couldn't blame Ryan for not wanting to leave Allison's side, but she didn't know how he handled that depressing hospital for so many hours on end. She wished he'd at least come home and spend some time with Josh. The poor little guy didn't understand. He didn't need to be hurting and sad.

She bent down to kiss Josh's cheek and then tiptoed from the room and down the stairs. Her dad had hired someone to clean the house, and the lingering smell of blood had dissipated, but Savannah couldn't enter the foyer without cringing. She could still see Allison splayed across the tile, bloody and unconscious. Would the image ever leave her? Would her sister recover?

She blinked several times and shuffled through the open area. She heard the television blasting downstairs. Noah and her dad were watching yet another sporting event. They both smiled a greeting when she entered the room, but with all the worry for Ally spinning in her brain, she couldn't sit. She hurried to her room and returned, wearing her favorite dri-fit running shirt and skirt.

Noah sat up straighter. He looked up and down her frame, his mouth ajar.

"Where are you going?" her dad demanded.

"I have to run, Dad. I can't sit around after eating those stupid candy fish." *Or worrying about Ally and her family,* she added in her mind.

Noah grinned. "Can't believe you stole candy from a baby."

She laughed, grateful for the release. "You shoved the stinking things in my mouth!"

Noah winked. "We both know you liked it."

Her dad's eyebrows rose.

She blushed. "Does anyone want to go running with me?"

Frank stared at Noah. Noah shook his head. "No way. Not me."

Her dad smiled. "Well, I'm not going. I haven't been able to keep up with her since she was seven."

Savannah whipped her hair into a ponytail. "No one has to come with me. I'm fine by myself."

Her dad looked outside. "Honey, it's too dark out there. Noah is going to watch over you."

"Why don't we just tell her she can't go?" Noah asked.

Savannah straightened and glared at him. "Because I'm going with or without you. Unless you want to hold me down."

Noah grinned. "I'd like to try that."

Her dad's mouth opened, but he didn't say anything.

Savannah bent to tie her shoelaces, ignoring them.

Noah groaned as he stood from his comfortable seat. He glanced at Savannah. "Can you wait two minutes?"

"Only two," she said.

She watched him walk from the room, loving the breadth of his shoulders. Turning, she caught her dad studying her.

"Go easy on him, Savvy," her dad said.

Savannah nodded. "Uh-huh. You bet. Just like I do with you."

"No, seriously. I like him. You be nice."

She wondered how much he'd like Noah if he knew he had accused Savannah of hurting Allison. "You're confusing me, Dad. Usually you run off any men I date with a pitchfork. It's like you're encouraging Noah." She reddened. She'd just admitted to her dad that she wanted to date Noah.

Her dad pressed his lips together and nodded. "I know I'm too protective of you. After Daxon . . ." he sighed. "I've had a hard time letting anyone near you."

She shuddered. Her ex-fiancé's face crossed her mind—dark-skin, eyes, and hair, and a perfect smile. She shook her head, perfectly evil. She'd shunned men for a year after their violent breakup, but even though she'd healed and returned to the dating scene, her dad had never stopped being overly protective.

"Noah's not like him, Savvy. I can trust you with Noah."

Noah reentered the room. His T-shirt stretched taut across his chest. His shorts brushed his kneecaps, revealing toned calves. Savannah could hear Mrs. Chambers voice, "that rock, hard body." She flushed.

"If we're not back in an hour, come find me," Noah said to Frank.

"What about me?" Savannah asked.

His eyebrows furrowed. "If we're not back in an hour, you won't be around to find."

Savannah grinned. "Let's go."

She raced up the stairs. Noah pounded behind her. She flew out the front door, down the driveway, and was halfway through the block before Noah caught her. He was already panting for air. She slowed her pace until he could keep up without gasping.

They didn't talk as Savannah guided him out of Allison's subdivision and through the fields between Hyde Park and Smithfield. The sunset over the mountains to the west was spectacular. Red and orange hues burned streaks through wispy clouds like whipped cream swirled with Jell-o.

They ran a loop along the southern edge of Smithfield, then turned and headed back south. The snippets of conversation all originated from Savannah. Noah could barely grunt a response as he panted for air. After five miles they turned east. Savannah took pity on him and slowed to a walk for the last uphill mile to Allison's house.

"Thanks," Noah said between gulps of oxygen.

"Thanks for going with me," she said. "I didn't really want to run alone."

Noah nodded. "You know I wouldn't have let you come alone, but I should've thought to follow you in a motorized vehicle."

"Of course you wouldn't let me be alone." She hated that it always came back to him not trusting her.

He drew in a long breath. "I couldn't live with myself if something happened to you."

Savannah turned to look at him. It was nearly dark. His gaze was on her. She gulped, suddenly out of breath herself. She dredged her mind for some way to change the mood before she forgot how he really felt about her and attacked those tempting lips.

He stopped walking. "Do you mind if we turn down this block for a minute?"

Was there a quiet park nearby? Maybe Noah wanted some time alone with her before they went back to her dad. "Sure, why?"

"I haven't been home in a couple of days. I'd like to check on my house."

Savannah's lips formed an O. "I didn't know you lived this close to Ally's."

"Didn't I tell you I was on my way home when I received the call to check on Allison's house?"

She hated to think about that night.

They walked through a quiet, well-kept neighborhood, stopping at an unlit two-story house. It was a restored Victorian, with white, clapboard siding, black shutters, and a wide front porch adorned with wood rocking chairs. The yard was large; the lawn short. The flowerbeds were filled with wood chips and trimmed with red and green bushes.

Savannah turned to look at him. "This is your house?"

Noah walked up the sidewalk. "Yep."

"Like your parent's house?"

Noah laughed softly through his nose instead of his mouth. "No, like my very own house. My parents don't live around here."

"How did you afford a house like this?"

He arched an eyebrow. "How do you know what I can and can't afford?"

Savannah gulped. "I'm sorry, I didn't mean it like that. I just thought a cop . . ."

He turned his back, reaching above the doorjamb for a key and inserting it into the lock. "An investigator makes a little more than most cops, and I got a great deal on the house. It was really run down when I bought it. I've spent most of my spare time the past couple of years fixing it up."

He swung the wood and clear-glass door wide, waiting for her to walk inside. He flipped on a switch to the right of the door, flooding the front hall with light. Savannah ran her hand along a curved oak banister. The stairs rose from the left in a steep arc to the second floor and an open balcony. On her right was an office with a glass transom above the door. The floor was a dark, distressed hardwood with fine grooves cut into it.

"It's amazing," she murmured.

"Thanks," Noah said, swinging the door closed. He moved through an arch, down the hallway, and into the back of the house. She followed him. He switched on lights as they walked. "It was built in 1904. The wood floor, stairway, banister and transoms above the doors are all original, but I've had to replace almost everything else."

"You're handy," Savannah said.

He turned to look at her. "Does that move me up your list?"

Her lips twitched. "It's definitely a plus." She lifted and lowered her eyebrows. "But didn't I already say you could be at the top of my list?"

Noah rolled his eyes. "Thanks." He turned and walked away.

Savannah trailed behind him. "You know I'm teasing about the list," she said. "I don't have some little black book."

Noah grunted, not looking at her. "No, you probably have a 300-page autobiography with notes and tabs besides each man and his list of good and bad qualities."

They moved into the wide kitchen and dining area adorned with cherry cabinets, a rustic curio cabinet, and a huge butcher block table.

She laughed. "Maybe I'll have to compile that someday."

Noah smiled. "You could sell it to all the desperate women in Cache Valley: *Savannah Compton's List of Worthwhile Men to Date*."

She shook her head and ran her hand the length of the table. The smooth surface was cool beneath her fingertips. She imagined Noah seated at the head of the rectangular table, laughing and talking with five or six children.

"Planning on a large family?" she asked.

Noah looked at her, his lips soft and slightly parted. "Someday."

He walked to the fridge, opened the door, and retrieved two water bottles. He tossed her one.

"I love this table," she said.

"Thanks. I made it."

Her head snapped up. "You made it?"

"Yeah. That, the curio cabinet, the entertainment center in the living room . . ." His voice trailed off and he looked away, seeming embarrassed by his admission.

"You really are handy."

He winked. "Make a note of it for your book." Smiling, he brushed past her. "I'll be back in a minute."

Wes idled down the block from Noah's house, hidden by the darkness. It had been easy to trail them running, but he never thought they'd end up here. It was bad enough watching Shumway stay the night at Savannah's sister's house, but now they were going into Noah's lair. Wes conjured up horrible images of what they might be doing. He couldn't take much more.

He opened the console and withdrew the Springfield pistol. He rotated it to his left hand and then back to his right. He would give Noah and Savannah ten minutes, then he was going in there after them.

Allison grinned at him. "Josh will be asleep in about an hour."

Ryan wrapped his arms around her and nuzzled into her neck. She smelled like baby lotion. "What'd you have in mind?"

She winked, trailing her fingers up to his shoulders. "I'm sure we can think of something."

"You sure Josh isn't ready for bed now?"

She gripped his shoulder hard. He jerked.

"Ryan?"

"Ally?"

"Ryan." It wasn't her sweet voice. It was gruffer, deeper. The vision faded. "Ryan, I'm sorry, but I need to check her vitals."

He sat upright. He was in the hospital. Allison wasn't smiling at him. She lay covered with tubes and attached to beeping monitors. No.

He swiped a hand over his face. Standing, he moved out of Ilene's way. He watched her work in silence. Ilene turned to face him. He didn't know what was wrong, but could tell by her eyes it wasn't good.

"They drew blood a bit ago."

He nodded.

"The Midazolam is there again. She's swimming in it."

The room swayed. Ryan sank onto a chair. "But the doctor said it was almost gone."

"She got another injection." Ilene scowled. "Possibly a double injection."

He looked over at his wife. "That's why she looks so bad."

Ilene nodded.

"I don't understand. I've been here almost the whole day. The only people who've messed with her IV have been you guys." He looked at her. "You think one of your nurses is doing this?"

Ilene reddened. "I sure hope not, because if they are, they'll have me to answer to."

"I've got to call Noah and Frank."

Ryan explained the situation to Frank. After threatening to come down to the hospital and move Ally himself, Frank finally calmed down. Ryan promised him he would stay with her through the night. He told him to get the information to Noah and ended the call.

Ilene studied him. "Listen. I know you're upset, but these things have a way of working out. We'll find out who's hurting her."

Ryan didn't respond. Ilene came over and clapped him on the shoulder.

"Now you go get some rest. I'm here all night again."

"I'm not leaving her."

"You need some rest. You were asleep on her bed."

"I know, but somehow she's getting that drug in her system. Noah can't seem to find who's doing it. I know he said the security and a policeman would be in and out tonight, but I can't trust someone else to protect her. It's my job."

"We're not supposed to let family stay in these rooms."

Ryan said nothing, just begged her with his eyes. She couldn't send him away. He had to be here with Ally.

She pursed her lips, studying him. Finally, she nodded. "All right. I'll get you a roll-away."

He exhaled. "Thanks, Ilene."

She clucked her tongue. "Wish I could do more."

Savannah wandered through a wide arched doorway and into a comfortable living room, taking a long swallow from the water bottle. The television was shut up in a mahogany entertainment center. She traced the routed lines of wood. Noah had made this. Amazing.

The sofa, loveseat, and overstuffed chair were upholstered in dark brown leather, comfortable and classic. Large windows covered the back of the house and landscape portraits adorned the opposite wall.

She wandered over to an end table and picked up a silver-framed picture. A beautiful blonde middle-aged woman had her arm wrapped around the neck of a younger and thinner Noah. Though their hair color was different, it was obvious the woman was his mother. In the photo, Noah gazed up at the woman, his expression a mixture of embarrassment and love. She was laughing, her blue eyes sparkling like Noah's did when he really smiled. Savannah wondered what had happened to this vibrant woman. Why did Noah scream her name at night and never want to talk about it?

Noah's heavy tread thudded into the room. Savannah turned with the picture in her grasp. "Your mom?"

Noah nodded, grimly taking the picture and setting it on the table. "We'd better get back before your dad starts searching for us."

He took her elbow and escorted her from the house, shutting off lights as they went. They entered the warm summer night together. Savannah inhaled freshly watered grass and wet concrete. She wanted to ask him about his mom, but refrained.

A vehicle started its engine and drove out of the neighborhood. The sound startled her. She jumped.

Noah chuckled. "It's just one of the neighbors."

Savannah smiled up at him. "I know. I just didn't expect it. Do you want to run home to get there quicker?"

Noah grimaced. "If your dad is that worried he'll call one of our cell phones."

"I didn't bring mine," she said.

His jerked his head up. "That explains it. I thought I'd missed hearing the annoying ring because I was concentrating so hard on my misery."

Savannah ignored his comment about her phone. "You really hate to run?"

"Pretty much."

"Why?"

"I played football in college to pay my way through school. I got so sick of running sprints I promised myself I'd never run again." He smiled at her. "Look at the things I do for you."

Savannah flushed. She wished it were really for her and not because he had to protect her or protect others *from* her. "Let me guess—you were the quarterback."

He scowled. "Wesley Richins was the quarterback."

She stopped walking. "Aha. Now that's interesting."

Noah's pace increased. His strong shoulders lowered. Savannah jogged to keep up with him.

"So what position did you play?"

"Center."

She raised an eyebrow. "Really? Isn't it the center's job to protect the quarterback?"

"Yep."

Savannah laughed shortly. "I bet that went over well seeing how much you like Wes."

He looked into her eyes. "I did a good job protecting the quarterback, even though I don't like Richins. I never let emotion get in the way. I always do my job."

She gulped. "You've never failed?"

He studied her, searching each crevice and cranny. "Never."

Ice trickled down her neck. "I hate how you make me feel like I'm on trial."

Noah's lips straightened further. "Should you be?"

She didn't answer—she just walked away. He followed her. Savannah counted the blocks until they would reach the house and she could leave his judgmental side. They'd been getting along so well. She could almost believe he didn't think she'd hurt Ally. Then he made stupid comments like that. She was sick of him thinking she was a bad person and there was nothing she could do to change his mind.

Noah grabbed her arm. Pulling her into his side, he sprinted toward a nearby house. She flailed beside him, trying to keep up.

"Noah, wha—"

"Shhh."

They raced around the side of the house, hidden from the streetlight. Noah waited. His eyes darted over the street. His grip on her arm tightened. Savannah's breath sounded like the roar of hurricane force winds. She tried to hold it. Her hands trembled, so she clenched them. Her throat was raw. Her mind filled with worst-case scenarios. People with guns? A psycho intent on harming them? A man with a machete and ski mask?

"The attacker?" she whispered.

"Shhh," Noah covered her mouth with his hand. His other hand wrapped around her waist, pulling her closer.

Around the corner an average-sized man with brown hair panted into the street. Pausing, he gulped for air and searched each direction. Shaking his head in frustration, he jogged up the subdivision. His face came into full view under a street lamp. Savannah gasped with recognition. The man from the grocery store.

Noah released her, and she felt exposed without his protection.

"Stay here," he whispered, sprinting from their hiding spot. The man whirled at the sound of approaching steps. His eyes widened. He pivoted and ran. Noah tackled him, easily subduing the smaller man. Savannah crept from the hiding space. She could hear Noah questioning him.

"Why are you following us?"

"I-I wasn't," the man said.

Noah pulled him to a standing position. He used one hand to pin the man's hands behind his back. "Right. I saw you this morning at the restaurant. I saw you this afternoon at the grocery store. Now I see you walking down the street behind us. What a coincidence, huh?"

Savannah approached. Noah's head whipped around. "I told you to stay there."

"I figured you had it under control."

Noah sighed. He turned to face the man. "Do you want to tell me what's going on now or down at the sheriff's office?"

"I can tell you now. I haven't done anything wrong."

Noah lowered his chin. "Uh-huh. Why were you following us?"

The man tried to elevate his shoulders, but they didn't move much with Noah's hand holding his arms. "Somebody paid me to. I've been taking pictures of your girl for the past couple days."

Noah's glanced at Savannah, then turned back to the man. "Who paid you?"

Savannah shivered with fear and hope. Why would someone want pictures of her? Was it the man who'd hurt Allison? If they found him they could protect Ally, and Noah would finally believe in her.

"I don't know," the photographer said.

Noah laughed. He released one of the man's arms, gesturing up the road. "Course you don't. We can talk about it at the sheriff's office."

The man lifted his camera. "Look. I'm serious. I was just supposed to take the pictures. I left them in the mailbox of an apartment. There was money waiting for me. Some lady called me yesterday morning and asked me to do it. Ten pictures yesterday. Ten today. I get a hundred bucks per picture."

"A woman?" Noah asked. He looked at Savannah. "Why would a woman want pictures of Savannah?"

The man's lips shifted. "How should I know? I just snapped the pictures, developed them, and collected the money."

"There wasn't a name on your caller ID?"

"It was blocked."

Noah started walking, pulling the man along with him. He dialed a number with his right hand, his left still gripped the man. "Jason, meet me at the Mendez house as soon as you can."

"Are you taking me in?" the man asked when Noah closed his phone.

Noah shrugged. "We'll see. It depends on if your story checks out and if I think you've told me all you know. Were you supposed to do a drop-off tonight?"

"No. Tomorrow morning. Eight o'clock. I only had seven good ones so far today. I was going to snap a few more of her tonight."

Savannah walked alongside Noah, listening to this insane conversation. Someone was paying to have pictures taken of her? A woman? She glanced around the dimly lit neighborhood. The night took on a sinister feel. She shivered, grateful for Noah's comforting presence.

"Where were you supposed to drop the pictures off?" Noah asked.

The photographer fished around in his pocket and pulled out a wrinkled paper. "1360 North 220 West, number four."

Savannah stopped. Her heart jumped into her lungs. She couldn't catch a full breath.

Noah looked back at her. "Savannah?" His eyes widened. "You okay?"

She shook her head.

Noah rushed to her, dragging the photographer with him.

Sweat broke out on her forehead. The asphalt was rolling and pitching. Noah was talking to her. "Savannah? Talk to me. What's wrong?"

She couldn't answer. Her tongue was thick in her mouth like a roll of cotton from the dentist's office. Noah wrapped an arm around her. She looked up into his blue eyes. They were full of concern. When he found out the truth, they'd be full of something else entirely.

Savannah panted for air. It felt like an elephant was stomping on her chest. She couldn't get any oxygen. Noah's lips were moving. She couldn't hear what he was saying. *Oh, Noah.* He'd never believe her now.

Everything went black.

⚜

Savannah woke to the sensation of floating through the air. Noah's arms surrounded her. She looked up into his face. He sensed the movement and glanced down at her. He smiled.

"You're awake." He brushed his lips across her forehead.

Savannah sighed. She leaned into his sweaty cotton shirt, wondering why sweat didn't stink on him. It smelled like salt and a good kind of antiperspirant. "You make me feel safe."

Noah chuckled. "That's interesting because you scare the crap out of me."

Savannah remembered. The photographer claiming he was supposed to deliver the pictures. She gulped. Did Noah already know the truth? "Why's that?" she squeaked.

He shook his head. "Lots of reasons."

She blinked at him.

"How am I supposed to take care of you if you pass out when I'm hauling in a criminal who could help us find Allison's attacker?"

Savannah's head swam. He didn't think she was the attacker anymore. She swallowed. That would change soon. "The photographer? Where is he?"

Noah jerked his head. The man plodded alongside them. "He decided to stay with us, rather than run and be in more trouble."

Savannah exhaled. She looked around. They were almost to Allison's house. "Are you going to that address?" She tried to keep her tone level.

Noah nodded. "A patrolman already checked, nobody's home. We'll be there in the morning for the dropoff. Right now, I'm going to meet Keller at Allison's house and have him take care of our friend here so I can take care of you."

Savannah snuggled into his arms. She might as well enjoy this until Noah found out the truth about where the photographer was delivering the pictures. "I can walk," she said against his chest.

Noah laughed. She felt the rumble of it against her face.

"I'm sure you can, but not until I find out why you passed out."

Savannah swallowed against the acid climbing her esophagus. She didn't answer. Her brain scrambled for some chronic condition that would cause her to faint. What was that heart condition called? Think, think. Aortic stenosis—that was it. Noah would believe she had a chronic heart condition.

She bit her lip. Unfortunately, her dad would not. They were almost to Ally's house. A red Jeep roared into the drive and a man jumped from the vehicle. He hurried to them.

"Are you okay?" he asked Savannah.

Savannah nodded.

"Savannah, you remember Jason?" Noah asked. "We work together."

"Of course she remembers me," Jason said.

Savannah smiled. "How could I forget?"

Jason grinned, but then concern filled his dark gaze. "What happened?"

"Panic attack," she said. Brilliant. The truth was good.

Noah set her on her feet, but kept an arm around her waist. She pressed herself into his side, knowing this might be the last chance she'd get to feel him next to her. Her dad raced out the front door and down the porch steps.

"Savvy! What happened?"

He rushed to her side. Noah released her. Savannah staggered. Her dad caught her in his lanky arms. She felt the comfort of familiarity instead of the excitement of Noah.

"It was a panic attack," she said.

"A panic attack?" Noah asked. "Do you get those often?"

"Um, not often," Savannah said. She glanced at her dad. He didn't say anything, but his gaze spoke volumes.

Savannah rushed to explain. "It must have been all the stress of thinking Allison's attacker was following us and the run was tough so the blood flow to my brain was probably reduced. Then when he said that someone paid him to take pictures of me." She shivered. "It was too much."

Noah, Jason, her dad, and the photographer all stared at her.

Savannah shook off her dad's hug. She walked unsteadily up the porch steps. All the men trailed her. Savannah turned around. They were like a semi-circle of vultures waiting to swoop on her.

She held up a hand. "Don't worry about me. I'm fine. I'll feel a lot better after a shower and some rest. I'm sorry if I scared all of you."

"No way, Savannah," Noah said. "We're going to the emergency room. It isn't normal to pass out like that."

Savannah's head shimmied. "No. I'll call my doctor. He has an after-hours emergency number. I'm fine. You guys do your thing. I'll see everybody in the morning."

She whirled on their shocked expressions and fled into the house. She was going to shower and sleep in a comfortable bed before Noah discovered the truth about that address. Tomorrow night, she could be sleeping in a jail cell.

⁂

Noah and Jason fired questions at the photographer, Kelly, for over twenty minutes until they were convinced he was innocent. They released him after verifying his address and phone numbers. Jason volunteered to find out who the apartment belonged to. A home address would have been easier, but Jason would have the information soon, Noah was sure of it. He trailed his friend to his Jeep.

"So, what was all that passing out stuff?" Jason asked.

Noah shook his head. "Don't know. Panic attack? It didn't fit. If she was going to have a panic attack about being chased wouldn't it have happened five minutes earlier?"

Jason climbed into the open-air vehicle. He whistled. "Beautiful piece of work—maybe she's whacked out."

Noah raised his eyebrows. "Or maybe she hurt her sister and she's playing me for all she's worth."

"Oh." Jason's mouth opened wider. "Never thought of that. But somebody's paying to have pictures taken of her."

"Could be, but Kelly claims that somebody who paid him is a woman. Would Savannah do something like that, have him chase us to throw me off?"

Jason snorted. "Dang, man. I don't know. You think she faked the passing out stuff?"

Noah thought back to her crumpling onto the asphalt. It had terrified him. He could still feel her softness in his arms. "I hope not. It seemed real to me." He frowned. "I don't know what to think with her."

Jason laughed. "She's a good one, that's for sure."

He stared at his friend. "What do you mean?"

"She's got you all confused. She's dragging you along."

Noah wrapped his hands around the Jeep's doorframe. "You're the expert on women. What would you do?"

Jason popped his gum. His lips spread wide. "I'd watch her close for two reasons." He held up a finger. "Number one: you want to make sure she's not going to hurt anybody if she is our suspect." He held up his second finger. "Number two: if she really did pass out she's going to need supervision throughout the night. You'd better stay in her room and make sure she doesn't have another panic attack."

"Great advice, Jason." He exhaled. "I'll just march in there and tell her dad that I'm going to spend the night in her room to make sure she's okay. He should love that."

Jason reached for the key dangling in his ignition. "You're the law around here. You make the rules." He turned the key. The engine roared. "If you can't do your job I'd be happy to take over."

Noah slapped his hand against the door. "Thanks, but I've got it under control."

Jason grinned. He jammed the stick into first, pumping his eyebrows. "Good luck tonight. Call me."

He pulled away. Noah was left with more questions than answers. Had Savannah really passed out? Why? He thought of Jason's advice. There was no way he'd sleep in Savannah's room, but he was worried about her. He trudged up the steps and through the front door.

Frank was waiting for him inside. "I've been waiting to talk to you, but I didn't want to talk in front of the photographer or upset Savvy. I wanted to be able to tell her in person." He paused. "Ryan called about an hour ago. They ran another blood test on Allison tonight." Frank's cheeks sagged. "She's full of Midazaloam again."

Savannah climbed from her knees. She hoped her prayers for Allison were doing some good. Faith, not fear, she repeated several times. Please help Ally, Lord. The words ran constantly through her head. Please help Ally. Maybe tomorrow would be the day her sister would awaken. Maybe then she could convince Noah she hadn't hurt her sister. She felt guilty even thinking that. She wanted Allison awake for the right reasons, but sadly clearing her name was also climbing the list.

Her door thudded with a soft knock. Her stomach fluttered. *Noah?* "Come in," she said.

The door swung open, and her dad leaned through the doorway. "Hey, sweetie, have you got a minute?"

Savannah nodded. She sank onto the bed. Her dad sat next to her. "What's going on, Savvy? You haven't had a panic attack that I've ever heard of. You're the least panicked person I know."

Savannah looked up at him—his tall, willowy strength; his graying hair; his dark, concerned eyes; the wrinkles forming on his craggy face. She wanted to lean against him and confide everything. She shook her head. He didn't need any more stress.

"It was weird, Dad." She tucked her knees into her chest and wrapped her arms around her shins. "I think everything just caught up with me. Worrying about Ally and thinking that guy was going to hurt us."

Frank's lips compressed. "I can't imagine you being too scared with Noah there."

Savannah took a deep breath. The only thing that scared her about Noah was how she felt about him and the way he was going to hate her once he went to that apartment in the morning. "It was scary, Dad. I'm sorry I acted like such a wimp."

"Oh, no, honey. I didn't mean that. Did you call your doctor?"

Savannah licked her lips. "Yeah. He wasn't on call, but the lady who was said I should make an appointment to talk with him, but she thought I'd be fine tonight. So that's good news. The last thing I want to do tonight is go back to that stinking hospital."

Her dad's eyebrows shot up.

"I mean . . ." Savannah swallowed. "I shouldn't have said that."

Frank shook his head. "No. I understand."

For the first time tonight, Savannah felt she could be truthful with her dad. "I hate it there. I hate seeing Ally like that. It reminds me of when Mom . . ." She swallowed and started again. "I just want Ally to be okay. I want her back." She leaned into his side, biting her lip. The tears came anyway. "I miss her, Daddy."

"I know, baby, I know."

Her dad held her, both of them lost in their sorrows and fears.

He pulled away and stared at her. "Honey, Ryan called earlier. The drug is back in Allison's blood. There's more of it than before."

The air whooshed from her lungs. "No. Oh, no." She gripped her dad's arm. "Is she ever going to be all right?"

He shook his head. "Wish I could answer that."

"What can we do?"

"Nothing tonight. Get some rest, and we'll just pray Noah can find whoever is shooting her full of drugs."

Noah. Would he think she'd put the drugs in Allison? Her throat constricted. He'd left her alone a couple of times today. What if he assumed she'd done something then?

Her dad kissed her goodnight and left. She sat on the bed thinking of Ally. Who was hurting her sister? Would the drugs do permanent damage? Minutes later, the door pounded, threatening to shake off its hinges. Savannah jumped to her feet as the door flung open.

"Noah," she whispered.

His eyes gleamed. "Do you think I'm an idiot? Where did you get the drug, Savannah?"

"What?" She stepped back. Her legs hit the bed frame. "I'd never even heard of Midaza . . . or Versed or whatever that crap is called until the other day."

Noah strode to her, his face set. He towered over her. He was so big he blocked out the overhead light. His eyes glinted an azure blue. His jaw couldn't have been cracked by a jackhammer.

"How much did you shoot down her today? I left you alone." He shook his head. "How could I have trusted you?" His eyes widened. "That's why you looked so guilty when I came to get you from Allison's room and then when you came back from the bathroom, you wouldn't meet my eye and you were shaking." He jammed a hand through his hair. "Oh, man. I am an idiot."

Her head swung back and forth. "No, Noah. I wouldn't hurt Ally. I'm as sick as you are about this."

He glared down at her.

"Noah, you have to believe me. Allison and I have a pact we made up when we were kids. We take care of each other, we stand up for . . ."

Noah held up a hand. "Save it. A childhood pinky swear isn't going to convince me."

Savannah swallowed and tried again. "I promise you I don't have any drug." She held up her arms. "Search me. See if you can find anything."

His eyes traveled the length of her body. She shivered at his look. He didn't touch her. "You're pretty smart, Savannah. You know I need a search warrant to search you or the house, or the evidence I find can be thrown out. I'm not falling for that. I'll get a warrant tomorrow to check this house and your apartment."

"You won't find anything." She folded her arms across her chest. "Will that prove I'm innocent?"

"No, but it would help your case."

"There has to be some way to prove I didn't do this."

His eyes softened. "I wish there was." He groaned. "I don't know where else to look. I've interviewed and checked backgrounds on every one of the ICU staff. Jason has been looking for another suspect and he hasn't found anything. The security cameras from the hospital have been monitored. Granted, they're pathetic, but they haven't seen anyone suspicious." He shook his head. "The nurses say no one has been in to see Allison but you, your dad, and Ryan. You are the only one we can place at the accident scene and you don't have an alibi." He flung his hands in the air. "You figure it out, Savannah."

Savannah stood her ground. She wouldn't let him intimidate her. She was terrified for her sister, and he kept trying to place the blame on her. "You've got to keep looking for him. There has to be someone else. Someone who wants you to stop looking. We have to find him before he kills her. Please, Noah. I wouldn't hurt Ally. I didn't do this. Please believe me."

He reached a hand out to touch her, then pulled it back. "I wish I could." His eyes narrowed. "Why did you look so guilty when I came to get you from her room this morning?"

"I was trying to get Ally to wake up. I-I pinched her arm, hard. It left a red mark. It was something she used to do to torture me when we were kids. Well, she only did it twice, but it hurt."

Noah arched an eyebrow. "That's the best you can come up with?"

Savannah exhaled. "Noah, please. Think about the time you spent with me today. I felt like we really got to know each other. You can't believe I'm capable of this." She stepped closer, placing her hand on his arm. He didn't move from her, but his eyes darkened. "Please. I can't handle you thinking I'm a criminal."

A muscle in his jaw twitched. His eyebrows lowered. "Why do you care what I think?"

"Because I care for you."

His face softened for an instant. His hand lifted and brushed her cheek. He yanked it back like she was an electric fence. "Stop with the games, Savannah."

"What?" She pulled her hand from him. "You've got to trust me. We've got to work together to protect Ally."

He studied her for several, terrifying seconds. Finally, he shook his head. "It all fits, Savannah. I left you alone today and now Allison is full of the drug again. I can't trust my instincts. I never should have. I wish . . ." He sighed and turned away. "Hopefully, we'll find something at that apartment tomorrow."

Her eyes widened. She was glad he wasn't looking at her. "Hopefully," she squeaked.

He turned to face her. His eyes searched her face. She squirmed and looked away.

"Goodnight, Savannah."

"Night."

She glanced up. He gave her one more look, then he turned, and his broad shoulders cleared the door. She withered onto the bed. Someone was continuing to hurt her sister, and Noah would never believe it wasn't her, especially after he went to that apartment in the morning.

***

She'd only been asleep a few hours when she heard it.

"Mom, Mom, I'm coming."

Savannah was fully awake in seconds. She threw back the covers and raced toward the room Noah was staying in, grateful her dad slept upstairs. She opened the door to Noah's bedroom and crept to the bed. His massive form twisted and writhed. The covers wound around his legs, his torso strained against his T-shirt. She wished she had the time to just admire him.

Savannah grasped his shoulder. "Noah." She shook him. "Noah."

"Mom?"

"No." She leaned closer, placing a hand on his face. "It's Savannah. Wake up, Noah. You're having another nightmare."

He shot up in bed, grabbing both her wrists and pulling her onto his lap. "Who are you?"

She gulped for breath, telling herself he wouldn't hurt her. He wasn't like Daxon. Her dad said he could trust Noah. She pushed against his chest to free herself. "Noah. It's Savannah. Please let go. You're hurting my wrists."

"Oh, Savannah." His grip lessened, but he didn't release her. Instead he tucked her into his chest. Letting go of her wrists, he wrapped one hand around her back and entwined the other in her hair.

She leaned awkwardly against him, one of her hands trapped beneath her leg. She didn't dare move for fear he'd wake fully and release her. She shouldn't want to be close to him, but she couldn't force herself to move.

Noah stroked her hair, shuddering from the after-effects of his nightmare. She shifted to get more comfortable, freeing her hand. He pulled her closer. His body stopped shaking. The room felt like a tropical island. The worries over tomorrow morning fled. The anger and fear she'd felt tonight dissipated. Noah might only be holding her because he was half-asleep, but she didn't care. She let herself enjoy each second without thinking too far into the future.

After several wonderful minutes with her head pressed against his warm flesh, she couldn't hold her tongue any longer. "Why do you have the nightmares? What happened to your mom?"

Noah stiffened, but didn't release his hold on her. "What happened to yours?"

Savannah wrapped her arms around him in case he had any plans of letting her go soon. She stroked his back and murmured into his chest. "Breast cancer."

Noah rested his chin on her hair. He kept one hand entangled in her dark locks. His other hand covered her waist. "I'm sorry. I'd hate to watch someone I love suffer through that."

"Yeah. It was awful. It was . . ." She paused. "I wouldn't wish that kind of pain on Hitler."

He laughed softly, and his chest rumbled against her face.

"Okay. Maybe on Hitler."

"I'm sorry," Noah whispered. Gently rubbing her back, he placed a soft kiss to her forehead.

Savannah sighed. Her forehead tingled.

"How long was she sick?" Noah asked.

Savannah bit her lip. Leaning against him, she found the strength to talk. "She was diagnosed when I was eleven. I wasn't old enough to really understand. They sheltered me from most of it, but I remember things being pretty tense and Allison even snapped at me a couple of times. Allison rarely gets angry, so I knew something was really wrong. But then Mom started improving."

Noah kept stroking her back. His hands worked on the tight muscles as she talked.

"I remember celebrating when she had her last test and they said the cancer was gone. We went to The Pie for pizza. Daddy took us bowling after and for frozen custard at Nelson's. I was thirteen. It was a great night." She shook her head. "Mom didn't even say anything when I ate three slices of pizza and an ice cream cone."

Noah's hands stopped moving. "Why would your mom care if you ate three slices of pizza?"

Savannah blinked. What had she said? "Um. She was kind of a health nut."

He nodded. "Like mother, like daughter, huh?"

"Yeah." Not really. She'd never make her child feel the way her mom used to make her feel. Not that she resented her mom. She'd dealt with those issues. Mostly.

"When did the cancer come back?" Noah asked.

Savannah could still see her mom exhausted from the chemotherapy and trying to stay awake to talk with her, begging Savannah for forgiveness, begging Savannah to believe in herself. "A few years later . . ." Her voice trembled. She cleared her throat and tried again. "She went into relapse, and they didn't catch it in time. They tried chemo, but it just made her last couple of weeks miserable." She shrugged. "At least we got to say goodbye."

The room was silent for several minutes. She leaned into his strength. He rubbed her back. Finally he spoke, "No wonder your dad is so edgy about Allison."

Savannah nodded against his chest. "I don't think any of us could survive losing someone else. Well, I guess we could survive, but we wouldn't want to. Ally is so much like my mom: patient and happy to care for everybody else. I was only fifteen when Mom died. Ally took over. She raised me, took care of Dad and the house. Ryan's loved her since high school, but she made him wait to marry her until I started college."

Noah moved his hand to her jaw. He tipped it up until she stared into his eyes in the moonlit room. "Allison's going to wake up."

Savannah licked her lips, studying his firm mouth just inches from her own. She shook her head to clear her thoughts. She was a bad person to be thinking of kissing Noah when her sister was in a coma, she'd just shared the details of her mom's death, and he still thought she was a suspect.

"Don't shake your head," Noah commanded. "Once the drug clears she'll be fine."

"I hope so." Savannah didn't want to talk about Allison. Her heart couldn't break any wider. "What happened to your mom?"

Noah pressed his lips together. "I guess it's only fair if I share too."

Savannah nodded, but didn't speak.

"She was killed."

Savannah gasped.

"I was sixteen." He tried to smile. It came out flat. "What a coincidence, huh? I was out late partying with my buddies. Mom and Dad came searching for me." He looked through Savannah like she was a pane of glass. "Dad was drunk. I guess Mom begged him to let her drive, but he was such a pigheaded . . ."

"Jackie?" Savannah supplied.

Noah's eyes focused on her again, he actually smiled. "Jackie works." His fingers trailed down her face, his thumb caressing her cheek as he spoke. "My dad and brother are alcoholics, like everyone else in my hometown. They always have been, always will be."

Savannah held her breath, afraid of what was coming.

"Dad drove them head-on into a semi truck. Mom was killed instantly. Unfortunately, Dad survived. Isn't it funny how the good ones are always taken?"

She couldn't formulate any words.

"It was all my fault," Noah continued. "If I hadn't stayed out so late, drinking with my stupid friends. Her blood is on my hands. Maybe that's why I have the nightmares."

"Oh, Noah . . ."

His finger moved to her lips, still caressing but also silencing her. "Don't. I know you're sorry. I'm sorry about your mom, too. There's nothing we can do to change it."

Savannah held her breath. "There is one thing."

He leaned closer, their foreheads touched. "What's that?"

She prayed he wouldn't think her silly. "We both understand how hard it is. We can comfort each other."

His fingers trailed along her jaw and back into her hair. His hand on her waist pressed her closer into him. "No one else has been able to take away my pain."

Savannah worked her hands up his back, loving the feel of his musculature under her fingertips. "No one else is me," she whispered.

"You're right about that." He smiled.

Savannah's hopes fell. He was laughing at her. She released her hold on him and tried to move from his lap, but his arms around her prevented her escape. Her head jerked up in surprise. Entangling his hand in her hair, he moved her face within centimeters of his own. Her lips parted in anticipation. His other hand tucked her against his chest.

Closing the distance between them, Noah kissed her. Savannah collapsed against him, responding to the movement of his lips and the feel of his hands. She forgot every worry as his warmth surrounded her. She pressed closer, wanting more.

Without warning, he broke away. He hefted her from his lap and onto the bed like a sack of flour with weevil in it. "I'm sorry, Savannah. I-I don't know what I was thinking."

Savannah rose to her feet, unsteadily putting some distance between them. He didn't know what *he* was thinking. She shuddered. What on earth was *she* thinking? He thought she was drugging her sister. Why had she planted herself in his arms? The problem was, if he gave her any indication that he wanted her there, she'd be back in his embrace.

"Maybe you can get some rest now," she said, embarrassed beyond belief.

"Thanks for checking on me," he muttered.

Savannah closed his door and leaned against it. Her erratic breathing didn't calm. She could hear him talking to himself. "What am I doing? I can't be like this with a suspect. I've got to keep my distance."

Savannah was ill. A suspect. Of course. That was how he thought of her and after tomorrow morning there would be no way to convince him otherwise. She teetered on unsteady legs back to her room. Noah obviously didn't want her, and he was the only thing she could think about. Sleep wasn't an option. She lay on her bed and remembered Noah holding her until her alarm buzzed at 5:30.

Twelve

The drive into the gym was awkward the next morning. Noah glanced at her, wondering what she thought of him, and what she thought of last night. She'd woken him up. He'd been caught up in the moment and muddled by her touch. She'd shared personal information. He'd shared too much personal information. But that was still no excuse. She was there and so intriguing, and he'd taken advantage of her. Or was it the other way around? He still wasn't convinced that the she was as innocent as she professed. Who was the real Savannah? The gorgeous angel he'd held last night or the conniving liar who was drugging her sister? He wasn't sure he wanted to find out.

His cell phone rang: Keller. Noah flipped it open. Savannah stared straight ahead.

"Yeah?" Noah said.

"Good, you're awake. Thought you'd want an update. I couldn't find a name on that apartment. The owner of the building lives in Millville; his answering machine says he's on vacation. I couldn't get anybody at the city utilities' office and the phone company claims the person I need to speak with won't be in the office until eight." Jason blew out a loud breath. "I'm headed to the apartment now. I'll watch for any action until you get there. Speaking of action, please tell me you got some last night. I'd love something to keep me happy this morning."

Noah squirmed in his seat. He squinted out the window at the pre-dawn lit road. "Nope, nothing yet." *Like he was going to tell Keller about last night with Savannah sitting right next to him.*

"Are you kidding me? Why haven't you kissed her? You've had enough opportunities. "

Noah sped up. "Opportunity isn't the problem."

"Come on. Are you a man or a moose? You're killing me, bro."

"I'll call you later."

"Wait a minute. You're giving me the brush-off and it's not even 6 AM? Is she sitting right there?"

Noah turned right. "That's affirmative."

"Affirmative? Give her the phone."

Noah laughed shortly. "Why would I do something as dumb as that?"

Savannah turned her head. Confusion filled her dark gaze.

"I can't get a straight answer out of you. Maybe the beauty will fess up to a late-night kiss from the beast."

Noah sighed. "At least you got the characters right. Talk to you later." He hung up the phone amidst Jason's protests. He caught Savannah's gaze. "Jason, um," he cleared his throat, "needed to give me an update."

She didn't respond, returning her gaze to the window. Suddenly, Savannah's phone rang. She picked it up, looking at the caller ID. She shook her head. "I don't recognize the number."

Noah reached over, stealing the phone from her hands, he glanced at the number on the screen to confirm his suspicions, then flipped the phone open. "Keller, how did you get this number?"

"In her file. You didn't do a very good job, buddy. There's no address or home phone written down, just her cell phone in the contact info. But I'll overlook it if you let me talk to Savannah. If you're not going to make a move on her, I'm taking her to dinner."

Noah ignored Savannah's stunned expression. "Keller. Don't call her again or I'll . . ."

"You'll what? I'm the one doing you a favor here. Now you listen to me, buddy. You better get that kiss by tonight, and you'd better let me know, or I'm knocking on that woman's door first thing tomorrow morning."

Noah hung up. He pulled into the gym parking lot. Savannah's eyes were wide. She didn't exit the car.

He grabbed his bag from behind the seat. She still didn't move. He opened the door. Savannah reached across him and pulled it shut. Noah had to force himself not to grab her and keep her close. She returned to her side of the vehicle and stared at him.

"What's going on, Noah?"

He shook his head. "Would you believe a wrong number?"

She arched an eyebrow. "Not even Josh would believe that was a wrong number."

Noah exhaled. He grasped the steering wheel for support. "It was Jason again."

She nodded. "Why was he calling my number?"

"He's a screwball. He has to do something to entertain himself." Noah tapped his watch. "And you'd better hurry. You don't want to be late for your client."

He jumped from the vehicle and walked into the gym. Richins was already there, leaning against a cardio machine. He winked at Savannah as they entered. Noah clenched a fist. The pompous jerk hadn't changed much since high school and college.

Living with his aunt, uncle, and six rowdy cousins in Cache Valley for the last two years of high school had taught Noah about Christ and kept him from a future of alcoholism, but there hadn't been any extra money to provide him with much more than food and a mattress. Wes took every opportunity to make fun of Noah's clothes, bike, haircut, and anything else he could think of.

Noah thought when he earned the football scholarship to Utah State, Wes would finally respect him, but he just made more subtle shots when their coach and fellow players weren't around. He also succeeded in stealing any girl Noah showed even the slightest interest in. Even a college of 12,000 students hadn't been big enough to escape Wes's influence.

Noah shook off the memories. He was past all that. He couldn't let it eat him up inside, but when he saw Savannah with Wes. . . . He'd never been so tempted to misuse his job title.

"Have a good workout," Savannah said as she breezed from his side. "How are you, Wes?" she called, linking her arm through his.

"Yeah, I'll have a great workout," Noah muttered.

He pushed through more weight than he'd done in months with his anger as a motivator. Savannah's tinkling laughter and Wes's suggestive tones gave him all the drive he needed to accomplish several extra repetitions of each lift, but he still couldn't shut out their voices from across the weight room.

"What are you doing later today?" Wes asked.

"I don't know." Savannah changed the pin on the lat pull-down machine, brushing across Wes. Noah wanted to scream at her to be careful where she moved.

"What'd you have in mind?" she said. Her eyes roved to Noah, but her smile was all for Wes.

Noah cringed. *What was she thinking?*

Wes trailed his fingers up her arm. "I could fly us to Vegas for dinner and a show."

Savannah giggled. "That sounds fun, but you'd better lift your weights first."

Maybe Noah could throw her in jail to keep her away from Wes.

"Come on, Anna, say yes."

"Lift your weights," she said, smiling.

"Not until you say yes."

Oh, lift your stinking weights, Noah thought.

"I'll let you know," Savannah said.

The conversation continued. Noah walked to the other side of the weight room. He got far enough away from the two that he couldn't hear much more than Savannah's tinkling laughter. He counted each minute of the hour-long training session. Finally he could take no more.

He marched up to them. "Savannah, are you about ready to go?"

Wes glanced up at him, a satisfied grin on his face.

Savannah's mouth dropped open. "Noah. I'm working here."

Noah looked at both of them. "I can see that."

"Ah." Her mouth fell open. "I will be done at seven," she said, turning her back on him.

Noah narrowed his eyes. "Check the clock. It *is* seven."

Wes's grin widened. Noah spun on his heel and marched toward the locker room. He'd shower and waste a few minutes in there, at least he could shelter his ears from the assault of their playful banter.

Savannah watched Wes finish his last repetitions on the seated row. She wouldn't really consider leaving her sister's side to go to Vegas, but she had known Noah was listening to the conversation, so she encouraged the flirtations. She knew it was petty, but she wanted to make Noah jealous.

She frowned. *Why was Noah such a jerk?* He acted like she was the one in the wrong. He was the one who thought of her as a "suspect." He was the one who'd turned her away last night. She blinked away the painful memory.

At eight o'clock this morning Noah would have another piece of evidence against her. A big piece. Maybe she *should* ask Wes to fly her away from here. No. She wouldn't leave her sister, even if she had to visit the hospital in prison orange.

She walked with Wes toward the front doors. "I'll see you tomorrow."

"Are you sure it can't be tonight?" he asked, trailing a hand down her arm.

She shivered, forcing her head to shake from side to side. "Maybe tomorrow night. I'll see what I have going."

"Okay. Maybe I'll have to find you in a bathroom again." Wes winked.

She playfully slugged his shoulder. "Just don't scare me so bad next time."

He laughed and strutted away.

Wes entered the locker room as Noah exited it. The men brushed past each other, saying nothing.

Savannah studied Noah. He looked amazing in a Polo shirt and jeans. But the look on his face marred the image. The disapproval written there made her squirm for a second, but just one. She spun on her heel and marched away from his condescending glare.

Flinging open the front door, she raced toward her car. Noah was so close he clipped the heel of her shoe. "Don't you need a longer shower or something?" she snapped.

"I didn't get worked as hard as your client," he said, breathing down her neck.

Savannah twisted to face him. "I was just doing my job."

Noah nodded. He leaned toward her, making a clucking noise with his tongue. "Didn't realize prostitution was legal in Utah."

"Oh!" she gasped. She raised her hand to smack him. He caught her fingers between his. She wrenched them free. "How could you even say that?"

Noah towered over her. His size became more intimidating because of the glower on his face. "He's paying you. You're all over him. How much is it going to cost Richins to take you to dinner?"

Savannah punched his chest as hard as she could. He didn't flinch, but her hand ached. "It's going to cost him a lot more than you could ever afford!"

His lips thinned. "Thanks for proving my point. I knew money was all that mattered to you."

"I-I hate you!" Savannah screamed. She whirled from him, running across the asphalt.

Noah caught her in seconds. He grabbed her shoulders and spun her around. "Grow up, Savannah. Not every man is going to kill himself to get an ounce of attention from you."

She stepped back, and his hands fell from her shoulders. "Especially not you."

He folded his arms across his chest. His biceps bulged. "That's right."

Tears of anger and frustration threatened. She choked them down. The silence lengthened as she stared at him. Couldn't he see that if he'd give her that ounce of attention she'd never look at Wesley or any other man again?

She shook her head. "You know what?"

Noah smirked. "No. Enlighten me."

Savannah glared at him. "I think I've figured you out, Detective Shumway."

"Oh, really?"

She moved closer to him, refusing to be cowed by his huge body. "You couldn't care less about me." She poked him in the chest. "That is until someone else expresses an interest."

He elevated an eyebrow. "You don't need me to care about you. You just need every man you meet to fling himself at your feet so you can add them to your stupid list."

Savannah's jaw clenched. "You are such a Sobie!"

"A Sobie?" Noah blinked. "Is that another one of your abbreviated swear words?"

"Yes." She flung her hair over her shoulder. "But for you I'll spell it out. You're a son of a—"

"I get it," Noah said, holding up a hand. "Can we stop the name-calling and just get to the source of the problem."

She wrapped her arms around her abdomen. If the source of the problem was that he couldn't care less about her, she didn't want to hear it. "Which is what?"

He studied her for half a minute as if debating whether to speak. Finally, he opened his mouth. "Why can't you come clean with me, Savannah?"

"Come clean with you?"

"You claim you didn't hurt Allison."

She clenched her arms tighter, but her stomach still pitched. They were back to this. "I-I didn't."

"You know I might believe you if you'd stop playing all these games with me. Every time I make you mad, you either hit me or swear at me."

Her jaw dropped. "I don't swear."

He rolled his eyes. "You use made up swear words. Then you come to my room at night, rescue me from my nightmares, and get me all riled up."

He paused and it was Savannah's turn to raise an eyebrow.

"You flirt with Richins. Why? Just to make me mad or is that what you're really interested in? It's obvious you're enamored with wealth. Are you shallow enough to hurt others to get what you want? What did your sister do to push you over the edge?"

Savannah's mouth flapped. Tears sprung to her eyes faster than a busted water main. She whispered, "So that's what you think of me? A conniving, two-faced hooker?"

His lips pressed together. "I didn't say that. I just can't read you."

"You did say that."

She moved toward the car as if in a daze. Noah was speaking, but she couldn't understand what he was saying. She tried to reach her door handle, but a large hand covered her own.

"I didn't mean it like that," Noah said.

"You just called me a prostitute," Savannah spat out, stealing her fingers from his grasp. "Guess you didn't mean that either?"

"No, I didn't mean that." Noah exhaled. "I shouldn't have said that. I was . . . upset." He rolled his head, unclenching his fist. "Guess you're not the only one who reacts in anger."

Savannah sniffed, swiping the tears from her face with the back of her hand. "Guess not."

"Don't cry." Noah pursed his lips. "Oh, Savannah, come on. Please don't cry." He opened his arms to her. "C'mere."

She should've turned away or at least hesitated. She didn't. She collapsed against his chest. He smelled clean, like a bar of Irish Spring.

Noah stroked her back. "I'm sorry, okay?" he murmured into her hair. "I should never have called you a prostitute or said you were shallow. I don't think either of those things are true."

Savannah nodded against him. "Dang straight, but you're still going to have to do some amazing groveling to make up for that."

Noah tilted her chin with one hand. His cheek crinkled. "I don't grovel."

Air forced itself through her nose in an unladylike snort. "Big surprise." She leaned away from him, looking into his eyes. "You don't grovel, you don't compliment, you don't make me feel like you care at all."

Noah stiffened. "I'm not like Richins if that's what you're after."

She ground her teeth. "What do you care what I'm after? All you do is tell me how horrible I am."

He tossed his head. "Come on, Savvy."

"Savannah," she corrected.

His arms dropped to his sides. "How could I forget?"

"I heard you last night," she whispered. "I heard you call me a suspect." She stepped back, searching the cornflower blue depths of his eyes. "How can you think of me like that?"

His lips thinned, and he lifted a shoulder. "How can I not?"

Savannah wrenched open the driver's side door, slipped inside, and slammed it. Noah stood outside the door with his mouth open and his hands empty.

Wes chose that moment to saunter up to her car. "Looks like you're doing a fabulous job with women, as usual."

Noah slowly rotated his head and stared at Wesley. Noah had the advantage of a couple of inches and at least forty pounds of muscle. Savannah wondered what would happen if Wes made Noah mad enough to fight. She could almost hear Noah trying to control himself.

"Thanks for watching Savannah for me." Wes smirked as he brushed past Noah.

Noah grabbed his arm, forcing the smaller man to face him. Wes's face stiffened. He tried to shake off Noah's arm, but couldn't.

Noah carefully enunciated each syllable. "Stay away from her."

Savannah gasped at the threat. Noah released Wes and stalked around to the passenger side of the Accord. Wes leaned down to her window. He winked and mouthed, "Bye, Anna," then sauntered away as if nothing had happened.

Noah slammed the door. She turned to look at him. "What was that about?"

He stared straight ahead and tossed her the keys. "Just start the car, Savannah. We need to go meet Jason."

Savannah seethed. She shoved the key into the ignition. Noah's implications that she was hurting Ally were enough to make her want to kill him. But the fact that he was immune to her when she would do anything to be in his arms, that fact devastated her.

Savannah pulled up to the familiar apartment complex. The white stucco on the two-story buildings looked like frosting swirled on a cake. Noah turned to look at her. "You need to wait here," he said. "Will you be okay?"

She nodded, unable to speak.

With one last glance at her, Noah climbed from the car. Savannah watched him. She clenched the leather seat with her fingers. What was he going to do when he found out whose apartment this was? She wilted against the seat. How had this happened? Somebody was setting her up. Why? How did they find this address? Why would they pay a photographer to follow her and then make it look like she was doing it? That same person was probably the one injecting Allison with the drug. How could Savannah protect her sister and prove her innocence?

Noah and Jason sauntered up to the apartment door. Savannah watched them retrieve an envelope stuffed with money from the mailbox by the door. Then she saw Noah sorting through the mail. She knew what they would find: her electric bill, her *Women's Muscle & Fitness* magazine. . . . She sank deeper into the seat.

Noah's head slowly pivoted. He stared at the car. Savannah considered starting it and speeding away, but she couldn't move.

Shoving all the papers into Jason's hands, Noah muttered something to his friend and stomped toward the car. Savannah turned her head so she couldn't see him. The driver's side door flung open.

"Move," he said.

Savannah scrambled to the passenger seat. Squeezing her eyes shut, she prayed this was all a bad dream.

He climbed in and slammed the door. Savannah opened her eyes. Noah gripped the steering wheel with both hands, a muscle working furiously in his jaw. He turned to look at her. He opened his mouth and then closed it. He spun forward, turning the key in the ignition.

Savannah was surprised the key didn't break from the pressure he exerted on it.

She cleared her throat. "Um, that was fast," she said.

Noah glared at her. "Jason's going to take care of the formal search and fill me in on the incriminating evidence he finds."

"He won't find anything," she said.

Noah ignored her and jammed the car into gear. The silence hung in the car like the heavy draperies in her grandma's house that nobody liked.

He gritted his teeth. "Why, Savannah?"

She swallowed. "I didn't do this, Noah. Somebody's setting me up. I promise."

Noah guffawed. "Uh-huh. What TV show did you get this idea from?"

Savannah grabbed his toned forearm. "Please believe me. Someone's setting me up, so you won't find who's really hurting Ally. You've got to believe me, so we can protect her."

His eyes squinted at her fingers on him.

Savannah felt like a parasite. She took her hand back and clutched both of her hands together to keep them from shaking. "Please, Noah. I didn't do this. I wouldn't hurt my sister. I didn't pay some guy to take pictures of me. I'm not some whack job."

He didn't look at her as he flipped on his blinker and turned south.

"Where are you going?" Savannah asked, fearing the answer.

"Where do you think I'm going?" He released a pent-up breath. "Hope you have a good lawyer."

Savannah's hands clamped onto his arm. "No, Noah. Please. Don't do this. You've got to believe me."

Noah shook her off. "If you're innocent, why didn't you tell me the address was yours last night? Why can't you be honest with me?" His jaw hardened. "I'll never be able to believe you, Savannah."

Her throat filled. She clenched her fingers together again. Tears stung at her eyelids. She wouldn't cry. She wouldn't let herself be a wimp. *I'll never be able to believe you.* The words echoed in her brain until she wanted to scream.

"Can you at least let me see Allison one more time?" she whispered, blinking at the wetness building on her eyelids.

"Why, so you can shoot more medicine into her?"

One tear escaped down her cheek. "You can sit right next to me, just please let me see my sister."

Noah looked at her and blew out his breath. "Don't cry," he said.

"Please," she whispered.

He darted into the left turn lane. "Don't ask me for anything else."

Savannah shriveled against the door. He drove toward the hospital. She should thank him, but all she could hear was the betrayal and anger in his voice. Even if Allison woke up and Savannah didn't get thrown in jail, she'd never have Noah. He'd never believe her. She couldn't change that.

Ryan startled awake in a strange bed. His cell phone was ringing. He flipped it open.

"Ryan." Frank's voice was thick and distorted. "We're in the cafeteria. Can you come eat breakfast with us?"

Ryan could hear Josh happily chattering in the background. He looked down at Allison covered with thin blankets. Her face didn't look as pale. Ilene stood outside the door.

"I hate to leave, Ally."

"Please, Ry. Josh needs to see you."

"Okay." Ryan hung up the phone and glanced at Ilene leaning in the doorway.

She nodded. "You can trust me. I won't leave her room."

Ryan touched Allison's cheek, stood, and walked to the nurse. "I don't know how I'll ever thank you."

"Just doing my job."

"No. You're doing much more than that." He hurried from the room before she saw him get emotional. Arriving at the cafeteria, Ryan stopped outside the door.

"Mommy, Mommy," Josh chanted. "Me plays with Mommy."

"Daddy will be here soon," Frank said.

"Daddy, Mommy." The baby's song continued. Ryan leaned against the wall, lacking the strength to stand on his own. His poor little boy. Why couldn't Ally come back to them? How much longer did they have to suffer?

Ryan straightened. He hurried into the cafeteria, eager to hold his son. "Bubba! How are you?"

Josh stood on the chair and vaulted into his dad's arms. "I happy, Daddy! I happy! Play with Mommy today!"

Ryan grimaced. He looked at Frank. "Did Papa buy you a donut?"

"Yeah!" Josh said, leaning into his dad's shoulder. "I eat it. Then me plays with Mommy."

Ryan exhaled. He patted Josh's back, shaking his head helplessly at Frank. Tears stained his father-in-law's cheeks. He'd obviously been listening to Josh's happy chanting all morning.

"Daddy!" Josh said. "Me plays with Mommy today. Yes."

Frank inhaled sharply. Ryan couldn't answer, and before long he had stains on his face to match Frank's.

Savannah said nothing as they walked through the building and down the hall to the ICU. Noah was glad. If she touched him, she'd another tear, or said please again, he didn't know how he'd resist her. How could he let himself fall for someone who would do something like this? Her normally straight form slouched forward. Her dark hair fell across her olive skin, and her black eyes were pool of misery. Noah was torn. He wanted to kiss her and shake her and scream: Why?

His phone rang. "Yeah."

"Noah, it's Ryan."

"What's up, Ry?"

Savannah's head swiveled. She stared at him.

"Something's been bugging me, and I probably should've told you earlier, but I kept thinking it was nothing."

"What is it?"

"I've seen this same guy in the hospital a couple of times. Yesterday I followed him down the stairs, and then he ran from me. I chased him, but I couldn't find him." There was a short pause. "I don't know, it's probably nothing, maybe he didn't know I was trying to talk to him, but it's just weird that he would run from me."

Noah looked at Savannah. Could it be possible that she was innocent? Noah's heart thumped faster. Who was the man Ryan had seen? "What did he look like?"

"Tall, strong, dark hair and skin."

"Let's keep an eye out for him."

Ryan exhaled. "It might be nothing."

"Yeah, but it might be exactly what we're looking for." Noah disconnected.

Savannah stared at him. "What did Ry want?"

Noah didn't answer her. His mind spun. *Was Savannah being framed?*

"Why didn't you tell him you're taking me in for questioning?" she asked icily.

Dr. McQuivey intercepted them. "Detective Shumway. I need to speak to you."

Noah turned to look at Savannah. "You'd better come with us."

"If it concerns Ally, I'm going to be there," she said, looking at him, but not into his eyes.

They followed the doctor to his office. Dr. McQuivey started into the issues without wasting any time. "I just found some information that could help you."

Noah glanced at Savannah. Please let it prove her innocent. "What is it?"

The doctor flipped open a nurse's log book to the day after Allison's accident, there was a notation of a driver's license number and a name. Jonathon Mendez.

Noah ripped the file from the doctor's hands. Hope flared in his heart. Could it be the same man Ryan had seen? "Jonathon Mendez?" He turned to Savannah. "Do you know him?"

She shook her head and searched his eyes. "Ryan's brothers are Shane and Thomas. They both live in California. Maybe a cousin?" Her lips pursed. "No. Ryan doesn't have many cousins on his Mendez side. I don't recognize that name."

Noah caught a full breath for the first time that day. This was what he'd been hoping for. This could prove Savannah wasn't the culprit. He wanted to grab her in the doctor's office and swing her around. He shook his head. He had to work first.

"It's not a real name," he said. He thrust the papers back to the doctor and stood. "Who do you think wrote this?"

The doctor frowned. "Ilene talked with all the nurses. Rosie told her the man is Allison's brother-in-law and that he's estranged from the family. Ilene said she called Rosie in to work immediately. She should be here any minute." He looked at Savannah. "You're sure you're not related to a Jonathon Mendez?"

She shook her head.

"I'm sorry," the doctor said. "I guess he's come by a few times. I don't know why Rosie didn't make him sign in or say something to any of us."

Noah was already leaving the room. "Let's not waste time apologizing. I want get a sketch done and get this guy caught. Can you come with me, Savannah?"

They hurried from the room. Noah's cell phone rang. He flipped it open. "Jase, there was a nurse letting a supposed brother-in-law into the room and Ryan chased some guy out of here the other day."

"We've searched the apartment and Allison's house," Jason said. "Savannah is clean. No drug. No evidence. Her bank account doesn't show enough money to have paid that guy taking pictures. I asked our picture buddy, and he swears Savannah's voice sounded nothing like the woman who called him. I think someone is—"

"Setting her up," Noah finished. He glanced at Savannah. She walked by his side, watching him with eyes full of hope. "Get a patrol outside the hospital," he said to Jason. "I need you on the inside."

"Make sure you kiss and make up before you work," Jason said.

Noah couldn't withhold a smile. "I'm on it."

He flipped his phone closed and turned to look at Savannah. All of his questions hadn't been answered, but he was almost certain she wasn't his suspect. He grinned with relief.

He pulled her into his side, hugging her close as they walked. "I'm sorry."

Savannah blinked back tears, taking two steps to his one. "*You're* sorry?"

Noah was grateful she let him touch her. "Yes. I was wrong. Incredibly stupid and wrong."

Her eyes lit up at that.

"It looks like someone is setting you up. I shouldn't have accused you and said I wouldn't believe you. I was mad and confused and I'm an idiot and I understand if you never forgive me."

Savannah reached her arms around his back and abdomen. She squeezed him in a sideways hug. "It's okay." She half-laughed, half-sobbed. "I didn't know what to say to make you believe me. I understand why you acted like an idiot."

He smiled. "I've never been so glad to be wrong."

A couple of tears fell. "I've never been so glad to see you wrong."

He chuckled, his arm warm around her shoulder. "I'm sure you'll see it happen again."

Savannah gazed up at him, winking. More tears cascaded. "I hope so."

They reached Allison's doorway. Noah turned and took her fully in his arms. Savannah leaned into him, enjoying each second of the embrace. He tilted her chin up, tentatively touching her mouth with his. Savannah rose onto her toes, returning the pressure of his lips.

"I'm sorry," he breathed against her mouth.

"I'll forgive you if you try that again," she whispered.

He smiled, lowering his lips to hers. Seconds later, he released her and pulled away to look into her eyes. "Forgiven?"

"Maybe tonight you can keep working on it."

Noah chuckled. "You go stay with Ally while I find this . . ." He paused, grinning. "What kind of an abbreviation do you have for son of a motherless goat?"

She laughed as she wiped her cheek with the back of her hand. "We haven't made one up yet."

Noah nodded, gently tucking a long strand of hair behind her ear. "When Allison wakes up you two think on it."

Savannah gulped, smiling up at him. Noah opened Allison's door and ushered her inside. With one last grin at her, he shut the door and hurried away.

Savannah rushed to her sister's side, grabbing her cold hand. "Ally, we're going to figure out who's hurting you. Noah's not going to put me in jail! You're going to get better now and oh, Ally, he's such a good kisser!"

Thirteen

The day was filled with a flurry of activity at the hospital. Savannah, Frank, and Ryan watched Noah interview people, pace, and talk on his phone. Ilene and the other nurses apologized over and over again. It seemed the imposter had only visited when Rosie was there. Rosie said he'd convinced her he was alienated from the rest of the family but still wanted to be there for Allison. The man had begged her not to mention his visits to the family, and she felt awful that she hadn't.

Savannah wanted to strangle Rosie and she could tell by the look on Noah's face that he felt the same. He said they were going to watch Rosie closely. She'd lied to him once and she could be lying again.

Jason brought Noah dress clothes from his house. Noah quickly changed in an unused room. Savannah practically drooled when she saw him. She'd forgotten how good he looked in a shirt, tie, and slacks.

"I can't believe he's making me pose as a nurse," Jason said. "Do I look like a nurse?" He gestured with a tanned hand to his short, thick frame.

Savannah giggled. "Don't hold to stereotypes. They probably need strong types to lift the patients off their beds."

"Yeah," Jason winked at her with a twinkle in his deep-brown eyes. "They need tough men to wipe their butts after they carry them to the bathroom."

Laughing, she scooted closer to him. "You called my phone this morning. Why?"

Jason raised an eyebrow. "I was going to see if you were free for dinner,

159

but the big guy," he jerked a thumb toward the direction they'd last seen Noah, "he said you're already taken."

Savannah straightened. "He did?"

Jason leaned into her side, whispering. "I know he's an emotional mess, but give the sucker a chance."

"I'm trying."

Jason squeezed her hand. "Don't give up. Now just between us . . ." He tilted closer. "Has he kissed you yet?"

Noah entered the waiting area. "Jason," he commanded. "I've got scrubs for you."

Savannah smiled at Noah. He'd told Jason she was taken. Maybe there was hope for them. Maybe now that he knew she wasn't the perpetrator, they could develop a relationship. She waited for him to come talk to her, but he didn't. He gave her a quick smile and rushed from the waiting room to continue working.

Later that night, Ryan and her dad went to get Josh and feed him before coming back to spend the night. Savannah was glad she'd been left behind to sit with Allison one more time. The last time they'd tested her sister's blood, the drug was significantly lower. The horrible substance was leaving her system and everyone was hopeful she would wake soon.

Savannah talked to Ally like she would actually respond. "I really need some advice right now, sis. I'm confused. You haven't met Noah yet, but oh, Ally, you'd love him. He's strong and fun, well, most of the time he's fun."

She pictured his face as he teased her. "I don't really know how to describe him, but I guess intriguing would be the right word. Honestly, I think I might be falling in love with him, but he's making it so hard." She rolled her neck, massaging her upper shoulders with her fingertips. "You know how it is for me. Usually, I lose interest quick. I haven't committed to anyone since Daxon. Now I finally find someone I'm dying over and . . ." She sighed. "Noah just doesn't express himself. There's this guy named Wes that I'm training, and he says and does everything right but he's a bit too much. I just wish Noah could be a little more aggressive with me. Can you believe I just said that?"

Savannah stopped talking. Had Allison moved? She could've sworn she felt pressure from the fingers she was holding. She waited several minutes, but nothing else happened. It must've been wishful thinking.

"Anyway, Noah is like closed off. I can't get emotion out of that dude.

Most of the time he acts like he could take or leave me." She laughed. "Except when I wake him up from his nightmares. I just wish I could get Noah to open up like Wes. Wes leaves no doubt that he's interested."

Allison's fingers tightened around hers. Savannah jumped. "Ally?" This wasn't her imagination, Allison gripped her hand and her eyelids fluttered.

"Noah! Noah! Get in here," Savannah screamed, praying for more movement.

Allison's lips parted. The pressure on Savannah's fingers increased. Her sister was making a noise. Savannah leaned closer. "Ally. Ally. I'm here. Wake up, sweetie. Please wake up. We've been praying and waiting for days. Oh, Ally." Savannah didn't take time to brush the tears away as she wrapped her arms around her sister.

She was so close she heard the murmured words, "No, Wes."

"What?" Savannah cried out, jerking upright. She leaned in again. "No, Wes?"

Allison's lips moved, but her eyes stayed closed. "No, Wes."

Savannah shook her head in amazement. "Okay, no, Wes. What does that mean? Oh, who cares? You're awake! Ally, you're going to be okay!" Tears streamed down her cheeks as she hugged Ally tighter.

Ally's eyes flickered open and she stared at Savannah. "Promise me." She gasped as if formulating the words had taken too much effort for her recovering body. "Stay away from Wes."

"Okay, I promise, but how do you know who Wes is? Oh, Ally, you're awake! Noah, where are you?" she hollered. "Ilene? Somebody get in here!"

Allison squeezed her hand one more time. She shut her eyes, apparently exhausted. Noah rushed into the room. "What's going on?"

"She's awake! She's awake!" Savannah jumped into his embrace. "Noah. Ally woke up! It was the greatest thing. She talked to me."

Noah crushed her against him. Savannah gasped for air and prayed he'd never let go.

"That's great," he said. "What did she say?"

Savannah squirmed. She moved from his embrace. How could she explain to Noah what Allison had said or why she had been talking to Allison about Wes?

"She . . ." Savannah licked her lips. "She asked about Josh and Ryan."

Noah nodded. His eyes clouded, the disappointment thick in his gaze. Savannah wondered if he knew she was lying. She hated it when he looked at her like that.

"Okay," he said. His lips lifted. "I'm glad she woke up for a minute. That's great."

Savannah's head twisted back and forth. "No, she's still awake, look at her Noah." She dragged him to her sister's bedside.

But Allison wasn't awake. She'd drifted back into unconsciousness. Savannah wanted to shake her awake, but the doctor arrived and explained that rest was the best thing for Allison. Now that she'd woken once, it would happen again. And that was really something to be thankful for.

Ryan could hear Josh splashing and singing in the main floor bathroom. Frank watched him while Ryan scrubbed. He cleaned the counters, scrubbed the sink, even wiped down the microwave. Ally was going to wake up soon. He knew it. He had to have the house clean when she came home. He'd clean toilets if it meant having his wife lucid again.

He almost had the mess beneath Josh's high chair under control when the phone rang. He jumped, banging his head on the wood chair. He pressed against the future bruise and raced for the phone. "Hello."

"Ry," Savannah said. "She woke up. She woke up!"

"Ally!" Ryan was already sprinting toward the bathroom. "Frank! Josh! Mommy woke up!"

Josh jumped in the tub, landing in a splash of bubbles. Frank grabbed Josh, naked and soapy, and danced him around the small bathroom.

"I talked to her, Ry," Savannah said. "She was awake."

Ryan watched Josh and Frank's happy jig. He felt like dancing himself. Tears flooded his vision. "She woke up. Oh, Ally." He choked on her name. "Is she still awake?"

"No. I wanted to wake her back up, but the doctor said to let her come around on her own. He said she needs rest."

"Rest?" Ryan didn't want to let her rest. He wanted to see her eyes and talk to her and cry when she held Josh and kiss her until she made him stop. "We're on our way, Savvy."

"I figured you would be. I'll be in her room."

Ryan hung up the phone. Josh vaulted toward him. Ryan caught the slippery, bare bum. "Josh! Mommy's awake."

Josh grinned. "I say Mommy play today."

Ryan brought Josh's face close, kissing the soft cheek. "Yes, you did." He cried and danced Josh around the bathroom. "Good boy, Josh. Yes, you did!"

Ryan, Frank, and Josh returned to the hospital. Josh kept screaming, "Play, Mommy, play!"

Ilene kindly explained that the other patients needed quiet. Finally, Frank took Josh for a walk. An hour later, Josh was tired and cranky, and there was still no sign of Allison regaining consciousness anytime soon.

Ryan looked across the bed at Savannah. "Savvy, will you take Josh home and put him to bed? I'm going to stay the night here, and I think your dad wants to stay at least a few more hours if not the whole night as well."

Savannah nodded. She didn't want to leave either, but she'd been the lucky one to actually see and hear Allison awaken. Ryan and her dad both needed that chance. Savannah kissed Allison's cheek and hugged Ryan, then vacated the ICU.

Josh was in the waiting room, sleeping on her dad's shoulder when she arrived. He transferred Josh to her arms.

"Do you mind taking him home, sweetie? We could have someone come get him if you need to stay."

Savannah shook her head. "He's been shipped around so much. I'll take care of him."

He pressed the keys to Allison's Tahoe into her hand and kissed her forehead. "I'm so glad you got to talk to her. She's really going to be okay now."

Savannah nodded. "It's great, Dad. The Lord has answered our prayers."

Frank smiled grimly. "This time he has."

"I'm sure Mom is watching over her," Savannah said.

Frank closed his eyes for a few seconds. "I guess you're right. Of course you're right." He propelled her toward the elevators. "Go get some rest."

Savannah searched for Noah as she exited the waiting area and made her way to the elevators. She wanted to talk to him. Maybe he would go to Allison's house with her. No, that was silly. He was busy here. He no longer needed to stay by her side. She shuffled through the rotating exterior door of the hospital.

Twenty feet down the sidewalk she heard heavy footfalls behind her. She clutched Josh closer, quickening her pace to a speed walk. The footsteps got louder. She glanced over her shoulder as she entered the parking lot. A tall man trailed twenty feet behind her. A hooded jacket covered his face and hair, even though it was a warm summer night.

Her heart pounded in her ears. She started to run. The man increased his pace. She passed under a streetlight, exposed to her assailant. Savannah bent over Josh, shielding him from the man. Three cars away from Allison's Tahoe, she heard him calling to her.

"Wait! Hold up!"

Savannah ran harder, jostling her little bundle.

Joshua cried out.

"Hush, baby," she said between gasps for oxygen.

The car was within feet. She pressed the automatic lock button and reached for the door. She was going to make it.

Someone gripped her arm.

"Aaah!" She pulled away. "I've got mace and I'm not afraid to use it."

"Anna!"

Savannah whirled to face him. For some reason she should've felt better knowing it was Wes. She didn't.

He chuckled. Reaching up, he pushed tendrils of hair from her face. "Sorry, Anna. I didn't mean to scare you."

"You didn't. I'm just hurrying to get Josh home and into bed." Her voice trembled.

"I saw you leaving the hospital. I couldn't pass up a chance to see you."

Savannah tried to smile. "Checking on Grandma?" She needed to open the door and put Josh in his car seat, but he felt like a protective barrier between her and Wes. She slowly rocked him back and forth. He settled into her shoulder.

"Yes, she's doing much better." Wes reached out and touched her cheek. "You look tired. Is your sister okay?"

Nodding, she disengaged his hand. "Yeah. She woke up for a few seconds tonight. Hopefully in the morning she'll come around again." She shifted Josh to her hip to relieve the strain on her biceps.

Wes's face tightened. "Oh." He cleared his throat. "That's good. Did she say anything about who hurt her?"

Savannah thought about what Allison had said. She backed up a step. "No. She didn't."

Wes moved closer. He grabbed her arm. "Savannah. I hate to be too forward, but I think you know I'm attracted to you." The smile he mustered up stretched tight across his face. "The little bit of time we've spent together has been great. You're beautiful and fun and smart."

She hid a groan of frustration. She didn't want to hear these words from Wes. Why couldn't Noah say crap like this to her? She rocked back and forth. Josh's weight was increasing.

"I'm glad your sister is doing better, but I think you need a break." He winked at her. "Why don't we take your nephew to somebody tonight, and I'll fly you away from here."

She started shaking her head. What kind of a wench would consider leaving her sister's side and going somewhere with him now, especially after what Allison had said to her. "Sorry, Wes, but—"

"Anna," he interrupted, "You need to get away. You're worn out. The strain of all this has been too much for you. Come away with me just for tonight. I know an amazing spa in Jackson Hole. We'll fly there and let them pamper you—a massage, pedicure, facial, whatever you need."

Savannah was still shaking her head. "They have a spa open in the middle of the night?" The words *No, Wes* kept ringing in her head.

He nodded confidently. "They'll do whatever I ask them to."

Her stomach curled. Noah was right. Wealth wasn't appealing. Her priorities were elsewhere. Talking with Noah alone, seeing Ally open her eyes again, and sleeping were at the top of her list.

Wes rubbed her arm. "I don't want to pressure you, Anna."

She was beginning to hate that nickname.

"But I'm worried about you. I promise you can have your own room." He raised an eyebrow at her. "Unless you *want* to share."

She wanted to hurl.

"You can sleep in tomorrow, and then after breakfast in bed I'll fly you back to Logan. You won't miss anything, but you'll feel a million times better. Come on."

She mustered up a smile for him. "Wes, what I really need is a good night's sleep."

"You'll rest better after the spa treatments and sleeping on the highest quality mattress you've ever felt."

Her arms ached from Josh's weight. She shifted him to her left arm and opened the rear door with her right. "I really appreciate the offer, but I can't right now."

"I'm not letting you say no."

"You'll let her do whatever she wants to do," a deep voice said from behind her.

Savannah whirled with Josh still in her arms. "Noah," she breathed.

He glared at her then moved his eyes to Wes. "What are you doing here, Richins?"

"I'm talking to Savannah, Detective," Wes sneered.

Noah nodded. "That better be all you're doing." He moved to Savannah's side, took Josh from her, and settled him into his car seat. "Get in the car, Savannah."

Savannah bristled, but nodded. Noah took the keys from her fingers, opened her door, and stalked around to the driver's side. She looked up at Wes and took a step toward the door. Wes pushed the door shut. His arm wrapped around her back, pulling her in. His head descended toward hers. Savannah ducked her chin just in time. His lips brushed her nose.

Wes's lips tightened. He forced a smile, releasing his grip. "My offer stands. Whenever you're ready, I'll be there for you."

She couldn't return the smile. "Thanks, Wes, but what I need right now is my family." She turned toward the door. "Also, I hope it's okay if we don't train tomorrow. I don't want to miss a minute of being with Allison."

His lips pressed together. "I understand," he said through a slit in his mouth.

Savannah jerked the door open and slid in. One glance at Noah's angry face forced her gaze to the window. Wes stared at them, hands in the pockets of his jacket, his shoulders hunched. He didn't move, just watched them drive away.

The air felt icy on the drive home. Savannah tried a few times to start a conversation, but Noah's terse one-syllable answers sealed her tongue. He pulled into the garage and jammed the vehicle into park. Savannah opened her door and swung toward the back seat. Noah rushed around and held up a hand.

"Let me get him. He's almost as big as you are."

Savannah trailed Noah into the house and up the stairs. His stiff form in front of her made her want to scream and cry. She'd give anything to spin him around and kiss those firm lips. *Yeah. That would work.* He couldn't stand her.

Noah set Joshua in his crib and covered him with a blanket. Josh's eyes flitted open and settled on Noah's face. "Night-night, Noah."

Noah leaned down and brushed his lips across Josh's forehead. "Goodnight, little buddy."

Josh held out his hand—palm forward, thumb, first finger, and pinkie extended. Noah looked at Savannah with a question in his eyes.

She gulped. "It means I love you."

Noah jerked. He turned back to Josh. "I love you too, Josh."

Josh smiled, rolled over onto his stomach and stuck his bum in the air. Within seconds he was asleep. Noah tucked the blanket around his diminutive form.

Her heart ached at the scene. She knew Noah could be tender, just not with her.

Noah turned to look at her, and his face turned grim again. He brushed past her and took the stairs two at a time until he reached the basement. Savannah raced after him. She caught him ripping his shirt over his head in the girly bedroom. He didn't fit here. The muscles in his back rippled like wind-blown sand dunes. She should've been content to just watch.

"You don't need to be here anymore," she said to his backside.

His head whipped around. "What are you talking about?"

"You finally admitted I'm not the one who hurt Ally. You don't need to watch me anymore."

Noah jammed a hand through his hair. Moving across the room in three long strides, he stood out of touching distance. "You need me more than ever. Allison's attacker is still out there. He could come after you."

"What's the likelihood of that?"

"Better than I like to think about."

She moved closer, shivering. She reached up and touched his bulging pectoral muscle. "How are you going to protect me, Noah? Sleep at the foot of my bed?"

He leaned closer to her, catching her hand with his own. "You don't have to keep playing these games with me, Savannah."

She wrenched her hand from his. "What games?"

Noah glared down at her. "The games you're such an expert at. Confusing me. Trying to make me jealous of Richins."

Savannah planted her hands on her hips, stretching to her full 5'5" height. He still had her by a foot. "Maybe if you'd talk to me and tell me what you're thinking, I wouldn't have to play games to try and draw you out."

His brow furrowed. His huge form overshadowed her. "What do you want me to think? What do you want me to say?" He shook his head. "Do you want me to tell you I can't get enough of you? That you're all I think about? That I'd give my house away if it meant I could touch you? Is that what you need from me?"

Savannah's mouth flopped open. "No. I mean. I don't . . . That is, you don't . . ."

Noah grabbed her around the waist with both hands. Lifting her off her feet, he pressed her against him and covered her mouth with his own. Just as quickly as it began, it was over. He set her on the carpeted floor and glared at her. "Maybe that was as good as what Richins did to you in the parking lot."

He stormed past her to the bathroom, slamming the door behind him.

Savannah didn't move for several minutes. She put a hand to her lips. "You have no idea how good it was."

Fourteen

Savannah wasn't sure when she fell asleep, but exhaustion finally overtook her. In her dreams Noah was crying out to his mom again. Then he was calling for her. "Savvy! Savvy! I won't let him hurt you."

She woke, flung the covers off, and raced toward Noah's room. The moon was shrouded by clouds, the night so dark she could barely see his form entangled in the sheets.

"Savvy!" he called.

She grabbed his thick shoulder. "Noah. It's me. You're okay. Wake up."

He thrashed around, mumbling her nickname.

Savannah turned on a lamp. Soft light filled the room. She hoped the sudden change would wake him, but it didn't. He repeated her name and squirmed on the flowered sheets.

Savannah knelt next to him on the bed. She leaned on his chest and grasped his face with her hands. "Noah. Please wake up. It's Savvy. I'm here."

Noah jerked upright in bed, taking her up with him. He wrapped his arms around her. "Savvy, is it really you? He didn't get you?"

Savannah leaned her lips against his cheek. The bristly hair tickled her mouth. "You're dreaming again, Noah. I'm okay. Nobody got me."

He pulled her so close she could hardly breathe. He smelled clean. Slowly, his hold relaxed. She arched her head to look into his eyes.

"You're okay now," she said breathlessly, her lips brushed his cheek. "It was just a dream."

He nodded. His eyes focused on her mouth. She raised her lips to his. He covered the centimeters separating them, responding to her kiss with a passion that almost scared her.

Several minutes later his hands moved from her back to her face. He gently pulled her away, searching her eyes. "You're really all right."

She smiled. "I am now."

He kissed her again. He tasted like warmth and happiness. Their lips became one until she had trouble catching a full breath. She didn't care.

Noah broke the contact of their lips. He slowly kissed her chin, her cheek, her forehead. He rested his mouth against her hair.

"Oh, Savannah. I was so scared."

Now that he was fully awake, he didn't use her nickname. She wanted to correct him, to tell him he could call her Savvy. "What happened in your dream?"

He trailed his hands down her arms, wrapping them around her waist. "At first it was like all the others. Mom was bleeding and dying, then suddenly it wasn't my mom." He pulled her closer. "It was you."

Savannah shuddered, clinging to him.

Noah stroked her back. "I couldn't live with myself if something happened to you."

Gazing into his eyes, she hoped he'd open up. "Why, Noah? Why couldn't you live with yourself?"

His body stiffened under her hands. "You're my, my, responsibility."

"Because you're assigned to me?" She bit her lip, needing him to correct her. She waited, praying he'd say the words.

Noah exhaled, releasing his grip on her. "It's not like that, Savannah."

She disentangled herself from his arms, sliding off the bed. "I wish for once you could explain to me what it is like."

He looked up at her, but didn't move in her direction. "I, um . . ."

Savannah waited, but he couldn't spit it out. "Good crimony, Noah. You get mad about me being around Wes, but at least he can tell me what he thinks of me. All you can do is grab me when you're half asleep and then you close up whenever I try to talk to you."

His lips thinned, but all he did was stare at her.

Whirling from his gaze, she stomped down the hallway. The light from his bedroom dimmed and darkness engulfed her. She bumped her shoulder into a corner, yelping in pain, but the ache in her heart was worse.

Tears raced down her cheeks, she was almost to her room when Noah grabbed her around the waist. She screamed. He spun her around to face him.

"Savannah, I'm sorry."

She tried to focus, but couldn't clear her vision of the wetness clouding it. She leaned against the wall for support. Strong arms encircled her, lifting her off the ground. The arms cradled her like a small child. She leaned her head against his soft T-shirt.

"Oh, Noah," she whispered. "Why? Why can't you care about me enough to tell me?"

Noah tilted her chin up, forcing her to look in his direction, though she couldn't see much in the inky night.

"Savannah. Of course I care. Dang it, that's the whole problem. If I didn't care do you think I'd be here?"

"I'm your responsibility," she flung at him.

Noah didn't answer. He carried her to the living room and settled her onto the couch, leaning across her to turn on a lamp. Savannah squinted against the light. Noah's face was inches away. All she wanted to do was kiss him again. She bit her lip, containing a sigh. *Like kissing him would solve anything.*

"Savannah," he said. He took a deep breath, then plunged in. "I've never been assigned to a case or a person twenty-four hours a day. This isn't a normal investigation for me. I'm doing this on my own time. I don't know if you'll believe me, but I've wanted to be close to you from the first time I saw you."

She looked into the blue depths of his glance. "The first time you saw me, all you could look at was my tank top."

He grinned at her. The corners of his eyes crinkled. He touched the tip of her nose with his finger. "It's not such a bad duty being close to you," he said.

"You're not getting paid?" she asked.

Noah exhaled. "There are some things more important than money."

"Really?"

He shook his head at her. His eyes narrowed. "Really, Savannah."

She waved a hand in dismissal. "No. I don't mean about the money. I mean, you're really doing this because you want to be with me?"

Lifting her legs onto his lap, he brushed his lips across hers. "I have a hard time admitting it, obviously, but yes, I want to be with you." He sighed, reclining into the cushions. "I just wish I could read you. I wish I knew you were being truthful with me."

"What?" she cried out. "You know I didn't hurt Ally. What do you think I'm lying about now?"

He cringed. "I didn't say you were lying, but this whole thing with Richins and all the different men calling you all the time. I know you're into money, and I do okay, but I'm not what you would call rich."

Savannah blew all her air out. "You think all I care about is how much money a guy makes?"

Noah didn't answer.

She met his gaze with a level stare. "Money's nice, but it doesn't matter that much to me."

Tilting his head to the side, he studied her face. "Are you sure? I thought that might have been the reason you liked Richins."

"I couldn't care less about Wesley or his money." She took a deep breath, exhaling slowly. "One of the things I learned through my mom's sickness was money isn't important. My dad traded everything he had to try and save my mom. There are many things more important than money."

Noah nodded. "I'm glad to hear that."

They were silent for a minute. Then Noah said softly. "This might be the wrong time to bring this up, but why *did* you flirt with Richins?"

Savannah shifted away from him, embarrassed. "I shouldn't have. It's not that I was interested in him." She paused then tossed the words out. "I did it to make you mad." She held her breath, wondering how upset he'd be now.

Noah lit up. "Really? You were trying to make me jealous?"

Savannah laughed. "I'm glad that's good news for you. I thought you'd tell me to grow up again."

"Well . . ."

She punched him.

He caught her hand and pulled it to his lips. "Consider the jealousy issue over," he said against the skin of her palm. "I don't like wanting to hurt another man. Maybe we can find some sort of do-not-call list for all the men who have your number."

Warmth seeped into her like walking from an air-conditioned building into a ninety-degree day. "You really like me, don't you?"

His lips turned up. "More than I can express. What did you say, I'm emotionally closed off?"

A laugh escaped. She bobbed her head up and down. "Messed up, more like. I think we'll need many counseling sessions to work through your issues."

"I've been to counselors with the department to try and help me with my nightmares." He frowned. "I hated meeting with them. It didn't help."

Savannah placed her hand on his stubbly cheek. "I wasn't talking about another counselor. I was talking about me. We'll have to spend a lot of time together ,and maybe I can help you overcome your emotional problems. And maybe you can convince me that you care."

"You're pretty needy." He smiled and leaned closer. "I don't know if I'll be able to convince you."

She licked her lips. "I know one way you could try."

He beamed at her. Savannah couldn't hide her smile as his head dipped toward hers. His warm breath and lips overtook her, and soon the world was filled with only Noah.

Frank was sleeping in the hospital room Ryan had used several nights ago. Ryan should've been sleeping in the roll-away bed. Instead he was studying Allison's face in the partial darkness. He knew Savannah had talked with her, but it was still hard to believe she'd been conscious.

He prayed for a movement, a flicker of response. He missed her. He looked around to see if any of the nurses were watching. The coast was clear. He slipped his shoes off. Gently, he moved the sheets and tubes aside and climbed into the hospital bed. Lifting Allison's head, he tucked his arm underneath it.

She didn't smell like Allison. She smelled like some kind of soap his wife would never use. He ignored the smell, buried his face into her neck, and wrapped his other arm around her stomach. His tears wet her pillow as he prayed for some kind of response.

A movement at the door startled him. He looked up.

Ilene shook her head. "Ryan. What are you . . . ?"

He begged her with his eyes.

Ilene smiled and shut the door.

Noah was flipping pancakes when Savannah entered the kitchen with Josh the next morning. Savannah admired everything from his wide shoulders stretching a white T-shirt to his firm lower body encased in Levi's.

"Noah," Josh yelled. "Cakes-cakes, my best food!"

Noah ruffled Josh's hair and kissed Savannah for several wonderful seconds. Josh's giggle interrupted them. Savannah blushed and carried her nephew to his high chair. The second she buckled the baby in, Noah grabbed her from behind. He whirled her to face him and kissed her again.

"Did I pass the test last night?" he whispered against her lips.

Savannah leaned back, gazing into his azure eyes. "What test was that?"

"You no longer think I'm emotionally closed off?"

Savannah laughed. "You did well. Opened up like the prize in a cracker jack's box." She blushed as she thought of how much she'd revealed last night, telling Noah about Daxon's abuse, the reason no one but her future husband would ever call her Savvy.

"Cakes-cakes!" Josh screamed.

Noah pulled away, arching an eyebrow. "I better not ruin the little guy's favorite food."

While he flipped the pancakes, Noah hummed an Alan Jackson song. Savannah peeled a banana for Josh to placate him for a few moments.

"Why couldn't you open up like that before?" she asked.

He looked at her over his shoulder. "I didn't trust you before."

"Ouch." She turned her eyes to the tile floor. "That doesn't make a girl feel too good."

Noah turned. "But that was before . . ." One look at her face, and he hurried to her side. He wrapped his strong arms around her back. "Forgive me?"

"I don't know." She clucked her tongue. "I seem to remember you telling me you don't grovel."

Noah grinned. "Oh, I can grovel." He paused, his lips pulling down. "I think. Can you explain to me exactly what I'm supposed to do?"

Savannah leaned into him, lifting her face. "You figure it out."

Noah kissed her softly. His hands worked a magic of their own as the kiss deepened. "Forgive me?" he whispered against her mouth.

Savannah laughed. "Boy, you keep doing that, and I'll forgive and forget everything you've ever done wrong."

Noah arched an eyebrow and leaned down again.

"My cakes-cakes!" Josh cried out.

Jerking away, Noah winked at her and hurried to rescue the pancakes. He flipped them onto a plate while she found the syrup and poured juice. Noah stacked four on her plate.

Savannah shook her head. "You've got to be kidding. I'd blow up if I ate that much."

Noah directed her toward a barstool and drizzled syrup over the pancakes. "Eat."

She cut a small bite and chewed slowly.

Noah sat next to her after stacking Josh's high chair with pancakes. "What is it with you and food?" he asked.

The pancake lodged in her throat. She sipped some juice to clear it. "I have to be careful what I eat."

He looked her up and down. "Bull. You're perfect. You're actually too skinny."

She didn't answer. Noah touched her cheek, gently turning her face until she looked at him. "I thought you said I was the one with the emotional problems. Why don't you eat anything?"

She licked her lips. Staring into his eyes, she opened her mouth. "I was chubby." Her face reddened and she looked away. "Actually, I was more than chubby—I was a fat kid."

Noah didn't say anything until she glanced at him again.

"Savannah, a lot of people are chubby as kids. You grew out of it. You're light years from chubby now."

She exhaled and tried to explain. "My mom monitored everything I ate. Before she died, I was at a normal weight for my age, but I still craved food and snuck it whenever I could." She bit her lip. "When Mom died I turned to food. It made me feel so guilty, but it was almost like I could finally rebel. I got really big."

Noah didn't say anything, but his eyes filled with compassion and understanding.

Savannah continued, "One day a boy I wanted to date said, 'You'd be pretty if you weren't so big.' It broke my heart. I came home crying and Ally held me. Ally was the one who taught me how to exercise and eat right. You know that girl I pushed down the stairs?"

"Jenalee?"

Savannah picked up her fork and twisted it in her fingers. "After I'd lost my weight, I caught her teasing one of my friends who was a bigger girl. I started defending my friend, and Jenalee just wouldn't shut up. She pushed me, and I pushed her back. I didn't realize she was so close to the stairs until she fell." Savannah tapped the fork against her plate. "I'm pretty sensitive about people being overweight. It's a miserable place to be. I can't let myself be there again."

Noah's eyes were wide. He didn't say anything, and Savannah's face burned. She shouldn't have told him all that. She looked down at her plate of pancakes then pushed it away.

He slid it back in front of her. "You've helped me with my problems. Now I'm going to help you with yours." He stabbed a piece of pancake with his fork. "Open up."

She shook her head. "Don't, Noah. Forcing me to eat is not going to cure me."

"It's a start." He smiled and placed the pancakes by her mouth.

Savannah ate the piece of pancake. Noah set the fork down and wrapped his arms around her. "Listen to me, Savannah. You are the most beautiful woman I've ever seen."

She laughed.

"I'm not kidding," he said. "But you'll notice I didn't say pretty. Pretty is only on the outside. You're beautiful all the way through."

She blinked. *Noah getting poetic. Wow.*

"Food isn't your enemy, and if you eat you aren't going to blow up. Even if you did, the people who care for you are still going to love you and think you're beautiful."

She had to swallow before she could whisper, "Thanks."

He released her. "Let's work on getting you healthy. Okay?"

Savannah nodded. She was safe with Noah, in every way possible.

She couldn't remember eating the almost-burnt pancakes, but she downed three looking into Noah's sapphire gaze. It was the first time in her adult life she hadn't meticulously dissected and thought about every bite of food that passed through her lips.

They cleaned up breakfast side by side as Josh happily slopped pancakes and syrup around his high chair tray. Savannah sniffed something rotten. She opened the cupboard under the sink. Brown banana peels, molding orange slices, and wet diapers peeked out of the overflowing garbage.

"Whew." She lifted the liner and tied the drawstrings. "I thought

Ryan said he cleaned last night. He must not have made it this far."

"I'll take that out." Noah took the garbage from her hands.

Savannah stole it back. "No way." She pointed at Josh, squishing pancake goop into his hair. "You clean *him* up. I'll gladly take out the garbage."

He reached for the garbage bag. Savannah swung away from him and darted out of arm's length. "Too slow."

She sprinted past him. He caught her by the waist before she escaped. Pulling her in close, Noah kissed her. Savannah laughed against his warm lips that tasted of maple syrup, half-heartedly struggling to free herself. "You are not getting this garbage sack, mister."

Noah chuckled. "Never knew I'd be having so much fun fighting over taking the garbage out." He slowly released her. Looking over at the gooey toddler, he sighed loudly. "Okay, you win. I'll find some way to spit shine the little monster. Clean washcloths?"

Savannah hurried away before he changed his mind. "Second drawer down."

The garbage was outside the west-facing garage door. She skipped to it. The house shadowed the sidewalk from the morning sun. Smiling, she couldn't stop thinking of Noah's hands on her and dreaming of spending more time with him. She'd told him about being chubby, and he still said she was beautiful. What a perfect morning. Allison was recovering, and Noah was wonderful.

She dropped the trash lid and came face to face with a pair of dark eyes. The smile slid from her lips. "Wes?" she managed to whisper.

"Aren't we happy this morning?" he sneered. "I noticed Detective Shumway stayed all night."

Savannah slowly backed away. "He's been staying here to watch over us. I told you that."

Wes rolled his eyes, folding his arms across his starched dress shirt. "Something tells me he's doing more than his duty."

"No." She shook her head. "Nothing happened. Noah's not like that." She turned from his black glare, moving up the stairs to the door.

Wes guffawed, following her. "Yeah, right."

Savannah grabbed the door handle. "I need to get back inside to my nephew."

"No, you don't." Wes caught her arm and pulled her off the step to face him. "Not until we get something straight."

Savannah raised questioning eyes to him. Her throat was tight. "What?" she squeaked.

He stared down his nose at her. "You're going away with me, and I really am not taking no for an answer this time."

Her heart pounded. Her stomach was practicing the squat thrust without her legs. "I can't right now, Wes. I told you that last night, maybe some other time."

He smiled, but his eyes were cold. "I told you no wasn't an option, not if you want your sister to recover."

"What?" Savannah's eyes opened wider. She heard Ally's whispered words. *No, Wes.* Understanding flowed over her. "You're the one who hurt Ally?"

His face twisted in a scowl. "I never meant to hurt her. It was an accident. But now I see it all worked out right because now I get to be with you."

Savannah backed away. He tightened his grip on her arm, yanking her off her feet and into his chest. Savannah struggled. He wrapped both arms around her and whispered into her ear, "We're going to fly out of here in an hour. I've got someone ready to deliver a note to your family at the hospital. All you have to do is go inside with me and convince Detective Shumway that you chose me over him."

Savannah shook her head, wrenching from his grip. "He'll never believe that."

"Why not?"

"Because he knows how much I want him."

Wes's teeth clenched. His hand grabbed hers again. He pressed her fingers until she winced. "What did you say?"

"I want him," she repeated with a glare.

Wes shook his head. "No, you don't."

Savannah nodded vigorously. "Yes, I do."

"No, you don't," his voice raised several decibels, "and you better be able to convince him that you chose me. He won't be too surprised. It's happened before." Wes consulted his watch. "You have ten minutes."

Savannah tried to pull free of his hand. "Ten minutes for what?"

"Ten minutes to make Detective Shumway believe I'm the one you want."

She gulped. "What if I can't convince him?"

"If my employee doesn't get a call from me by 8:30, she will be

178

injecting something lethal into Allison's system."

Her mouth gaped open. "You wouldn't. You couldn't."

"I could and I will." He shrugged. "My employee is ready and will-ing. I'm paying her plenty. Once she's given Allison the shot or delivered your note, another fifty thousand dollars will be delivered into her brand new offshore account." Wes tilted his head, smiling like a shark about to devour a minnow. "So, what'll it be? How are we going to ruin Noah's day?"

Ryan woke early in the noisy hospital. He'd only slept a few half-hour stretches. He gingerly climbed from Allison's bed and stretched. He hoped he hadn't hurt her by sleeping with her. She looked good, though. He caressed her cheek. At his touch, her eyelids fluttered. Ryan jumped.

"Ally? Ally, girl?" He leaned closer. "It's me, honey. Wake up. Please, wake up."

As if on command, she slowly opened her eyes and gazed at him.

Ryan couldn't stop the tears racing their way to his chin. "Hey, baby."

Her lips lifted at the corners. She blinked a couple of times. "Hey," she whispered.

Gently touching the corner of her lips, he trailed his fingers along her jaw. "You don't know how I've prayed for this moment."

She cleared her throat to speak. "What happened? Where am I?"

He kissed her cheek. "You fell down the stairs. You've been in a coma for four days."

"Four days?" she croaked.

"Do you remember anything? We think somebody hurt you. Savan-nah found you."

Her eyes shuttered. She didn't answer his question. "I need a drink of water."

Ryan leaned back. "Ilene?" he called. "She's awake. She wants water."

The nurse rushed in. "She's awake. Oh, praise the Lord. She's really awake." She did a little dance and scampered back out of the room as quickly as she'd come.

Ryan stared into his wife's eyes. His vision clouded with tears. He flung them away so he could keep drinking in the sight of her.

Ilene reentered with a paper cup filled with ice chips. Elevating Allison's bed, she gently spooned some ice into her mouth.

"Thanks," Allison whispered.

Ilene beamed. "You can't have fluids just yet, but you hold these ice chips down, and in an hour I'll get you anything you want to drink."

Ilene left the room, and Ryan helped Allison with another spoonful of the ice chips.

She reclined into the pillow, sucking on the ice. Reaching up, she self-consciously patted her hair. "I'm a mess."

Ryan smiled. "You've never looked more beautiful."

He leaned in to kiss her. She lifted a hand, weakly pushing against his chest. "Don't get too close. My breath tastes horrible."

Ryan grinned. "Honey, I've never cared about anything less than I care about the way your breath tastes." With that, he kissed her until he was certain his wife was really back.

Shouts of glee from his father-in-law interrupted them. Ryan leaned back and let Frank hug his daughter and share in his tears of happiness.

Noah swiped the rag across Josh's face one extra time. "Clean enough. Don't you think so, big guy?"

"All clean!" Josh pronounced. "Let's play."

Noah smiled. "All right." He looked toward the back door. How long did Savannah need to take out the garbage?

His phone rang—Jason. "Yeah?" he answered.

"I've been dying for the details."

Noah lifted Josh out of his high chair and set him on the floor. "How's everything going?"

"Fine. Haven't seen anything from the perpetrator. I think Allison is stirring again, but it's hard to tell with the husband and dad hovering over her like they are. I'm hoping she's all right for their sakes."

"Yeah, me too."

"That's not why I called. I'm stuck in a smelly hospital thanks to you, and there's nothing to entertain me. I've been waiting for you to call."

"Chase me, Noah," Josh called, running away.

Noah jogged after the little boy. "I'm gonna get you, Josh."

Josh watched Noah over his shoulder as he pumped his legs forward. The little boy giggled as he ran.

"Has it happened?" Jason asked.

"What?" Noah asked innocently.

"That is one perfect woman. Now I promise I'll admire her from afar if you can only answer my question correctly."

"What question is that?"

Jason groaned. "Please tell me you've kissed her."

Noah followed Josh. His face broke into a smile. "Which time?"

Jason didn't say anything for a second then he hooted. "Which time? Oh, you've made my day. Okay. I'm back on the job. See you soon." He chuckled again. "Which time. That is great."

The phone disconnected. Noah shoved it into his pocket. He got on his hands and knees and chased the giggling toddler around the spacious great room. His knees hurt from the hardwood flooring, but he didn't care.

A few minutes later, he grabbed Josh from the floor, stood, and threw him into the air. Josh laughed and laughed. He heard the door from the garage slam and footsteps coming through the laundry room.

He tossed the toddler again. Josh giggled louder. Noah turned to see Savannah's reaction. His heartbeat paused. His eyes widened. What was he doing here? "Richins?"

Wes nodded with a tight smile. "How's it going, Shumway?" Wes's fingers gripped Savannah's hand possessively.

Noah wanted to rip the imbecile's hand from hers. He looked from Wes to Savannah. Her olive skin had gone pale. "Savannah?"

She smiled, pulling her hand from Wes's grasp. "I need to ask a huge favor, Noah. Can you take Josh to the hospital?"

Josh pulled on Noah's sleeve. "Throw 'gain?"

"In a minute, buddy," Noah murmured. He set Josh on the ground, and the little boy scampered off.

Noah stared at Savannah, trying to make sense of what she was saying. He glanced at Wes. "Did you invite him here?"

She nodded quickly. "Yes. I called him before breakfast. Wes and I have to run an errand, and then he'll drop me off at the hospital." She looked everywhere but in his eyes.

Noah shook his head. The confusion was leaving, and anger rushed in. Why had she called Wes? How could she betray him like this? "What kind of errand?"

"Wes needs his workout schedule printed out since I'm going to take a few days off to be with my family. It's on my computer at work. We'll run by the gym and see you in a few minutes."

Wes took Savannah's elbow and they both fled for the front door.

Noah stood stunned for a second before he rushed after them. He caught them on the front porch steps. "What's going on, Savannah?"

She looked back at him with a pleading gaze, the bright sun outlining her. "Noah, please. This will just take a few minutes. It's not a big deal. Please take Josh to the hospital."

Noah didn't know how to respond. He wanted to snatch her from Richins' clutches. *Was he overreacting?*

Wes grabbed her hand, dragging her toward his Hummer.

Savannah looked back over her shoulder. "Oh, and ask Ally about what she said to me when I talked to her last night."

"When you talked to her last night?"

"Yeah. She'll know what I'm talking about."

Wes shot her a strange glance, opened the passenger door, and ushered her into the vehicle. He shut the door, nodding at Noah with a smirk. He ran around to the driver's side and slammed his door. The motor sprang to life, and the Hummer jumped forward, racing away.

Noah stood frozen. He wanted to run after her, to beg her not to go. Why would she choose to go somewhere with Wes? Was the training schedule just an excuse? Was she trying to make Noah jealous again? Nothing was making any sense.

He ran back into the house, picked up Josh, and headed for the garage. Five minutes later he entered the hospital parking lot. He took the stairs two at a time and sprinted down the hall to Allison's room. Josh giggled as they ran, thinking it was all a big game.

Frank and Ryan were leaning over Allison's bed, talking, laughing, and crying with her. When Allison spotted her son, her face lit up.

Noah's stomach clenched. She looked so much like Savannah.

Josh screamed in delight, "Mommy! Mommy woke up!"

"C'mere baby. Come to Mommy!"

Noah hurried to the bed and placed the child in his mother's arms. Despite the worry and confusion over Savannah's actions, he enjoyed the tender scene. He even felt his eyes water for a second.

Allison cried, kissed Josh, and then cried some more.

Josh patted her cheeks and hugged her. He couldn't stop squealing, "My mommy! My mommy!"

Fifteen

Wes drove toward the airport. They met the nurse from the hospital in Wes's hangar.

"Rosie!" Savannah exclaimed. "How could you? You've been in on this the whole time."

Rosie squirmed. She wouldn't look at Savannah, but she glared at Wes with narrowed eyes. "Have you got the letter? I need to hurry. I'm supposed to report in to Officer Keller in half an hour. I want to be out of the valley before then."

Wes handed her the letter he'd forced Savannah to write. It had taken her five tries to write one that wasn't smudged by her tears.

"Thanks, Rosie. I'll deposit the balance into your account as soon as you call me with the delivery confirmation."

Rosie nodded, not smiling. "It's been a pleasure knowing you, sir."

Savannah didn't think anything about Wes was a pleasure. From the sarcasm in Rosie's tone, she imagined the nurse wasn't too thrilled either. Rosie left.

Wes turned to her. His smile made him look like a brown lizard. "It's just you and me now."

Savannah shivered, despite the warm day. She lifted her chin and swiped tears away with the back of her hand. "Don't remind me."

He ignored the snide comment, reaching up to stroke her cheek. Savannah swung her head away.

"It's okay. You don't need to be sad anymore, Anna. Allison's going to be fine, and you're going to love Costa Rica."

"Stop calling me Anna!" She swung at him.

Wes grabbed her hand. "If you can't cooperate, I'll have Rosie inject her instead of deliver the letter. How does that sound?"

Savannah gritted her teeth. She dropped her eyes to the cement floor and muttered, "Sorry."

"That's better." Dragging her by the wrist, Wes jerked her up the steps to his airplane. He settled her into a seat. Lifting her T-shirt a few inches, he took his time doing up her buckle. Savannah cringed each time his hands touched the exposed skin of her abdomen.

Savannah sat rigidly in her seat. She tried to appear hollow and uncaring, but inwardly she fumed, schemed, and begged the Lord to give her some way to escape. She knew once they were airborne, she'd never be free again.

⁂

Noah chafed with impatience as he stood to the side of the happy family reunion. He felt like a spectator at a baseball game who would never get the chance to participate. He didn't want to interrupt, but he couldn't leave until he asked Allison about the conversation that Savannah had been talking about. Maybe it would give him some clue as to why she would call Wes and choose to go somewhere with him. That thought hit him like a jab to the kidneys. He ached with the pain. *She'd gone with Wes. She'd chosen Wes over him. What about last night? Had it all been a lie?*

He shook his head. No. It couldn't be. Last night had been . . .

"Where's Savvy?"

His head snapped up. Frank had asked the question. They all looked to Noah for the answer.

"Um," he couldn't find his tongue. "She's coming."

"Where is she?" Frank asked. "Who's she with?"

"Wesley Richins," Noah could barely spit out the truth.

Frank and Ryan appeared confused.

Allison looked ill. "No," she murmured.

Ilene breezed into the room. "I'm sorry to interrupt, I have a note for the detective."

Noah stared at their beloved nurse. "A note? From who?"

She shrugged. "The greeter from downstairs brought it up. Sometimes people leave cards and flowers on her desk. Odd that it's to you and not the patient."

Noah walked out of the room. He searched for Jason. "Find out who delivered this note."

Jason nodded. "I'm on it."

Noah ripped open the envelope. Somehow he knew it was from Savannah before he even read the first line.

Noah,

    I've gone on a short trip with Wesley. He thought I needed to get away from all the stress for a little while. I think he's right. He's very considerate of my needs. Will you let my family know I'll be back in a few days? Tell Ally I love her and I'm glad she's awake.

    I hope you don't feel bad about me choosing Wes over you, but I'm sure you can understand why I couldn't refuse someone like him.

Take care of yourself,
    Savannah

Noah's jaw clenched. He crumpled the note in his hand. It couldn't be true. She wouldn't really choose Wes over him. A shudder ran through him. It had happened before, numerous times. Now it was happening again. Richins was the charmer. He was better looking than Noah, and he had more money than Donald Trump. Not really, but it felt that way.

Frank exited the room. He wrapped an arm around Noah's heaving shoulders. "Noah? What is it?"

Noah almost crumbled. The kind gesture from Frank was too much. Savannah's dad. *Oh, Savvy.* How could she do this to him, to her family? He couldn't speak. The only thing he could do was slowly release his hand, allowing Frank to take the note from his cramped fingers.

Frank read the note, then shook his head and reread it. He steered Noah into the room. Noah wanted to be anywhere but with Savannah's family as they listened to Frank read the note. Their kind faces weren't soothing, they were acid eating away at the concrete of his heart. Noah withdrew into himself. His pain was all he could focus on.

Allison turned on the television, muted it, and then handed Josh the remote. He played happily with the buttons, changing channels. Allison shook her head. "No, Daddy, no. I don't believe it. She wouldn't do this. This note doesn't even sound like her."

Frank ran a hand through his dark gray hair. "It's her handwriting. Why would she lie?"

"Daddy, I told her not to go with Wes. She said okay. Savvy wouldn't disobey me on something like that."

Ryan reached for his wife's hand. "Why did you tell her not to go with Wes?"

"Because!"

Josh whimpered. "Don't yell, Mommy."

"Sorry, baby." Allison pulled him close, kissing his forehead. "Because," she whispered with a fierceness that was reflected in her gaze. "Wes is the one who hurt me!"

Three pairs of eyes zeroed in on Allison. Noah felt like a bear waking up from hibernation. "What," he yelled. He moved closer to her. "What did you say?"

She looked from Noah to Ryan. "Wes came to our house that night. Josh cried out and I ran to get him. Wes followed me up the stairs."

Ryan's face hardened. Allison focused on Noah.

"I tripped, and he grabbed my arm, I don't think he meant to make me fall, but he was trying to . . ." She gazed at her husband again. "Do other things."

Ryan's hands clenched. His eyes narrowed.

"I'm sorry, babe," she said.

Ryan shook his head but he didn't answer.

Allison cleared her throat and glanced at Noah again. "The next thing I remember was waking up in the hospital and Savannah was there. I was probably incoherent, but I know I said, 'No, Wes.' I know she heard me. I remember her agreeing."

Noah grabbed Allison's hand. "Your last conversation with her, she told me to ask you about it. Do you think that's what she was talking about?"

Allison nodded. "She was telling me all about Noah and she mentioned Wes's name."

Noah gritted his teeth. *Why had she lied to him?*

"I told her 'No, Wes.' She promised me."

"Allison," Noah said. "How do you know it's Wesley Richins who hurt you, there could be dozens of Wes's in the valley."

"I-I don't know. I just feel like he's the same guy. She met him at the gym, right?"

Noah rocked back on his heels. He released her hand and ran to the nurse's station. Ilene was there.

"Do you have a sketch of the perpetrator?" Noah demanded.

Ilene found the sketch that had been done of the man who had been pretending to be Allison's brother-in-law. She handed it to Noah. Now that he looked closer, it did look like Wes. Why hadn't he seen it?

He raced back to Allison's room and held out the paper to Allison. "Is that the man that hurt you?"

She grabbed the paper. "Wes's face isn't so thin, his hair is longer, and he's better looking than this picture."

Noah grimaced. He could see his expression mirrored on Ryan's face.

Allison nodded. "It's not identical, but yes, I think this is him."

She grabbed Noah's hand. "Yes." There was no hesitation this time. She applied more pressure to his fingers, her voice increased in intensity. "Noah. You've got to find Savvy. Please. Don't let him hurt her too."

Noah nodded. He squeezed her hand, then dropped it and raced from the room. Jason was nowhere to be seen. He flipped open his cell phone and dialed. "Jason, I need you."

"I think Rosie dropped the note off," Jason said. "She's not answering her home number. I'm putting out an APB. We'll find her."

"Richins has Savannah."

Jason didn't say anything for a few seconds. Then he swore. "Richins? He's the one?"

"Yeah. I should've seen it."

"This isn't your fault," Jason interrupted. "It's Richins. You know what he drives?"

"A Hummer."

"Figures. Get a hold of the department secretary. She can get his plate number. We'll get everyone searching for his vehicle. I'll try and find Rosie."

"Okay." Noah disconnected. He took the stairs two at a time while dialing the sheriff's office. As he burst through the front door of the hospital, the department secretary answered.

"Shawna, it's Detective Shumway. I need a trace on a cell phone." He rattled off Savannah's number. "Also, I need to know everything there is to know about Wesley Richins. Get his license plate number and get everybody searching for his Hummer. Also, what properties do he and his family own? Other vehicles. Airplanes." Noah stopped talking. He remembered Wes asking Savannah to fly somewhere with him—he must have a pilot's license.

"Call me when you know something." He disconnected and sprinted for Allison's Tahoe. He put the vehicle into gear and sped down the street. He dialed Savannah's cell phone number. It rang five times before her voice asked him to leave a message. "Dangit." He slammed the phone closed. It buzzed seconds later. He looked at the display screen: Jason, not Savvy.

"I've got Rosie. A Logan City policeman caught her, and she spilled quick. Wes and Savannah are at the airport."

Noah took a deep breath. "I thought they might be."

"I put out an APB. We should be able to catch him before he gets off the ground. The officer is bringing Rosie to me. I'll be right behind you."

"Meet you there." Noah was less than a mile from the airport. It felt like twenty. Would he catch them in time? Even if he did, how was he going to stop an airplane from taking off?

⁂

Savannah tried to catch a breath, but acid lodged in her throat. Her neck throbbed with tension. *How could she get away from Wesley? What must Noah be thinking? Was Allison really okay or had Wes lied again?* She looked over at Wesley. She hated him.

Another plane moved into position to takeoff in front of Wesley's plane. He turned, tossing a wink in her direction. Savannah shuddered, brimming with revulsion. She wrapped her arms around her stomach and looked away.

Wes trailed his fingers down her arm. "Soon we'll be in paradise. Just the two of us."

Savannah swung around to glare at him. "Paradise would be purgatory with you."

His eyes darkened, hard as coal.

"Why?" Savannah jerked her arm from his creepy long fingers. "Why are you doing this? You could have any woman you want and you're forcing the only one who's not interested to go with you."

His eyebrows formed a V on the bridge of his nose. "You're the only one I want."

"Bet you said that to my sister, too."

Wes raised one eyebrow. His lips thinned. "It wasn't the same. I didn't know you then. I never would've bothered Allison. I'm sorry about this whole mess with her getting hurt, but you have to see that you're the one for me, Anna."

She stared into his black gaze. "That's a load of smack. The only reason you want me is because I don't want you."

Wes said nothing. He turned to watch the Cessna across the runway gunning its engines.

Savannah shook her head in disbelief. "You've really never heard the word *no* before, have you?"

Wes wouldn't look at her.

"No, Wes. I'm telling you no. I don't like you. In fact I hate you. I would choose Noah over you, and I would've the first day I met you. Noah is a million times better man than you."

His body was rigid. The other plane had risen into flight. Wes drummed his fingers on the dash. He ignored Savannah as he impatiently watched and waited for his plane's turn.

"How does that make you feel, Wes? My sister obviously told you no, and know I'm telling you no. No, I won't go with you. No, you can't force me to care for you. No, I would never choose you over Noah!"

"Stop it, Anna," Wes hissed between his teeth.

"Don't call me Anna, you spoiled rich piece of crap!"

Wes turned to her, anger distorting his features. He raised a hand. "Stop it!" He yelled.

Savannah jammed her body against the door.

Wes's phone rang. He slowly lowered his arm, exhaling several times before answering his cell.

"Rosie. Did you deliver it?"

"Great," he continued. "The money will be in your account within the hour." He paused, looking at the phone in confusion. "What? Give the phone back to Rosie. Who is this?"

His face paled. "Jason Keller?" I hate that guy." He shut the phone off, unrolled his window, and hurled his BlackBerry at a hay field. "See if he can trace it there."

Savannah's heart leapt. Jason. He'd captured the nurse who was supposed to hurt Ally. Ally was safe. Oh, thank heavens. Her sister was safe. She looked at Wes's thinned lips and set jaw. He had nothing to threaten her with anymore, if she could only find a way to get free.

Noah spun off the main road and raced through the airport. He heard the sirens of patrol cars chasing him. He watched a Cessna take flight. If the department secretary was right, the white Meridian Piper taxiing into position for takeoff was owned by the Richins' family. The propellers were rotating.

Noah sped onto the runway.

The plane moved slowly at first but quickly picked up speed.

Noah slammed the gas pedal into the floor, the Tahoe responded but not as fast as he would've liked. He had about two hundred more feet of runway. He had to catch that plane before it rose off the ground and Savannah was lost to him.

He gained on the airplane. Seconds later, he'd reached the wheels. Edging a few feet in front of the plane, he knew he'd only get one chance at stopping them. Noah braced himself against the impact. He looked wistfully at the seat belt hanging by his shoulder that he'd neglected to fasten. There was no time.

Turning sharply, he banged into the airplane. The Piper veered from the runway. The Tahoe bounced off the airplane, teetering onto two wheels and then rolling onto its hood with a sickening crash of glass and metal. The last thing Noah registered was banging against the roof, wondering if he'd done enough to save Savannah and wishing he'd taken the time to put the seat belt on.

❦

Wes cursed, watching Ally's Tahoe hit his airplane from the seat of his Hummer half a mile away. "Now they'll know we weren't on the plane."

The plane veered off course, bouncing to a stop in the dirt east of the runway. The driver Wes had paid to fly the Piper tried to keep the wheels rotating, but a chain link fence stopped him in front and a line of police cars coming from behind halted any chance of escape.

The Tahoe took flight instead of the airplane. The vehicle rolled several times before coming to a stop upside down.

"Noah!" Savannah screamed, rising out of her seat.

Wes jammed his Hummer into gear, muttering about incompetent help. Savannah glanced at his mottled face. The vehicle picked up speed on the country road where they'd watched the plane try and take off. She unlocked the door manually and pulled on the handle.

Pushing the door open, she saw the black asphalt flowing beneath them. It was going to be a bad fall, but anything was better than Wes. Savannah gritted her teeth and flung herself at the road. She didn't get past the running board. Her shirt was ripped from behind and she rammed into the middle console.

"What are you trying to pull?" Wes screamed. Reaching past her, he slammed the door shut. He locked it again as he veered down the road. "Don't ever try something stupid like that again."

He jammed the gas pedal to the floor, and the Hummer shot forward.

Savannah watched the sagebrush fly past her window. She whirled on him. "The stupid thing would be to go anywhere with you!"

Wes gripped her arm so tight it ached. "Sorry, girl, you don't have any choice in that. Not now. Not ever. That idiot Shumway stopped the plane, now they'll know we weren't in it. I thought if we faked an escape it would buy us a few hours." He released her arm, concentrating on the road in front of them. "Now they'll be watching for us to get out some other way. I don't know if we can make our flight out of Salt Lake."

He kept muttering about Noah messing up their plans. Savannah spun in her seat, watching the flashing lights surrounding the plane and the wrecked Tahoe back at the airport. *Noah!* Was he injured—or dead. Oh, please no. Not that. *Please, Lord. Please protect him and somehow find a way for me to get to him.*

Noah opened his eyes to flashing lights and Jason poking at his throat.

"Is that some kind of first aid move?" Noah whispered.

His friend jerked in surprise at the sound of Noah's voice. "He's not dead!" Jason cried out.

"Don't move him," he heard another voice say. "Wait for the EMT's."

"No," Noah croaked. "Forget the stinking EMT's. Jase, get me out of here!"

Jason had already pried the passenger door open. He took Noah's arm.

Noah groaned, writhing in pain. He felt like his body had gone through the spin cycle in an industrial washing machine. He made it out, crawling on hand and knees. The Tahoe rested on its roof. Noah looked at the airplane, pinned against the fence.

"Savannah!" Lurching to his feet, he staggered toward the airplane.

Jason grabbed his arm. "They weren't on the plane."

"What?" Noah shook his head, trying to clear the gray matter that had been mashed. "Who was on the plane? Where are they?"

Jason stopped him. "Sit down."

Noah sunk to his knees. Jason squatted next to him. Some other police officers milled around, staring at them.

"Apparently Richins paid some guy to take off in his plane. The dude claims he was just supposed to take it to Vegas and then come back. He acts like he knows nothing about the kidnapping. That's all they've gotten out of him so far, but I guess we'll see how involved he was."

Noah rotated his neck thirty degrees. He grimaced at the throb he created, using his fingers to massage it. "Where is she?" he whispered.

Jason shrugged. The movement was nonchalant, the look in his eyes was not. "Sorry, buddy. Nobody knows where they are. They traced Savannah's cell phone to Allison's house. Found it in the outside dumpster. And they found Wes's in a field north of here."

Noah's head pounded harder.

"The APB on Wes's Hummer is out, but we haven't heard anything yet."

"Well, obviously." Noah struggled to his feet. Pain radiated through his leg, but he ignored it. "Everybody's sitting around gawking at me instead of trying to find them. Give me the keys to your Jeep."

Jason followed Noah's stuttering forward momentum.

"Yeah, right." Jason laughed, but it was hollow. "Look at what you do to vehicles." He gestured toward the totaled Tahoe. "Whose buggy?"

"The sister's." Noah pressed his fingers against the tenderness in his side, just below his rib cage. The pain intensified, and he pulled his hand back again. He must've snapped a rib or something.

Jason nodded. "Quite a way to get in good with the family. Wreck the sister's car."

Noah blinked, squinting through the bright sun at his friend. He heard the approaching sirens of an ambulance. "Either give me the keys or start moving. We've got to find her."

Jason smiled. Dangling the keys out of Noah's reach, he sauntered toward his red Jeep.

Noah followed like a dog on a leash. They came face to face with Sergeant Malm.

"Shumway, what kind of a stunt are you trying to pull?"

Noah looked down several inches at his boss. "I'm trying to rescue the woman I've been watching. She's been kidnapped, sir."

"I realize that, but you should be in the hospital." He looked over Noah's scrapes and cuts. "Where does it hurt, son?"

Noah straightened his face, standing tall even though it was excruciating. "Never felt better."

Sergeant Malm shook his head. "Let's get you checked out, and then you can get back on this case."

An ambulance screeched to a stop beside them in a cloud of dust.

"Please, sir," Noah begged, "I need to find her. She's my responsibility."

Sergeant Malm looked him up and down. "Seems to me like it's turned into a lot more than that."

Noah gulped, knowing he could lose his job for becoming involved with a suspect. "You're right." He glanced into his sergeant's gray eyes. "Please let me go find her."

The man studied him, pursing his lips.

Noah fidgeted, aching to move even though it hurt. Every second was one more that Wes had Savannah. He wanted to beg his boss. "Please, sir," was all he could manage.

"Are you sure you're okay? That was quite a wreck."

Noah nodded, inhaling past the increasing pain in the upper part of his abdomen. "Everything's in working order, Sergeant. I'll get to the hospital after we find Savannah."

The ambulance personnel hovered around Noah like mosquitoes ready to draw blood.

Sergeant Malm swatted them away. "Let him go."

They backed away with uncertainty.

The sergeant turned to address the rest of the officers. "You've got the descriptions of the girl, the man, and the vehicle. Now go find them."

"You want us to leave this wreck?" a highway patrolman asked.

"Yes. Go find the girl!" He nodded to Noah.

Noah smiled in return, moving gingerly with Jason away from the wreckage. Jason stayed close, holding onto his elbow for support.

"I'm okay." Noah shook him off, rounding the Jeep and climbing in. He bowed his head and silently prayed he could find her.

Sixteen

Savannah held onto the middle console and the door as Wes careened around corners, racing through the narrow canyon road. She stared at the towering mountain walls, the batches of pine and aspen trees, and the Logan River cascading next to the road, but Noah was all she could think about. Would he be okay? The whole nightmare was her fault. If only she could have thought of a way to warn Noah or escape from Wes.

No. She couldn't have done either. She would never put Allison's life in jeopardy. But what if she'd killed Noah? How would she live without him? She groaned. Oh, Noah.

She turned to look at Wes's dark profile. Would he hurt her when they stopped? He'd raised his hand to hit her earlier today and he'd hurt Allison. He claimed it was an accident, but Savannah didn't believe anything he said.

He veered off the main road, darting down dirt ruts and heading north. Dust filled her nose and billowed behind them. Minutes later he turned onto a path barely wide enough for the Hummer. Sunlight filtered through the huge poplar trees covering the road like hands with interlocking fingers. Branches scraped against the vehicle, but Wes didn't seem to notice the damage to his custom paint job. Savannah gripped her supports tighter as they bounced along the rutted path.

"Where are you taking me?" she asked.

"Someplace safe," Wes muttered. "We'll stay there until they stop searching for you and then we can escape."

"No place is safe with a snake like you," Savannah shot back.

Wes glanced at her. "Be careful, Anna, I'm all you've got now."

The Hummer hit a huge tree limb. Wood cracked and metal groaned. Savannah cried out. Wes floored the vehicle, bouncing up and over the obstacle.

Savannah clung to the armrest. Maybe when they got wherever they were going she could escape. She'd never seen Wes run, but she was betting she could sprint faster. If only she could get free for a second. She could run to the road and then make her way to Noah.

Noah and Jason sped toward Wes's condominium. The authorities at the airport, train, and bus stations had been alerted to watch for anyone matching Wes and Savannah's descriptions. The valley and surrounding canyon roads were crawling with cops searching for the Hummer. Officers were assigned to search the Richins' mansion up on Cliffside, the family's business buildings, and the numerous rental properties they owned. It could take all day to make it through the rental units.

The Richins also owned homes or condominiums in Park City, Jackson Hole, Palm Springs, and several international residences. The local law enforcement at each spot had promised to secure those locations, but Wes and Savannah couldn't have made it farther than Park City.

Noah got a search warrant to check out Wes's condo. He and Jason arrived at the front door. Pressing his ear against it, Noah heard nothing. He rapped with his knuckles. "Open up!" No answer. He tried the doorknob—locked.

He looked at Jason. Jason grinned, white teeth gleaming against his dark skin. "Is it my turn?"

Noah gestured. "Be my guest."

Jason backed up, drawing his Sig from inside his shirt. He quickly shot numerous rounds into the deadbolt and door handle. He kicked the wood door with his heel. It swung open. The apartment beckoned like a sinister cave full of bats, bears, and all things unpleasant.

Jason bowed to Noah. "After you."

Noah grunted. "Thanks a lot."

He stepped onto the gray tile flooring. His eyes adjusted to the dimness of the spacious condo. Fractions of light seeped through the drawn blinds. Noah flipped a switch, illuminating the room. The open kitchen and living area brimmed with black and stainless steel. The beige walls contrasted with black leather sofas, a black entertainment center, and black granite counter tops. All the appliances, framed pictures, and other decorations were stainless steel. The kitchen cabinets were walnut and almost as dark as everything else.

"Cold guy," Jason muttered.

Noah and Jason silently searched the rest of the condo. It was empty. The décor was consistent, except for in the master bedroom. Instead of landscape prints dotting the walls, they were covered with pictures of Savannah: walking out of the gym, eating lunch with Wes at Angie's, standing next to her Accord, on the porch of Allison's house playing with Josh.

Jason whistled. "Creepy." He examined the pictures. "These were all taken recently?"

Noah studied each one. He reached toward Savannah's face, catching his hand before he touched the print. His throat caught. He shook his head and turned from her image. "Looks like it. Our little photographer friend, remember?"

Jason nodded.

"I wish I would've noticed him sooner," Noah said.

Jason lifted an eyebrow. "Give yourself a break. You were a little wrapped up in the woman."

Noah dug his fingers into his palms. "Who we need to find."

Jason offered Noah a set of plastic gloves. They carefully searched through drawers, under beds, and in the recycling bin. They found nothing telling them where Wes might have taken her. Twenty minutes later, they exited the condo.

Noah called the crime scene investigators and asked them to catalog the pictures as evidence and check the apartment thoroughly.

"Where to next?" Jason asked.

Noah leaned back, letting the sun wash over his face. The fresh air helped cast off the sinister feel of Wes's home. He felt like an inmate being removed from solitary confinement.

He inhaled several gulps of clean oxygen. "We've heard nothing from Park City, Jackson Hole, or the airport. I feel like they're close."

He shuffled toward the Jeep, holding his ribs to keep them from bouncing. "Let's go talk to his dad. Maybe he'll have something for us."

"You're just going to march into his dad's house and demand to know where his psycho son has taken your girlfriend?" Jason climbed into the driver's side.

Noah stared at his friend. My girlfriend? He gulped. *Oh, Savvy, if I ever find you, I'll do anything to make that phrase come true.*

He withheld a groan as Jason slammed the Jeep into drive and they bumped down the road. There might have been a worse vehicle to ride in, but right now he couldn't think of one.

"Head up Cliffside," Noah said. "His dad was always nice to me."

Jason raised an eyebrow. "Whatever you say."

"What?" He angled his body to face his friend.

"I remember the old man screaming at you every time his baby boy got sacked on the field. It was like you were the only member of the line."

Noah snorted. "The wimp didn't get sacked very often."

Jason smirked. "That's true, but I still remember Wes's dad being pretty protective of his kid."

Noah looked out at the million dollar homes sliding past the Jeep. "I never told you, but his dad talked to me after the last home game of our senior year. He told me he was grateful for how hard I'd worked. He also sent me a card and a check for five hundred bucks when I graduated from college."

"Really?" Jason arched an eyebrow. "Didn't know the politician had a heart. What do you think about all the rumors? I heard someone's black-mailing the old man with pictures of him dressing up in women's under-wear."

"Sounds like a funny picture, but who knows if it's fabricated or not." Noah shook his head. "Either way it could keep him from the governor's mansion."

The Logan City police were just exiting the Richins' enormous home when Noah and Jason burned through the circle drive. They climbed from the vehicle.

"What's up, boys?" Jason asked.

An older officer with a craggy face and thinning brown hair shook his head. "Keller. Haven't had the pleasure since I skunked you at that golf tournament last summer."

Jason grinned. "That's okay, Palmer. When I'm old and can't do anything else I'm sure I'll have time to perfect my golf game too."

"Hey, Shumway." Palmer studied him. "Word is it's your girl who's missing."

Noah cleared his throat. "Yeah. Did you find anything?"

Tom's features tightened. His head rotated from side to side. "Not here, and the senator was livid about us searching. Kept saying his boy would never do something like this." Palmer rolled his eyes. "It's always the spoiled rich ones whose parents think they're perfect."

Noah nodded. "We're going in to talk to him."

Palmer lifted an eyebrow. "Good luck."

The two uniformed officers climbed into the patrol car as Noah stumbled past the water feature and up four steps to the columned front porch. The spot where his abdomen and chest connected ached, slowing his oxygen intake. His head could explode from the pressure, and he'd be better off. His legs were barely functional. He pressed the button on the paging system, staring at the wood and etched glass door.

"What do you want now?" A gruff voice demanded. "Is there no respect in this city for your state leaders?"

"Mr. Richins. It's Noah Shumway. You might remember—"

"Noah. Of course I remember you, son. You protected my Wesley more times than I can count. What can I do for you?"

Jason's lips twitched. "Son?" he mouthed.

Noah shook his head at him. "I'm here with the Cache County Sheriff's office."

"Are you here to help me figure out this mess with the cops? You know Wes. I mean the kid's an irresponsible putz sometimes, but you know he'd never hurt some girl."

Noah glanced at Jason who was trying to keep from laughing. Noah motioned to the cameras. "Um, sir, could we come in and talk to you for a few minutes?"

"You can. I don't need that other bozo in my house unless you have another bogus search warrant."

The door buzzed. Noah pushed on the handle and swung it open. He turned to his friend.

Jason smiled. "The other bozo will wait in the Jeep."

Noah walked through the eight-foot door, looking up at a massive crystal chandelier dangling above him. Stairs adorned with graceful cherry railings hugged each side of the cavernous entry, sweeping to the wide second-story balcony. Cigar smoke laced the air.

"Come in here, son."

Noah swung to his right where a door stood open a few feet before the staircase began. Walking through the portal, he saw Wes's dad, seated behind a massive mahogany desk. The room's floor to ceiling north-facing windows overlooked the houses below and the entrance to Logan Canyon. The room was classic and sharp, containing little besides the desk and a bookshelf.

Noah nodded to the angular, dark-haired man behind the desk. He was dressed in a black suit and burgundy pinstriped tie. "Thanks for letting me in, sir."

"You always did have decent manners, unlike those other cops who just barged in and demanded to search the place." Mr. Richins gestured to a leather chair across from his desk.

Noah sank onto the edge of the firm seat.

"What's going on here, Noah? Wes won't answer his cell phone, and these cops are claiming he took some girl." He guffawed, waving his cigar through the air. "You know as well as I do, no woman has ever said no to Wesley. Why would he even think of taking a girl against her will?"

Noah bit his lip. "Maybe one finally did say no and he couldn't believe it."

Mr. Richins straightened. "You're not here to help Wesley."

Noah held his gaze. "No".

Mr. Richins rose to his full six feet and pointed to the door. "Then get out!"

"Please, Mr. Richins." Noah stood, towering over the man. "Hear me out."

His cigar trembled. "Why should I?"

Noah started talking and fast. "Sir, Wes took the girl." He held up a hand at the father's protests. "We have witnesses. He hurt her sister four days ago and put her in a coma. He's been drugging the sister, using a medicine called Versed that has kept her in the coma and was supposed to cause amnesia."

Noah held Jamison Richins' angry gaze. "I'm guessing he was hoping to buy himself time to get to know Savannah and hoping no one would find out about him hurting Allison. But Allison woke this morning and she knew exactly who'd hurt her. Wes had an inside informant at the hospital. He took Savannah and ran."

The senator lowered his arm, dropping the cigar in a pewter ashtray. His eyebrows lifted, smoothing out some of the embedded wrinkles underneath and deepening the wrinkles above. He didn't say anything.

Noah took his silence as permission to continue. "He paid off a nurse at the hospital. He paid someone else to fly his plane and make it look like they were trying to escape by air." Noah exhaled, and then slowly took another breath. "Wes took Savannah Compton against her will. I came here, sir, to see if you know where he might have gone."

Mr. Richins collapsed onto his studded leather office chair. His head lolled. He looked like a dejected child cradled in a giant's hand. After a few minutes he raised his gaze. "You really think he could've done this thing, Noah?"

"I know he did, sir." Noah nodded. "Please help me find them."

"He told me he was dating a Savannah."

Noah snorted. "He wishes."

Mr. Richins' eyes flashed. "You care for the girl?"

Noah's head bobbed again.

"I seem to remember you two competing for a few different girls back in high school and college. Are you just trying to win this one, Noah?"

Noah cleared his throat. "No, sir. I actually love this one." The words sounded foreign on his tongue, but he knew they were true.

The older man didn't answer. He reached under his desk, jerking out a tray with a computer keyboard. His fingers danced with the keys.

Noah shifted to ease the ache in his upper abdomen. He watched the clock on the wall, hating the wait. Every minute he wasted here was one more that Wes could be taking Savannah further away or hurting her. He couldn't stand the thought of Wes touching her, let alone . . .

Mr. Richins looked at Noah with a scowl. "He's moved a lot of money in the past twenty-four hours. I show at least three million transferred or withdrawn. Funds deposited in accounts of a Rosie Sanchez and a Damon Bosworth."

Noah leaned forward and looked at the screen. "The nurse and the pilot."

Wes's dad massaged his neck with long fingers. "I'm having a hard time believing any of this. Why would Wes do something so crazy? He could go to prison. He knows I'll cut him off financially." His eyes narrowed. "None of this can get out. This is an election year."

"Sir, if you help me I can try and keep the names from the press."

"I can't endanger my only son."

"He's endangered himself. He made himself a criminal."

Mr. Richins groaned, thin lids sliding over black eyes. "My son, a criminal." He passed a hand over his face and then opened his eyes and stared at Noah, his expression hollow and filled with sadness. "He asked me the other day what I'd do if he got into trouble. I thought he was joking." His mouth flapped open, but his voice came in a whisper, "Maybe it's all a big misunderstanding and you'll be able to clear it up for him. Will you do that if you can, Noah?"

Noah kept his facial expression neutral. "Hopefully that will be the case, sir."

Mr. Richins leaned toward him. "Will you do all you can to help him?"

Noah pressed his lips together. He wanted to do all he could to hurt Wes, but his job was to protect and serve. "Sir, I'll do all I can for Wes, but if he is found guilty he'll be put in prison."

The older man swallowed. His head bobbed up and down once. "I understand."

"Please help me find them. I'll ask everyone involved to keep the case quiet for as long as we can, so you can prepare damage control."

Mr. Richins pursed his lips, closing his eyes against Noah's pleading stare. He rubbed his eyes with his fingertips for a few seconds before focusing on Noah. "I'm going to have to use this."

Noah stared. "What do you mean?"

Jamison Richins' lips turned up. "I hate to do this to him, but it will work. It has to."

Noah's stomach rolled. *Had the senator lost it?* "Sir?"

"Don't keep it quiet, Noah. Let your officers talk all they want."

"Seriously?"

Senator Richins hesitated. "Dangit, Wesley," he muttered. He pursed his lips, showing spiderwebs of worry wrinkles. His eyes closed.

Several minutes passed in silence. Noah shifted in his seat. As the pause stretched past uncomfortable, Noah prayed the senator would volunteer some information. If he didn't, Noah knew his self-control would soon disappear.

Seventeen

Savannah watched Wes scurry around the small cabin. He'd carried her from the vehicle, not letting her study the exterior of the cabin for long. She'd ascertained that they were less than a quarter mile from a cliff on the north side and framed by batches of pine trees on the east and south.

Once inside the cabin, he'd tied her hands with a thin kitchen towel and settled her onto a musty couch. Then he proceeded to open windows to try and better the air quality.

His movements were jerky. Savannah didn't know if he was nervous they would be found or if maybe his actions of the past few hours were finally producing some guilt. She stared at him without apologizing. She wanted to make him squirm.

Wes retrieved a rag from the kitchen and started wiping down the dusty countertop. He glanced at her. "You didn't know I was so handy, did you?" He tried to chuckle, but it came out as a gurgle.

Savannah didn't answer. She prayed he'd stay in this embarrassed, busy mode. If he tried to touch her . . . Her stomach curled at the mental image she conjured. She'd go down fighting, of that she was sure.

She blocked out the dusty log walls, plaid furniture, and industrial, green carpet. In her mind it was last night and she was in Noah's arms.

Wes slammed a cupboard, jerking her back to reality. "I didn't think about bringing food or anything." He shoved a hand through his hair. "I thought we'd be on a plane to Costa Rica by now." He sighed, giving her a tired smile. "Are you hungry?"

Savannah shook her head. Hungry? Even though it was late afternoon, her stomach was still distended from the pancakes she'd eaten this morning. Pancakes. She thought of Noah flipping them, grabbing her for a kiss, smiling at her over Josh's head, telling her she was beautiful inside and out.

"Well," Wes interrupted her daydreams again, "if you get hungry there are some cans of fruit, chili, and a box of stale crackers. The water's really good here, so that's a plus. We'll be okay until it's safe to travel."

Savannah didn't return the smile or answer him. Wes flinched. Turning away from her, he opened the oak cabinet door and retrieved a glass. He rinsed it in the sink and filled it with water.

Every time he turned his eyes from her, Savannah picked at the towel binding her hands.

He took a long drag from the glass. "At least the well is working," he muttered. He went around trying light switches again, as if the electricity would suddenly spark. "The generator probably needs to be started, wonder if it has any gas in it."

Please let him go and start the generator. He didn't move to the door. Didn't give her any opportunity to be alone. Instead he went to the cupboard, rinsed another glass and filled it up. He moved to her side. Not meeting her gaze, he held out the glass.

Savannah rolled her eyes. "How am I supposed to take it, Wesley? You tied my hands."

Wes's eyes flitted from her hands to her face. "Oh. I . . ."

He held the glass to her lips. Savannah took a long drink. Cool water slid down her throat, spilling over onto her chin and thin T-shirt.

Wes set the cup on a pine end table. He moved closer to her on the couch, their legs touching. Savannah shifted away from him.

"Look, Anna," he began. "I didn't mean to hurt Allison."

"So you keep saying."

Wes stood and began pacing angrily from one side of the living area to the other. "I made a mistake."

"True, but how did we get here?" She held up her bound hands. "You could have any girl you want. Why are you doing this to me?"

Wes knelt in front of her. "I saw you teaching aerobics the day after Allison's accident . . ." He shook his head, reaching tentatively for her hand.

She recoiled from his touch.

He exhaled, jamming a hand through his hair. "I saw you teaching and I've never wanted anyone as bad as I wanted you. I had to have you, and when you didn't respond to anything I tried and you liked Shumway better than me . . ." He clenched his fists. His lips thinned. "I guess that's how we ended up here."

Savannah felt a little pity for him. "Wes, you can still make this right."

He rocked back on his heels, arching an eyebrow. "How do you figure?"

"Take me home. Turn yourself in. Admit you made a mistake."

Wes shook his head furiously.

She groaned. "Come on, Wes. They'll go easier on you if you turn yourself in. I bet you'll hardly get any prison time."

"Are you kidding?" A harsh laugh bubbled from his throat. "We're not going back. I'm not letting Shumway win."

Savannah jerked. This was all a competition to him.

"Besides, my dad would kill me. We're sticking to the plan. I won't spend any time in prison." His eyes roved over her body. "Even though I messed up getting you here, I'm still glad you're here. After a couple of years you'll love me so much you'll forgive me for everything I've done wrong."

It was her turn to laugh. "How in the world do you think you're going to keep me by your side for two years?" She lifted her bound hands. "I think this will raise a few questions when we go out in public. Every chance I get I'll try and escape from you. What kind of a relationship is that?"

Wes leaned into her again. Savannah arched back against the couch. Wes's body pinned her legs. She had nowhere to go.

"Oh, Savannah."

He raised a hand to her cheek. She tilted her head away. Wes stood, giving her a minute of relief from his touch.

"Come on, girl. Would you look at me?" With a big smile, he turned a slow circle. His khaki pants encased trim hips. His blue dress shirt stretched over broad shoulders. His dark coloring and sculpted face had caused many a second and third lingering glance.

He completed the circle and winked at her. "No woman has ever turned me down. Ever. You'll learn to love me a lot faster than you think."

"My sister turned you down."

"Only because she was married." He grabbed her arm and jerked her to her feet. "Let's go check out that dusty bed. I'll show you what you've been missing. I'll demonstrate to you why you will never walk away from me."

Savannah's stomach plunged. She yanked against his grip, but couldn't free her arm. "Are you ready to add another crime to the list? When Noah finds us he'll prosecute you for everything he can."

Wes held tight to her wrist, but stopped dragging her. He sneered at her, his mouth twisted in an ugly S curve. "What crime is that?"

"It's called rape, Wes."

He chuckled softly. "Can't rape the willing."

"I am not willing," Savannah screamed. Her heartbeat resounded in her ears.

She flung back, managing to drag her arm free. Whirling, she sprinted for the exterior door. She was mere feet from the handle. Wes grabbed her from behind and spun her into his chest.

"Aaah!" she yelled, watching freedom slip from her once again.

"Don't even try it."

Savannah kicked his shin as hard as she could with her leather sandal. It felt like she broke a toe. Wes grunted, but didn't release her. Wrapping her in his steel embrace, he forced her face up with one hand. He planted his lips on hers and tried to elicit a response. She bit his tongue.

Wes yelped. "What'd you do that for?"

"Don't touch me! Let me go!"

"I'll never let you go."

He flung her over his shoulder like a fifty-pound sack of sugar. She flailed and kicked. Wes carried her through the bedroom door and tossed her on top of the squishy bed. Savannah flipped onto her side and scrambled off the mattress. Grabbing her arms, he pinned her down with the weight of his body.

Savannah squirmed and fidgeted. She strained with every ounce of muscle she possessed. She couldn't move an inch. His head lowered toward hers. She prayed for help. She had to do something and fast.

"Wes, please. Look at yourself. You just admitted you made a mistake and you were sorry. Don't make another mistake." Her voice trembled. "Please don't do this."

He paused and loosened his grip on her arms but didn't release her.

"If you really want a relationship with me do you want to start it by forcing me to do this? I'll resent you. I'll hate you. You'll never make me love you this way."

He released one of her hands, slowly outlining the contours of her face. "How can I make you love me, Savannah?"

She wanted to wrench her face from his touch and explain that he could never make her love him, but she couldn't risk making him angry now. The only time he was reasonable was when she got him talking and feeling a little guilt about what he'd done. She was no match for him physically. She'd have to win her way free with a battle of wits.

She lay still while he touched her, though it made her ill. "You could start by treating me like you actually care for me instead of like you just want a piece of my backside."

He smiled and slowly released her, helping her sit up on the bed. "Well, both are true," he said.

Relief weakened her. Without meaning to, she leaned against his side. Wes smiled. "You need me to take it slow?"

Savannah mustered up a believable grin. Maybe she could talk her way out of this. "Yes. Very slow. Why don't we go back in the living room and talk? I hardly know you, Wes. Maybe once I get to know you better, I'll start to feel differently and then, who knows?"

Wes's smile grew. "See, now you're being reasonable."

She held up her hands. "Do you think you could undo the towel?"

He bit his lip. "Do you promise you won't try and escape?"

She couldn't give him a straight answer. "It's not like this towel is keeping me from escaping, it's just making me uncomfortable, and it will make it hard to express myself if I start feeling differently about you." She winked at him.

His eyebrow and the corner of his mouth arched. "Well, all righty then."

Slowly untying the knots, he trailed his fingers up her arm and back down. "I love how toned you are," he whispered.

Savannah shivered. It was all she could do to not reach her hand up and slap his perfectly tanned face.

Wes took her hand, stood, and pulled her from the bed. He guided her toward the family room.

Digging in her heels, she tugged on his arm. "I need to go to the bathroom. Which one should I use?"

Wes paused and looked down at her. Savannah gazed up at him with wide, innocent eyes. He directed her into the master bedroom and the attached bath. Dusk was approaching and the small bathroom looked grim. The solitary window was high and narrow. Wes studied the window and grunted in satisfaction. He smiled at Savannah as he shut the door.

Four footfalls sounded, then stopped. He wasn't going far. Savannah turned on the water and flipped the lock on the door handle. The window was just above her head. It was small and frosted, but it had two panes and could be slid open.

Savannah grabbed a wooden magazine rack and carried it to the wall. If she stood on top of it, she could reach the window. She clicked the latch softly and slid it all the way open. There wasn't a screen. The opening was probably less than two feet wide and not quite that high, but it was enough.

She clawed the window frame and scurried up the wall. She took a breath of fresh air as her arms and chest found freedom. Pausing for a moment, she looked down at the ground six feet below her. Her breath caught. It was going to be a hard fall, but it would be worth it. Her hips wiggled through the opening.

Wes pounded on the bathroom door. "Savannah," he called.

Her heart pounded fiercely. "I'll just be a minute," she screamed back.

Gripping the opening with her fingernails, she twisted her body the rest of the way through. Her backside hung out of the opening. She dragged her legs toward independence. She was almost there when her foot caught and she lost her grip. She clawed at thin air and bounced off the ground, settling amidst pinecones and dirt.

She grunted and bit her lip to keep from crying out. Her legs and rear hurt.

"Savannah!"

Her head whipped up. Wes scratched at the master bedroom window, staring at her in shock. He turned and ran. She leapt from the ground. Night screamed toward her as she sprinted from the cabin into the thick grove of pine trees to the west.

"Savannah!"

He was coming fast.

Dodging the scratchy pine needles, Savannah increased her pace. Footsteps pounded behind her. She twisted her head to gauge the distance between them. His longer strides narrowed the distance. Fear increased her pace. She couldn't let him catch her.

Two sets of headlights bounced along the rutted path from the west. Friend or foe didn't matter at the moment. She raced toward the vehicles, but tripped on some undergrowth.

The ground came rushing up to meet her. "Ooomph!" she cried out as broken branches, pine needles, and dirt were embedded in her hands and knees.

The lights careened past her. They were barely twenty feet away but they couldn't see her sprawled on the ground. Savannah struggled to her feet and forced herself to keep moving. The vehicles stopped at the cabin. She heard doors open and slam. People calling her name. She was almost there.

"Savannah! Savannah!"

Joy filled her. "Noah!" she screamed in return. She pushed against the tree limbs that kept her from him. "Noah," she called again, his name a strangled cry on her lips.

Noah whipped around. He looked so good to her—strong and handsome and safe. A tear slid down her cheek. Her strength left as she struggled through the last few trees that separated them.

Strong arms encircled her waist. "Help!" she screamed before a hand clamped over her mouth.

"Shut up," Wesley whispered harshly.

"Savannah," Noah called.

Tears of desperation clouded her vision. She caught one last glance of Noah storming in her direction before Wes half-dragged, half-carried her back into the pine tree dungeon.

❦

Allison held Josh against her chest in the stiff hospital bed. Her baby slept soundly, his soft lips pursed, his hair tousled. She glanced up to see Ryan studying her. He reached out his hand, and she clung to it.

"How are you feeling, sweetie?" he asked.

Allison shrugged. "I'd be a lot better if I knew what was happening with Savvy."

Pressing his lips together, his cheeks tightened. His eyes searched hers. "Your dad and I decided it would be best not to worry you."

She almost laughed. "Come on, Ry. My sister has been kidnapped by the jerk who hurt me, and you think I'm going to sit here and not worry. I haven't stopped praying since Noah left."

Her husband nodded. "I understand. You're just going through so much trying to recover. I thought it would be good for you to enjoy Josh, and take your mind off Savvy."

Allison sighed. "Don't think for me. Okay, babe?"

Ryan jerked and released her fingers. "I'm sorry, I . . ."

She held up her hand. "No. Don't apologize. I know you're always trying to protect me, but I'm a big girl. I can handle things. I love holding Josh, and yes that has helped, but I need to know what's going on with my sister."

He bit his lip. "Okay."

Waiting was torture. "And?"

Her husband stood, jamming a hand through his dark, wavy hair. "Honey, I'm sorry. I don't know much more than you do."

She shook her head, grimacing at the lingering headache that intensified from the movement. "Bull. Out with it."

Ryan sighed. "They've been searching for them everywhere. Noah called and said he's hoping Wesley took her to a cabin that his dad used to take him to." He shrugged. "That's all I know. Right now it's just a waiting game."

Allison nodded, her stomach tumbling. "What's Dad doing?"

The corners of his mouth lifted. "Going crazy. He's out in the waiting area, calling Noah's phone every two minutes and Noah's sergeant every three. He keeps pacing and praying."

Allison knew her dad's pain. She wished she could be pacing and calling. All she could do was pray and cry. "Why didn't Dad go with them?"

"Noah wouldn't let him. He ordered me to take Frank's keys and make him stay and take care of you and Josh."

"Somebody that can make Dad relinquish control over his baby girl?" Allison smiled, despite her stress. "I think I like this guy."

Ryan nodded. "We all do." He paused. "Well, we'll see if Frank still likes him after tonight."

"Does Savvy like him?"

He grinned. "You should've seen them together. She was standoffish and smart alecky and she couldn't quit checking him out. Yep, she definitely liked him."

Allison laughed but sobered quickly. "Oh, Savvy. Do you think they'll find her before Wes hurts her too?"

Ryan sank onto the chair next to her bed. "I don't know."

She took a gulp of air, brushing the fluid from her cheeks. "It's all my fault."

"What? Honey, don't say that. None of this is your fault."

"It is. If I hadn't flirted with Wes at the gym, and then he came to our house and . . ." Allison stopped at the furious expression distorting her husband's face.

His next words were carefully measured and slowly enunciated. "You *flirted* with him?"

Allison gulped, clinging to her son. "Yeah," she whispered.

Ryan's look of anguish broke her heart. "Why would you do that?"

"I-I . . ." She leaned her head into the stiff pillow, closing her eyes to avoid his gaze. "Oh, honey. I'm sorry."

"Why?" he repeated softly.

"Well, you were gone all the time, and I was lonely. He was always complimenting me, and you rarely do. I know that's not your way, and none of this is your fault, and I'm not really trying to place the blame on you, but . . . oh, I don't know!" She opened her eyes, staring into the brown warmth of her husband's gaze.

"I don't tell you how pretty you are?"

Allison blinked. "Not very often," she whispered.

"Oh, Ally." He shook his head. "You're the most beautiful woman I've ever seen."

Allison nibbled at her chapped lips. "I'm sorry. I never should have flirted with him."

Ryan frowned, gripping the side bar of the hospital bed. "Dang straight you shouldn't have."

Her eyes opened wider. "I'm sorry, Ry. I promise it won't happen again."

"It better not."

She swallowed. "It was stupid, and I never meant anything by it. You know I'd never be interested in anyone else."

Ryan held up a hand. "I know that, Ally."

Several quiet seconds passed as Allison studied her husband. He kept his gaze focused on the window. Finally, she could take it no longer. "I'm sorry," she said again.

Ryan's eyes found hers. He nodded. "It's okay." He caught her hand between both of his. "I'm sorry I've been neglecting you."

"No. I shouldn't have said that. None of this is your fault."

"It's not yours either. Of course he would've hit on you, who wouldn't? If your husband is too dumb to appreciate what he has, maybe the idiot needs a wake-up call."

Allison smiled. "I love you, Ryan."

He leaned over the bed and kissed her thoroughly. "I love you. You gorgeous neglected thing."

She enjoyed his kiss until he released her and straightened. "I'd better go check on your dad. Do you need anything?"

"Some orange juice sounds good."

Ryan bent and kissed her one more time. "I'll be right back."

Allison watched him leave, grateful for his forgiveness. She hugged Josh closer, unable to stop worrying about her little sister. Somewhere out there her sister was being held against her will. Was she afraid, hurting, praying for help? Allison did the only thing she could do. She prayed with all her heart.

"Savannah!" Noah cried out. He sprinted in the direction she'd disappeared. Footsteps pounded behind him as Keller and two other officers followed.

Noah searched, but couldn't see her in the dark forest. Where could she have gone? "Savannah, Savannah," he called.

He ran through the pine trees, their branches scraping at him. What had happened? How could she have vanished minutes after he'd found her? "Oh, Savannah." He groaned. Where could she have gone? And where was Wes? Did he have her? Was he hurting her?

Knowing he needed a flashlight and some help, Noah prayed silently as he ran back to the cabin. His friend Jason, the wiry Officer Daines, and the baby-faced patrolman known only as Sharks all watched him expectantly. Noah took command. "Daines, you stay with the Hummer and the cabin, make sure they don't double back here and get away in the vehicle. Keller, you and Sharks help me search."

They retrieved flashlights from their vehicles and started a slow, thorough search. They each went a different direction, calling Savannah's name. Noah didn't know what to do to find her. They were so close. He'd heard her. He knew he had. He was certain he'd seen her small frame moving toward him. Then nothing. Suddenly she'd disappeared.

Savannah's mouth and abdomen ached. Wes wouldn't stop pulling her. She bit at his hand, but couldn't get a good angle on it. He was running hard, panting as he dragged her away. Noah's voice faded. She couldn't hear him calling anymore. She ached from the pain in her stomach and mouth, but she ached more from the loss of Noah.

At least he was all right. He'd survived the rollover. He was here looking for her. *Oh, Noah. Please find me again.*

Wes slowed, releasing his hand off her mouth. He jerked her next to him and heaved great gulps of oxygen.

Noah was probably too far away, but Savannah took a deep breath and gave it her all. "Noah! Noah! I'm here. No . . ."

Wes's hand covered her mouth and nose, cutting off her words and her breath. She moaned against the pain, thrashing and kicking at him, but her movements slowed. Her limbs felt weak. She couldn't think clearly. She couldn't feel her extremities. She was certain her head would explode, and then mercifully the darkness took her.

Eighteen

Savannah opened her eyes, but still saw black. Her head ached. Wes's fingers dug into her forearm. His measured breathing was the only sound in the terrifying darkness. She turned toward the man holding her. She didn't dare squirm, even to alleviate the ache in the small of her back.

The surface underneath her was rough and unforgiving. It wasn't a tree trunk; it was some sort of rock. Where were they? It was so dark. No stars. No moon. It must be a cave or tunnel.

Holding her breath, she gently pried Wesley's fingers off her arm. She prayed the entire time. Lifting his limp hand, she set it softly on the ground. He didn't move.

Cautiously, she crept backwards like a centipede until she bumped into the opposite wall. She rose to her feet. Stretching to her full height was bliss. She used the stone wall to guide her. Foot by agonizing foot she continued to distance herself from Wes. Ten halting steps and she accidentally kicked a rock. It's rolling thuds sounded like a string of Black Cat firecrackers in the silent cavern.

Savannah stopped and held her breath, waiting, praying. She heard pebbles scattering.

"Savannah?"

She didn't hesitate. Using the wall as her compass, she raced into the inky gloom. She wasn't sure if she was running deeper into the darkness or out of it.

"Savannah! Come back here. You could get hurt!"

His footsteps pounded behind her. She rounded a corner and cried out in excitement. A faint glow beamed twenty feet ahead of her. Forcing her legs to rotate faster, she sprinted for the light.

She reached freedom, exiting the mouth of the deep cave. Wesley screamed her name from behind. The moon had risen, a half-sliver in the pinpricked darkness. She could see a few feet in front of her. She wished she could stop and make sure she was going the right direction, but stopping wasn't an option. She couldn't waste any time. She wasn't going to let Wes catch her.

She raced forward in what she hoped was a southern direction. From what she'd seen earlier, the cliff was north of the cabin. She hoped the cave Wes had taken her to was part of that cliff.

"Savannah, Savannah."

Wes's calls were softer; either he was running out of oxygen to scream or she was running faster than he was. Savannah hoped both were true. The only thing that really mattered was getting away from him. If she missed the cabin, at least she'd eventually come to the main road. She could flag down a car or maybe a miracle would happen and she'd find Noah again.

After several frustrating hours, Noah met back at the cabin with Keller, Daines, and Sharks. Officer Daines said a search and rescue team and more police officers were on their way, but they couldn't count on finding anything until morning when they could track footprints and organize a productive search.

Noah rubbed the sore spot between his stomach and chest. His legs were tired, but still able to carry him. The ibuprofen he'd downed had alleviated most of the pressure in his head. "They haven't come back for the vehicle. Unless he had another car stashed somewhere they can't be far. I'm going back out to look."

Jason nodded, his face lined with exhaustion. "I'm right behind you."

Sharks looked tired enough to drop where he was. Daines took the flashlight from his slackened grip. "You stay here, Sharks. We need you to watch for the rescue teams."

Sharks dropped onto the couch, nodding his gratitude.

The three men exited the cabin and resumed their search. Noah's throat was hoarse from calling Savannah's name. His injuries from the wreck with the airplane continued to ache, but he ignored the physical pain. It was nothing compared to his agony over Savannah. He needed to find her, to hold her. She had to be okay.

He trudged through the woods, lifting his feet just high enough to clear the underbrush. He listened for some kind of human sound, praying and hoping.

Then he heard it, footsteps pounded in his direction, and a man's voice cried out Savannah's name. It wasn't Keller or Daines. This call was faint, but it was an urgent scream, not a repetitive hope. Noah jumped over a tree branch and took up a call of his own.

"Savannah! It's Noah. Where are you? Savannah?" He flashed the light crazily as he ran. "Look at the light. Can you see it? Come on, baby. Come to me."

A small figure hurtled through the beam of light. Savannah flung herself into his arms. Noah caught her, dropping the flashlight.

"Savvy!" he cried.

"Noah!" She clung to him.

He wrapped her in his arms. "Oh, baby. I've got you. It's going to be okay now."

She trembled in his arms. Reaching up, she grabbed his face, kissing him long and hard.

Noah responded. He lifted her off the ground, cradling her closer.

She released his mouth and snuggled into his chest. "Oh, Noah. You're okay. I was so worried."

Noah tried to laugh. It came out like a chortle. "*You* were worried? Oh, baby. If something had happened to you."

He kissed her again. Everything would be okay now.

Suddenly, she was ripped from his grasp. Noah was flung in the opposite direction. He twisted to retrieve her, but his foot caught a root and slammed him into the ground.

"Noah!" she screamed.

He jumped to his feet. Wes was carrying Savannah away from him.

"No!" Noah grabbed his enemy from behind, dragging him to a stop.

Wes tossed Savannah like a child's toy. Noah released his hold on Wes and hurried after her. Wes jammed a shoulder into him from behind. Pain shot through Noah's back. He fell to the ground face first. Wes dove on top of him. Noah cried out as Wes's weight drove his injured ribs into the earth. Noah twisted under Wes, rolling over with a groan of agony.

Wes punched him in the face again and again. "Why, Shumway? Why can't you just let me win?"

"Noah," Savannah cried out. She scrambled to her feet and yanked on Wes's shoulders to distract him.

Noah rebounded. He elbowed Wes in the chest, driving him off of him. Savannah jumped out of the way. Noah gasped for air through the shooting pain, then pounced onto Wes and started throwing some punches of his own. They rolled on the hard ground, hitting each other.

Wes gained the upper hand after a vicious kidney punch stopped Noah for a moment. "Savannah's mine," Wes screamed. "There's nothing you can do about that."

"No!" Savannah threw a jab at Wes.

He deflected it with an elbow and glared at her. "Stay out of this, Savannah. As soon as I finish with Shumway, I'll take care of you."

"You'll never touch her again," Noah yelled. He dug deep, finding strength to fight through the pain and flipping Wes off of him.

Wes tried to scramble away, but Noah grabbed his ankle, dragging him through the dirt. Noah jumped onto Wes. He finally had him pinned. He shoved Wes's no longer smug face into the earth with his right hand, using his left to jerk Wes's arms behind his back. He pressed one knee into Wes's back, digging the other knee into his shoulder blades. Pushing with all his strength, he buried Wes's face into the spongy ground.

Wes tried to raise his head, but Noah pushed harder. He could hear Wes's muffled screams for help, but his only response was more pressure on the back of Wes's head.

Wes squirmed and shimmied but couldn't budge Noah.

"Noah," Savannah whispered.

His head snapped up. He looked at her smudged cheeks. Her bruised lips. Her tousled hair. She was beautiful.

She shook her head at him. "Don't do this." Her voice cracked. "Please, just let him go."

Noah's mouth fell open. They weren't the words he'd been waiting to hear. He glanced at Richins, flailing under his weight. *What was he doing?*

Letting go of Wes's arms, Noah released him. Wes lifted his head, gulped for air and rolled over with a groan. Noah grunted to his knees, slowly standing. Jason and Daines sprinted to them. Jason ripped the panting Wes off the ground and wrenched his arms behind his back.

"You have the right to remain silent," Daines began.

Jason winked at Noah as they walked past. "Good job, buddy."

Noah didn't feel like he'd done a good job. If Savannah hadn't stopped him, he could've injured Wes severely, maybe even killed him. Noah hung his head. He'd promised Wes's dad that he'd do all he could for him, and he'd promised himself that he'd do his job. He'd promised the Lord he would love his fellow man, but he'd failed. The last time he'd felt this ashamed was when he realized it was his fault his mom had died.

Jason nodded in Savannah's direction. "You got her?"

Noah's head swiveled toward Savannah. He nodded once. Savvy—she could heal the pain in him. She was okay, and that was all that mattered. Sometime soon, he could sift through the confusion over his calloused treatment of another human being. Right now he needed her. Holding Savannah in his arms would ease every ache.

Slowly, he staggered toward her. Her eyes were wide and frightened. Her mouth soft. Noah stopped several feet from her and opened his arms. She shook her head with uncertainty once, and he jerked in surprise. She blinked, tears rolling down her silken cheeks. She shook her head again, this time with a firmness that terrified him.

Noah's arms dropped like twin anchors in the sea. Slowly, deliberately, Savannah walked a wide arc around him.

He gulped at the bitterness gurgling from his throat and filling his mouth with acid. He pivoted and helplessly watched her go. She picked her way through the trees, following Keller and Daines. Jason turned at the sound of her footsteps. He looked past her to Noah. Confusion filled his face, but he took her arm and escorted her toward the waiting vehicles.

Noah wanted to chase after her, beg her to let him hold her, but he couldn't move.

What had happened? Where had he gone wrong? He fell to his knees in the damp forest. Oh, Savannah. His Savvy. Why? He'd saved her and she still hadn't chosen him.

Nineteen

Noah woke early. His ribcage was tightly bound, and he was drugged up with more Percocet than he'd ever thought he would take, but the medication didn't alleviate the deepest ache.

He was on leave for a few more days. He'd spent the past two days trying to rest and working on easy jobs around the house and yard that didn't make his injuries worse. He painted the trim in the spare bedroom upstairs, mowed the lawn, and even pulled a few weeds. Mostly, he prayed, reflected on all that had happened, and wondered how he was ever going to live without Savannah.

He fixed himself a bowl of raisin bran, but hardly tasted it. He washed most of it down the disposal. Looking out the window at the leaves swaying on his maple tree and the towering mountains to the east, he thought of his dreams the past two nights. For the first time in longer than he could remember, his nighttime visions weren't nightmares.

The first night his dreams had been filled with Savannah, laughing and kissing him. He could picture her face. He missed her.

Sighing, he retrieved a dishrag and swiped at the counter. Last night he'd seen his mom in his dreams. She was beautiful and vibrant. Her blue eyes shone as she smiled at him. He could still hear her voice. "We all make mistakes, sweetie. You're going to be okay."

He gripped the countertop. His mom had said he was going to be okay. Was he? Even if he could forgive himself for what he'd almost done to Wesley Richins, could Savannah forgive him? He thought of the story of her fiancé. She'd broken up with him because of his violent behavior.

Did she believe Noah was like that?

Noah sighed. She had to see what Wes had driven him to. She had to know that he would never do something like that again. Would she give him another chance? And if she didn't, would he ever really be okay?

The television blared the morning news in the living room. Noah went to shut it off. A caption read, "Candidate for Governor Apologizes to Family." Noah's eyes focused in on Jamison Richins. Instead of switching off the set, he turned it up.

"My deepest apologies go out to the Compton family. I'm happy to tell all of you that both daughters are recovering and have accepted my regrets for my son's actions."

Noah's jaw dropped.

Senator Richins smiled grimly into the camera. "Sometimes, after all we do, our children still make poor choices." He paused. "I'm sure many of you have suffered as I am. I pray you'll join me in praying for the family . . ."

Noah shook his head as the man continued to speak. *I'm going to turn this around*, Mr. Richins had said to him. Now he knew what the senator was talking about. Jamison Richins had sacrificed his son for his career. He was going for the sympathy vote. What a snake. Noah actually found himself feeling bad for Wes.

He pushed the off button, his thoughts sliding to his mom. He felt peace in knowing that his mom understood and forgave him. She loved him. Maybe his nightmares were finally over. Maybe he could have a future with Savannah. He walked into the bathroom and started the shower. The only way he'd know was if he tried.

<hr>

Savannah pushed Josh on a swing in Allison's backyard. Ally rested in a lawn chair. She'd been released from the hospital earlier that day and had begged to be allowed to sit in her yard and breathe fresh air.

"What's the deal with you and Noah?"

Savannah's head pivoted toward her sister. "I don't know. He hasn't called."

Allison studied her. "Why haven't you called him?"

Savannah could picture his strong body, his blue eyes, his lips descending toward hers. She shook her head. "Ally. Do you think I'm mental about food?"

"Whee!" Josh cried. "Higher, Savvy." Savannah gave him a stronger shove, and he giggled.

Allison's eyebrows rose. "Where did that come from?"

She shrugged. "Noah told me I was beautiful inside and out and that I could gain twenty pounds and still be teeny. He said even if I did gain weight the people who love me still would."

Her sister smiled. "All true. Guess he picked up on your eating disorder?"

Savannah straightened. "I don't have an eating disorder. I have to be careful."

"You might not have a full-blown disorder, but you're borderline. Do you really have to be a size two? Do you have to monitor every bite you take?"

She exhaled. "You've seen what I can do to myself. I'm afraid if I slip a little I'll pork out again."

The swing was barely moving. "Out, Savvy," Josh said. She lifted him from the swing and set him on the grass. He toddled off to dig in the sand.

Savannah sank into a chair by Allison. Her sister grabbed her hand. "You're an extremist, Savvy. Do you remember how much you ate to become big after Mom died?"

Savannah closed her eyes. "I try not to remember."

"Well, it was a lot. Dad and I knew you were grieving. We didn't want to be mean to you." Allison looked away. "I was almost glad when that boy made you feel bad. You needed something to wake you up."

She nodded. "But I get big so easily. I was a fat kid."

"Baloney." Allison snorted. "Mom went overboard on you."

Her eyes opened wider.

"Sweetie. We all loved Mom. She was great, but she messed you up." Allison held up a hand. "Don't look at me like that. Just because she's dead doesn't mean she was a saint. So you were chubby as a child. A lot of kids are. You just hadn't hit a growth spurt. You would've grown out of it. You were so beautiful." She shook her head. "Mom just wanted you to be perfect."

"Like you."

"What? I'm not perfect."

"To me you are."

Allison hugged her. "Thanks, but I'm far from it. Anyway, you aren't prone to be fat, and you don't need to be as thin as you are. Why don't we concentrate on making you healthy?"

Savannah smiled. "I could try that. My friend at work is a dietitian. Maybe she could help me."

"Good. Go talk to her, and if you still need help, we'll find a good psychiatrist."

Savannah nodded.

Allison grinned. "I'll take care of you like you took care of me." She extended her pinkie. "Sister pact."

Savannah wrapped her pinkie around her sister's then pulled her into a hug. "I missed you."

They finally pulled apart and Ally broke the silence, "Okay. I know you don't want to talk about why you aren't with Noah, but I need something." Her eyebrows rose. "Tell me about your first kiss."

Savannah laughed. "You think I'm easy? I haven't kissed him."

"Yeah, right. Spill it, sis."

Noah walked from Sergeant Malm's office to his desk, but Jason intercepted him. "What's going on? I thought you were still on leave."

Noah looked around. The department secretary and several patrolmen watched them with interest. "Jase, can I talk to you outside?"

"Sure."

They exited the back door and made their way through the parking lot. Jason leaned against his Jeep. Noah stood a few feet away.

"What's going on?" Jason asked.

"I just turned in my badge."

Jason's body went rigid. "You *what*?"

"I'm done, Jase. I don't like being an investigator." Noah pushed his hand through his hair. "This was your dream. I just tagged along because I didn't know where else to go."

"But we work so good together."

Noah shook his head. "No. You work hard at catching my mistakes."

Jason glowered at him. "You're a good cop. Everybody makes a mistake once in a while."

"That's not okay for me." He held up a hand to stop Jason's protests. "I might be an okay cop, but that's not good enough. I want to be great at something. I want to love what I do."

Jason's eyes widened. "I assumed because I love it, you must too. Guess we've been friends too long."

"Nah. I'm just tired of watching your back."

Jason chuckled. "First day of junior year. I'm getting pounded by Nicholas Gentry and all of the sudden this big dude lifts the punk off of me, says something, and old Nick runs for the ladies' room."

"Yeah. I thought Nick was the bully. If only I'd known you'd insulted his mother ten seconds before I walked on the scene."

"The kid was a jerk."

"You loved picking fights."

"Especially when you protected me." Jason laughed, and then sobered. "So what are you going to do now?"

Noah took a deep breath. "I'm going to restore older homes and build furniture."

"You're good at that." Jason smiled. "Actually, you're great at that."

"I love doing it. I've already got a home restoration lined up and four orders for entertainment centers."

"That's cool, man." Jason pushed away from the Jeep and clasped Noah's hand. "I'm going to miss seeing you everyday."

"I'm changing jobs, not dying."

"I know, but it won't be the same." Jason pounded him on the back and then released him. "So, what's up with the woman?"

"The woman?"

"Don't give me crap. You know what I mean."

"Haven't seen her."

Jason shook his head. "I told you how it's going to play. Make your move or I'm giving her a call."

Noah's stomach clenched. "And I told you to stay away from her."

"I love seeing you all possessive and stuff." Jason laughed. "Go get her, buddy. So I don't have to pick up your slack."

Savannah rinsed the last dinner plate, loaded it into the dishwasher, and then started the machine.

Straightening up, she glanced out the front window of Allison's house. Another summer day coming to an end. Another day without Noah.

Savannah sighed, ignoring the happy sounds of her family behind her.

Three days. Three of the longest days of her life. She'd met with a dietitian and a psychiatrist who specialized in eating disorders. She remembered Noah saying he would help her get healthy. She shook her head. She was going to get healthy, but she was going to do it alone.

She spent each minute wishing Noah would call. She dreaded every time the phone rang, wondering what she would say to him. Then she'd cry after she hung up from talking to any man who wasn't him and she'd curse when the phone didn't ring at all.

The separation was her fault. She was the one who'd walked away from him that horrible night. She shook her head. Why couldn't she have fallen into his arms? He wasn't like Daxon. He'd never hurt her. She knew that. Why had she acted like a scared little filly and scurried away? Why hadn't she called him since?

A white truck pulled into the circle drive. Savannah blinked to make sure it wasn't a figment of her imagination.

She could hear her dad and Josh wrestling in the background. Ryan was teasing Allison about letting Savannah do all the housework. She knew they expected her to join in, to come up with a snappy reply, but a crane couldn't have pried her from the window. All she could do was stare at the jean-clad legs climbing from the Chevy truck and taking long strides across the sidewalk and up the front porch steps.

She drank in the sight of him. His dark blond hair, his firm jaw line, his startling blue eyes, his full mouth, his well-built chest and shoulders. She didn't realize she was gripping the counter so firmly until her dad came up behind her.

"Savvy?" he asked quietly. "You okay?"

She didn't answer. She just pointed out the window. The doorbell rang.

Her dad studied her. "You haven't said one thing about Noah. He hasn't called. What happened with the two of you?"

She wrenched her eyes from Noah and glanced at her dad. She could hear Ryan opening the front door and that deep, mellow voice asking how Allison was feeling. At the sound of his voice she was filled with longing.

"I don't know what happened," she muttered to her dad.

Her dad raised an eyebrow, waiting for more. Ryan and Noah appeared in the great room.

Savannah's breath caught. Oh, he looked good.

He wore a half-smile, half-grimace.

223

Her dad left her side and went to shake Noah's hand. "How are you, Noah?"

Noah nodded. "I'm fine, sir."

Frank touched his shoulder, looking him over carefully. "Did you get hurt in that accident?"

"Not too bad. Bruised a few ribs, banged up my leg a bit. Nothing a little time won't heal." His gaze moved to Savannah's face and held there. "My mom always said time will heal everything."

Savannah froze. She wanted to tell him so many things. She wanted to tell him that time wouldn't heal the ache she felt without him. Noah blinked and looked away. He walked around the couch and bent down to Josh's level. The little boy jumped into his arms.

"How's my buddy?" Noah asked.

"Good," Josh said. "Throw me, Noah!"

Noah tossed him into the air. Savannah noticed the muscles bulge in his arms. She watched the way his cheek crinkled when he smiled at Josh. She sighed loudly and turned her head. She caught Ryan and her dad exchanging meaningful looks.

Noah held Josh and talked quietly with Allison. Savannah only caught the last line, "I'm really sorry about your Tahoe. I'll pay for the insurance deductible and any rise you see in your premium."

Allison laughed. "No way! Did you hear this, Ry? The man who saves me and saves my sister is offering to pay for a stupid car. You have got to be kidding, Noah."

He smiled. Oh, Savannah loved his smile. Would it ever be aimed at her again?

"I am planning on paying for it," he said.

Ryan sauntered to the couch and slapped Noah on the back. "Don't even think about it. Your money's no good here."

They chattered for a few more minutes. Savannah might as well have been a robot. She watched mechanically as everyone but her enjoyed the man she loved.

Josh patted Noah's cheeks, talking a mile a minute. "Noah," he said. "You stay here?"

Noah grinned. "What do you mean?"

"You stay forever," Josh said, patting Noah's arm.

"Josh, that's up to Noah. You can't make him stay," Ryan explained.

Noah's gaze swung to where Savannah stood. Her mouth fell open.

She leaned against the counter so she wouldn't crash to the wood floor.

"I don't know, Josh," Noah muttered, studying her with a hopeful expression. "I, um . . . just don't know."

Every eye in the room zeroed in on her. They all waited in silence. Savannah's hand fluttered to her constricted throat. Her vocal chords were malfunctioning. She couldn't say anything.

Noah's face fell. He turned from her and kissed Josh's cheek. "I'll see you soon, little buddy." He set the small boy on the floor.

Ryan and Allison watched Noah with sad smiles. Frank's eyes never left his youngest daughter. She shrugged, lifting one hand. He pursed his lips and shook his head.

Noah glanced around the room, avoiding Savannah's gaze. "I'd better get going. I'm glad you're feeling better, Allison."

Allison grinned. "It's Ally to you and thank you." She grabbed his hand and pulled him into a hug. "Thank you for everything." She whispered something else in his ear that Savannah couldn't hear.

Noah straightened, locking his eyes on Savannah.

Her face filled with warmth.

He turned back to Allison. "You never know. I guess we'll see about that."

Noah moved toward the front entry. Savannah's entire being cried out for him, but she couldn't do anything to stop him.

"Savannah will walk you out," Frank announced as he shook Noah's hand again.

Noah's head swiveled. He studied her without blinking. "No, it's okay. I can find my own way."

"Savannah will walk you out," Frank repeated, commanding her like she was a five-year-old and he was telling her to get to timeout or else. "Right, Savvy?"

Savannah's legs rotated of their own accord. She walked rigidly around the bar. She couldn't look at Noah as she passed him. Her steps carried her to the foyer. She gripped the door handle like it was a flotation device for a drowning victim. She listened to Noah tell everyone goodbye.

Seconds later he was by her side. She could smell him, his clean, oh-so-appealing scent. She still didn't glance up. Opening the door, she stepped onto the porch and wrapped her arms around her stomach.

Noah shut the door behind them. He turned to her.

Savannah glanced up, gnawing at the inside of her cheek. His gaze locked on her face. His eyes were 100 percent puppy dog: scared and sad and hopeful.

She wanted to say so many things. She wanted to throw herself at him, but she stayed strong and held her ground. *Or maybe,* she reminded herself, *she was staying weak and losing the opportunity of a lifetime.*

He raised a hand as if to touch her face, but then his mouth and eyes hardened. He dropped his fingers.

"Goodbye, Savannah," he said.

He turned and trudged toward his truck.

Savannah watched him walk away with tears streaming down her face. His fingers reached for the door handle.

She ran down the porch steps, finally finding her voice. "Noah!"

He stopped. He didn't turn around.

"You can call me Savvy if you want to."

He slowly pivoted toward her. He squinted against the west sun, a half-smile creasing his face. "Really?"

Savannah's throat caught. "Boy, if you'll stay with me, you can call me anything you want."

He opened his arms. She rushed to him and threw herself into his warm embrace. He caught her in his arms and held tight. They said nothing as they clung to each other. Noah wrapped his hands around her waist. He lifted her from the ground, his mouth finding hers.

Savannah returned his kiss, pleasure exploding through her.

Noah released her mouth and gently slid her to the ground. Savannah leaned against his broad chest, planning to never leave this spot.

He tilted her chin up. "Savannah, I . . ."

She touched his lips with her fingertip. "It's Savvy to you," she corrected.

"Right, Savvy." He smiled.

Warmth flooded through her. He understood what that nickname meant.

"I need to say," he said. "That is I don't understand—"

She held up her hand. "Wait, Noah. I need to talk first."

He swallowed. "Okay."

He released her. She felt the loss down to her hair roots. Forcing herself to forget his warmth for a minute, she walked up the steps to the shelter of the front porch. She moved past the rocking chairs, settling onto a wide wooden bench.

Noah followed. She patted the seat next to her, and he gingerly lowered himself onto it.

"You're still hurting?" She wanted to kiss each sore spot.

He shook his head, no.

"Yes, you are."

He shrugged. "Maybe a little."

An awkward silence ensued. Savannah stared at Noah's profile as he looked over the green expanse of lawn. She started to speak several times, but couldn't find the right way to proceed. Finally, she plunged in. "I'm so sorry."

His gaze swung to meet hers. "You don't need to be sorry about anything."

She gulped. "Yes, I do. You rescued me and I acted . . ." Savannah's breath caught in her throat. She touched the smooth musculature of his bicep. "I was scared," she said.

"Yeah, I caught that," Noah said, his eyes tortured.

"I thought you were going to kill him," she whispered. "It made me think of the way Daxon . . ."

He stood, crossed to the porch railing, and wrapped his fingers around it. Savannah followed him. She cocked her head back and searched his handsome face, twisted in agony.

He cleared his throat, but didn't glance her way. "I'm glad you stopped me. I'm really glad." His knuckles were white where they gripped the banister. "I've never hurt somebody like that before. I told you about the history with Wes and I. We've never liked each other. And then you came along."

Noah raised a hand in her direction, but didn't look at her or touch her. "I can't explain how I felt when I found out he had you and I couldn't rescue you. I really did want to kill him."

He turned to her. Brushing his fingertips down her cheek, he tilted her chin and stared into her eyes. "When I thought of him hurting you, maybe doing other things to you . . ." His hand trembled. He whispered. "When I thought he was doing things to you that nobody but me should ever get to do."

Fire rushed through her. It began in her midsection and flowed out until her whole body was sweating. She raised her face as an invitation.

Noah leaned down and gently touched his lips to hers. He lifted his head. The way he searched her eyes told her he wanted so much more, but was willing to wait. He pulled away from her, dropping his hand from her face.

He spoke slowly. "When we were fighting I went into survival mode. All I wanted to do was hurt him. I don't think I would've killed him, but . . ." He flexed his hands. "I don't know what I would've done if you hadn't stopped me." He glanced at her with a nod. "Thank you. I'm glad you stopped me. I couldn't have lived with myself."

Savannah studied him, waiting.

"I'm sorry I scared you." His hands shook. He lifted one and covered her small fingers clutching the railing.

Savannah released the railing and clung to his hand.

"I promise you, Savvy," he said. "I've never been like that before and I would never hurt you or anyone else. I'm not like Daxon. I can swear to you that I would never do anything to hurt or scare you. If you're worried about that I can get counseling or—"

Savannah stopped him with a shake of her head. "I don't think you're dangerous, Noah, and I know you're not like Daxon."

He exhaled.

She continued. "I can't imagine what you must've been going through. I thought you were hurt in that accident and it tore me up inside. I could've killed Wesley for being the cause of that. I wanted you to hurt him, isn't that awful? He'd already hurt you and Allison—the people I love the most."

Noah jerked at that, but she kept going. "He caused all of us so much pain, but I knew if you killed him it would be awful and it would change you." She shrugged, carefully choosing her words. "After they took Wesley away and I knew I was safe, I wanted to fall into your arms again. I've never wanted anything so badly, but I was scared of how powerful you are, scared of what you're capable of."

Noah nodded. "I think I understand why you were scared. It was an awful night."

The breeze blew a lock of hair across her face. Noah lifted it away, tucking it behind her ear. Savannah leaned against his large hand. He cradled her face with his palm.

"So, where does all of this leave us?" he asked.

She moved closer to him and brought his hand around her back. Releasing his hand, she leaned into his chest. Noah pulled her closer.

She looked up at him. "Do you get angry often?"

Noah shook his head. "No."

"Have you ever wanted to hit your other girlfriends?" she teased.

He laughed. "What other girlfriends?" His face sobered. "I'd never hurt any woman."

Savannah nodded. "I know that." She wrapped her fingers around his neck, trailing them down to his shoulders. "So, I'm your first girlfriend?"

His blue eyes twinkled. "You are my first and only girlfriend."

"So do you think you'll stay? Forever?"

Noah's head bobbed up and down. "Oh yeah. I'm staying right here." He kissed her thoroughly. Lifting her off her feet, he spun her around kissing her and laughing. "I'm not going anywhere, Savvy."

Savannah tilted her head back and laughed. Out of the corner of her eye, she could see her dad, Ryan, Allison, and Josh, peeking through the kitchen window, clapping and cheering.

Discussion Questions

1. Savannah obviously had body image issues. How can we prevent ourselves, daughters, and granddaughters from being caught in the trap of believing we must look perfect to be loved?
2. Do you believe Savannah could have dealt with her eating disorder in a different way?
3. Have you ever felt jealous of a sibling because she was labeled as nicer, prettier, or better at sports?
4. Have you ever dealt with a loved one experiencing a serious medical issue? How did you cope?
5. Noah struggled with forgiving himself. With the help of the Lord can we learn how to forgive ourselves and others?

About the Author

Cami Checketts is a wife, mother, exercise scientist, and avid supporter of Cold Stone Creameries. Although clean toilets are a wistful memory, she adores her husband and three wild boys. Sometimes between being a human horse, cleaning up magic potions, and reading Berenstain Bears, she gets the chance to write fiction. Cami has a BS in Exercise Science from Utah State University. She currently has a thriving business as a pro bono fitness trainer. Cami's blog, fitmommas.blogster.com, offers fitness advice and strength training routines for busy women.

Cami lives with her family in the beautiful Cache Valley of northern Utah. During the two months of the year it isn't snowing, she loves to swim, run, and bike.

For more information about Cami and *The Sister Pact*, check out her website: www.camichecketts.com.

A portion of the proceeds for *The Sister Pact* will be donated to The Child & Family Support Center of Cache County, Inc. For more information on this worthy cause please visit www.cachecfsc.org